Dear Reader,

It happens to all of us. We're thrown into circumstances where we have to pretend to be someone else. Like when you graduate from high school, go to college, and pretend you're a college student. Or you get married and pretend you're a wife. Or you have a baby and pretend you're a mother. You ask for the instruction manual and everybody chuckles.

You're in dead earnest.

So you face the days, one at a time. First, you overcome the initial incompetence, the sense that you're the wrong person in the wrong place and everyone's going to know. Slowly you realize that people take you at face value and you learn how to do the tasks assigned to the new person you're pretending to be. Sure, you fall on your face a few times, but gradually you discover your strengths. Maybe you're not like all the other college students or the other wives or the other mothers, but as time goes on you fail less and less. Finally, you discover that while in the process of faking it, you've proved you're just as smart, just as good, just as witty, just as accomplished as anyone in the world! It's a great feeling, and it's happened to me, maybe . . . twice. But that feeling is all the more significant for being rare.

Madeline de Lacy, duchess of Magnus, faces just such a situation when she changes places with her companion and cousin, Miss Eleanor de Lacy. Madeline has to pretend to be meek, humble and competent with an iron. She is, of course, none of those things. Just when she thinks matters couldn't get worse, she meets her former fiancé, Gabriel Ansell, the earl of Campion—and they do.

I hope you enjoy *Scandalous Again,* and may all your dreams come true!

Warmly,

Christina Dodd

Also by Christina Dodd

CANDLE IN THE WINDOW
CASTLES IN THE AIR
THE GREATEST LOVER IN ALL ENGLAND
IN MY WILDEST DREAMS
A KNIGHT TO REMEMBER
LOST IN YOUR ARMS
MOVE HEAVEN AND EARTH
MY FAVORITE BRIDE
ONCE A KNIGHT
OUTRAGEOUS
PRICELESS
RULES OF ATTRACTION
RULES OF ENGAGEMENT
RULES OF SURRENDER
RUNAWAY PRINCESS
SCOTTISH BRIDES
SOMEDAY MY PRINCE
TALL, DARK, AND DANGEROUS
THAT SCANDALOUS EVENING
TREASURE OF THE SUN
A WELL FAVORED GENTLEMAN
A WELL PLEASURED LADY

CHRISTINA DODD

Scandalous Again

AVON BOOKS
An Imprint of HarperCollinsPublishers

AVON BOOKS
An Imprint of HarperCollins*Publishers*
10 East 53rd Street
New York, New York 10022-5299

Copyright © 2003 by Christina Dodd
ISBN: 0-7394-3351-2
www.avonromance.com

First Avon Books paperback printing: March 2003

Avon Trademark Reg. U.S. Pat. Off. and in Other Countries, Marca Registrada, Hecho en U.S.A.
HarperCollins® is a registered trademark of HarperCollins Publishers Inc.

Printed in the U.S.A.

To Heather MacAllister,
a dear friend and a great help.
You worked with me hand-in-glove
to give this plot the perfect touch.
Thank you!

Chapter One

~

Suffolk, 1806

"Now, Madeline, I realize you've only just arrived home from your tour abroad, and you
deserve to rest, but I'm afraid that's not possible."

Madeline de Lacy, the Marchioness of Sheridan,
the future duchess of Magnus, bit into the first
good English beef she'd had in almost four
years, chewed, swallowed and smiled beatifically
across the sunny breakfast table at the bluff, red-
cheeked bulldog of an Englishman. "Why is that,
Papa?"

"I wagered you in a game of piquet and I lost."

She stared. Placing her knife and fork carefully
beside her plate, she glanced at the dumbfounded
footman, frozen in place as he bent to pour Magnus his morning coffee. "That will do, Heaton.
Place the carafe on the sideboard. We'll call you if
we need you." When Heaton had left, she gazed
at her father and repeated—for she wanted no

misunderstanding—"You wagered me in a game of chance and lost."

He continued eating steadily, silverware clinking and flashing. "No use trying to soften the blow, I say. Not with you, m' dear. Sturdy girl. Sensible girl. Always said so. Glad of it."

Drawing on that famed sensibility, she said, "Perhaps you could give me the details of this extraordinary bet."

"Had the bad luck to play not knowing he had gained a pique, which reduced me to—"

Madeline took a fortifying breath. "No, Papa. I mean—why would you put me in a game as ante?"

"Well, *he* suggested it."

"He being . . . ?"

"Mr. Knight."

"And you agreed because . . . ?"

"I'd just lost our fortune and all our estates. You were the only thing left."

Amazing how rational he made his actions sound. "So in a run of bad luck, you wagered everything we have—and your only child?"

"Yes. At the time, it seemed a wise move."

Her brows rose. After the death of her mother seventeen years ago, when Madeline was five, her life had changed from that of a sheltered daughter to one of a girl dealing with the frequent disasters orchestrated by her beloved papa. By the time she was twelve, she knew how to direct a household, to plan a party, to deal with every kind of social disaster.

She was *not* prepared for this. Yet her heartbeat remained calm, her brow unwrinkled, her hands relaxed in her lap. She'd faced catastrophes of Olympian proportions before—almost all the result of her father's careless disregard. Her composure would not be compromised now. "How so?"

"At least if he won you, you'd be assured of having our estates under your control, or at least the control of your husband." Magnus chewed thoughtfully. "It's almost the same as offering the estates as your dowry."

"Except if the estates had been offered as a dowry, I would have the advantage of knowing my husband and agreeing to the match." It seemed a point her father should concede, although she had little hope of that.

"There is that, but really, what difference would it make if you know the chap? You were already engaged once. You loved him. And that proved a disaster! What was his name? Brown-haired fellow with those damned disturbing eyes." Gazing up at the gilded, cherub-decorated ceiling, Magnus stroked his chin. "He was a hundred times more suitable than this Mr. Knight, but you jilted him. Rendered London speechless for at least"— he chuckled—"eight seconds. Until then, didn't know you could lose your temper. *What* was his name?"

A crack appeared in her tranquillity; her hands curled into fists. "Gabriel Ansell, the earl of Campion."

"That's right. B' God, I'll never forget. Magnificent in your wrath! Reminded me of your mother on a rampage."

Madeline didn't want to hear this. She didn't like to be reminded of her rage, or her loss of control, or that night and what followed. Afterward, for the first time in her life, she'd tossed decorum aside. She'd gone abroad to forget, and hadn't come back until she'd achieved forgetfulness. She never thought of Gabriel anymore. She scarcely remembered his name.

"Your mother was just like you. Always level-headed except when she flew into the boughs, then the oceans quailed." Turning toward the closed door, Magnus shouted, "More kippers!"

Picking up the bell at her elbow, Madeline rang it. The butler answered. Heaton had undoubtedly raced to the kitchen to share the extraordinary news with the household. She addressed Uppington in a composed manner. "His Grace would like more kippers." Anything to fill his mouth and stop him from talking about Gabriel. About Lord Campion.

Uppington bowed. In his rush to handle yet another of Magnus's "situations," he had buttoned his tailed jacket askew. "Aye, my lady." He refilled their plates.

Madeline bent her attention to her meal. A less formidable woman would have had her appetite destroyed by Magnus, but if Madeline allowed her father to destroy her appetite every time he scrambled their fortunes, she would be a wraith. She saw no wisdom in that.

"Will there be anything else, my lady?" Uppington asked.

"Not . . . yet." Although, she reflected, perhaps she should ask for a cricket bat or any blunt object with which to beat sense into her parent. Actually, it was far too late. She knew that . . . or she might have tried it. She was accounted to have a good swing. "Papa, did you lose the queen's tiara?"

"No! Not mine to lose." Magnus actually looked alarmed. "It belongs to *you*, who will be a duchess in her own right. Your mother wore it in her wedding portrait. Elizabeth herself would come back and haunt me if I wagered the tiara."

The queen's tiara had been given to one of Madeline's ancestors, a lady-in-waiting to Queen Elizabeth the First, for saving Elizabeth's life. Solid gold and encrusted with jewels, the tiara was worth a fortune in cash and sentiment, and the queen decreed that, regardless of their gender, the eldest child of the family would inherit the title. Thus, in the last two hundred and twenty-two years, there had been dukes of Magnus, of course. But there had also been three duchesses of Magnus—girls born first in the family and who were thus duchesses in their own right.

She couldn't help it. She had to ask. "Do you swear it's in the safe?"

He huffed. "I swear it's in the safe, and the dukes—and duchesses—of Magnus always keep their word."

She hadn't.

"Don't know how I got along without you

while you were gone, my dear." Magnus provided a brief pat on her arm. "What shall we do today? Good day for hunting. Or perhaps you'd like to ride into the village and visit your old governess, Mrs. Watting."

"Watling," Madeline corrected. "I'd like to hear more about this wager."

Sincerely puzzled, he asked, "What else is there to know?"

"Perhaps the name of my new . . . husband? Or am I to be a mistress?"

"Mistress?" Magnus harrumphed indignantly. "Good God, daughter, do you think me totally without prudence and sensibility?"

Madeline refrained from answering that.

"Of course you're not to be his mistress! Chap is to marry you, or nothing!"

"Such a relief." She marveled at her father's equanimity in the face of what was economic and social disaster. "Do I know him?"

"No. He's an American, or at least he hailed from the Colonies."

"I believe they've achieved their independence," Madeline said dryly.

Magnus dismissed that fact with an airy wave. "It'll never last. No, Knight's family originated here, and he arrived in London last year. Been making a name for himself in the clubs. Not popular, but I had to play him. Couldn't resist."

And that was the problem. Magnus couldn't resist any kind of gaming challenge.

Magnus frowned. "He has the devil's own luck

with the cards." He said nothing more, as if that settled every curiosity she might have.

If one were unacquainted with Magnus, one might have thought him a monster of parental disinterest. Madeline knew better. He loved her as best his shallow personality could love, but he lacked both an attention span and a sense of responsibility. Fortuitously, Madeline had always been a strong-willed female of unusual prudence. "Is he old, young, a professional gambler, a merchant?"

"Well. Not worthy of a duke's daughter and a duchess in her own right, but damned hard to find anyone worthy of *us*, isn't there? Even your mother, God rest her soul, was only the daughter of a marquess."

"So he is a . . . gentleman? Or as much of a gentleman as any American can be?"

"Unexceptional. Dresses well, coats by Worth, cloisonné snuffbox, keeps a townhouse in Berkeley Square, handsome, popular with the ladies." Magnus dabbed a bit of yolk off his mustache. "Got that damnable accent, but men respect him."

Madeline correctly interpreted the last comment. "He can use his fists."

"Boxes. Punishing left. Good defense. Punched the hell out of Oldfield, and Oldfield can fight."

Madeline finished her meal in silence, thinking hard all the while. She had no intention of marrying . . . anyone. Her one venture into romance had ended disastrously. Glancing up, she saw Magnus watching her with a worried frown.

"See here, Mad, if you really object to marrying this fellow, you don't have to. I have a scheme—"

Well acquainted with her father's schemes, which usually involved gambling and ensuing disaster, Madeline exclaimed, "Heavens, no!" Realizing she had been less than tactful, and possibly had waved the red flag at her bull of a father, she added, "I have a plan, too. I'm going to go to London and explain to Mr. Knight it would be ridiculous for us to wed."

Chapter Two

"It looks as if the Red Robin has disintegrated since last we stayed here." Miss Eleanor de Lacy, Madeline's companion—and cousin—said as she peered out of the luxurious, well-sprung coach. Her voice quavered.

March's promise of daylight had faded with the onset of ocean fog, and the light that shone from the inn's windows blurred in the mist. Men's voices blared from the open door. From what Madeline could see, the yard was awash with filth. Yet her coachman wasn't shouting imprecations at the post boys, so they must be handling the cattle well.

That was really all the mattered. That their horses be well cared for so they could travel on to London the next morning. "We might have made the trip in one day if we hadn't had such a late start."

"We needed to pack the proper clothing," Eleanor answered, serene in her conviction. "Mr. Knight will listen to a handsome lady with more favor than a hoyden, and that's what you would look like if we don't mind our business."

"I suppose," Madeline admitted grudgingly. Eleanor was the expert about all matters feminine.

At the age of twenty-four, Eleanor was pretty, much prettier than Madeline herself. With shining black hair, a porcelain complexion and languishing blue eyes, Eleanor looked like a princess out of a fairy tale. Madeline shared the black hair, but her skin was tanned from a careless disregard for her bonnet, and her blue eyes did not languish, they danced. Yet the cousins were reputed to look alike, especially when both were dressed in dark traveling costumes as they were tonight.

Unfortunately, an early life spent in grinding poverty, coupled with the loss of her mother and her father's unfortunate remarriage, had made Eleanor timid and uncertain of herself.

Yet Madeline loved her dearly. Patting Eleanor briskly on the shoulder, Madeline said, "Chin up, dear! Compare this to that smuggler's inn in Portugal." Madeline gave her hand to her footman and descended the step.

"Oh, definitely." Eleanor followed. "But we had no expectations of that inn."

"And our lack of expectations were met."

For one moment, in the doorway of that rundown inn, the two cousins exchanged a grin. What else could one do, when one remembered an agonizing night spent with bedbugs, knowing all the while that the French troops downstairs might decide to take English prisoners? Though the cousins were completely different personalities, they understood each other. After spending four years almost constantly in each other's company in some of the most dangerous conditions ever known to an Englishperson of either gender, they had found their already sturdy bonds strengthened.

Dickie Driscoll, Madeline's groom and the man who had escorted them throughout Europe, hurried to her side. "Looks rough, Miss Madeline."

"Yes, but it's too far to proceed and too dark, too." Madeline glanced back at the coach. She had come in full ducal splendor, with a well-sprung coach, outriders, two footmen, her father's best coachman—and Dickie. That would assure her safety. That, and the loaded pistol tucked in her black velvet reticule.

She patted him on the shoulder. "Take the lads, go around to the kitchen and get yourselves a hot meal. It's four hours to London. We'll get an early start."

The women stepped into the common room. A blast of song and the stench of unwashed bodies made Eleanor quail, but Madeline caught her by the arm and hauled her forward into the chamber.

Mr. Forsyth, the innkeeper, hurried toward them through a cloud of blue tobacco smoke. "M' lady." He bowed cursorily, and spoke rapidly, blocking the sight of them from the room. "How good t' see ye again after so many years! May I urge you t' go back t' our private parlor?"

"Yes, please." Madeline craned her neck and scanned the tables, crowded with men of the type she recognized from her travels. Rough men, mercenaries, who loved to fight, to drink, to whore.

"This way." With scarcely a pause, Mr. Forsyth snatched up a candle and led them down the narrow corridor.

He didn't want them to linger in the common room, and in Madeline's opinion, that showed good sense on his part. "You'll care for my people?"

"Indeed I will, ma'am. Ye can depend on me and the missus, just like always." He cast a harassed glance behind him. "*They* promise t' be gone in the morning, an' that's none too soon fer me. I've got me daughter hidden in our bedroom with the lock turned, and begging yer pardon, ma'am, not that I want t' tell a lady o' yer quality how to behave, but I'll ask that ye remain in the parlor and when ye've finished yer supper, go right to yer chamber by the back stairway an' lock the door tight."

"Are they guests who are none too welcome?" Eleanor ventured.

"It's not as if I could have turned them away, an' they're paying very well, but they've been here four days an' they've made a pigsty out o' everything." Flinging open the door, he stood back to allow the women to precede him.

A merry fire burned on the hearth, with a comfortable chair and a bench before it. If only Mrs. Forsyth set a good supper on the table, everything would be flawless.

"What do you mean, you couldn't have turned

them away?" Madeline prowled toward the fire, towing Eleanor with her.

"They came in early to work for Mr. Thurston Rumbelow, the gentleman who has rented Chalice Hall for the year. They're to make sure nothing goes wrong at the Game of the Century."

Madeline turned swiftly on Mr. Forsyth. "The Game of the Century? Whatever do you mean?"

"Haven't ye heard, m'lady?" Pleased with the chance to impart such juicy gossip, Mr. Forsyth said, "It's all the talk, so I've been told."

Grimly, Madeline answered, "I've been out of the country."

"Gambling! A magnificent game o' piquet. It's exclusive. The players are allowed in by invitation only, an' must pay ten thousand pounds' ante. Everyone who is great an' who games is coming. Ambassadors, merchants, exiled French noblemen—rumor says even the highest of English noblemen! I suspect the prince himself, but others say different."

The highest of English nobleman? The prince was royalty, not nobility. The highest title for an English nobleman was that of duke, and dukes were rare indeed. There were Prinney's brothers, and a few ancient titles scattered about the country—and Madeline's father's, the duke of Magnus. Her heart sank. Worse, her father had said he had a scheme to rescue her from Mr. Knight. . . .

Well aware of Madeline's consternation, Eleanor helped Madeline remove her cloak, hat and gloves and said, "Mr. Forsyth, I'm not familiar with this Mr. Rumbelow."

Mr. Forsyth lit a branch of candles as he chatted merrily on. "Mr. Rumbelow is a rich gentleman—well, ye know he must have a fortune to lease Chalice Hall. 'Tis the largest house in the district!"

"But who are his people?" Madeline seated herself. "Where does he come from?"

"Quite the mystery, is Mr. Rumbelow." Mr. Forsyth stirred up the fire. "But a generous gentleman with the blunt. He's spared no expense for this party, laying in barrels of ale and wine, and buying through the local merchants instead of sending to London. He's hired village lasses to help the resident staff clean the hall—been a couple of years since it's been leased—and although I'm not happy with these men he's lodged here, he's making good—and some—on the damage they do."

"An enigmatic gentleman charges ten thousand pounds to enter a game at his house, and without knowing who he is, the gamblers are willing to pay him, and trust him to hold their ante safe." Madeline smiled with sphinxlike superiority. "I will never understand a gambler's faith in honor."

Mr. Forsyth looked disconcerted. Like every other man in the world, he wanted the fable of easy money to be true. "Well . . . but . . . he's invited the families, too."

Taken aback, Madeline said, "Really?"

"Aye, the wives and the daughters and sons. He's promised them entertainment, hunting and dancing. The orchestra is coming on tomorrow's post. 'Twill be a real house party, one like we've not seen here fer too many years." Mr. Forsyth offered a tentative grin.

Madeline had made him worry, and he was not to blame for her difficulties. "A good thing, then. What has Mrs. Forsyth prepared for dinner?"

Obviously relieved, Mr. Forsyth said, " 'Tis not fancy, fer we are feeding the great mob out there, but still a fine lamb stew with a white bread and a wheel of Stilton. Will ye have mulled wine?"

"Yes, thank you." Madeline waited until Mr. Forsyth had bowed his way out before leaping to her feet and pacing across the room. "The nobleman is Papa!"

In her most comforting manner, Eleanor said, "Now, Maddie, you don't know that."

"Who else can it be?"

"Someone else, for where would Magnus get ten thousand pounds?"

"Papa told me he had a scheme to remedy matters. All he knows how to do is gamble."

"And break your heart," Eleanor said in a low voice.

Madeline lifted her eyebrows. Eleanor seldom spoke her mind, and never had she indicated anything but the greatest of respect for Magnus. In a humorous tone, Madeline said, "A bit melodramatic, I think."

"Perhaps, but that's only because he hurt you so much in the past with his indifference. You're like a turtle, who sticks your head out only when it's safe."

Torn between amazement and astonishment, Madeline asked, "Are you calling me a coward?"

"Only about love, dear cousin." Eleanor bit her lip. "But I do beg your pardon. I had no right to speak so about your father. He has been most kind in allowing you to keep me with you for so many years." Her indignation broke forth again. "But—to wager you away! For shame!"

"You didn't say that to him, did you?" At Eleanor's guilty expression, Madeline said, "Oh, no. He'll consider that a challenge, too! Of course he'll be at the game of the century." She hardly knew what to think about Eleanor's accusation of cowardice. She hadn't thought herself protected against love. Why, only four years ago she had given herself wholeheartedly to a man reputed to be a fortune hunter. Surely that qualified as an act of courage.

Yet Madeline experienced a prickle of self-consciousness, and why would she feel that way unless Eleanor's accusation was true?

"Forget what I said," Eleanor begged. "I had no right to speak so about you."

"I have forgotten already." Or Madeline would, if she didn't know Eleanor had spoken from a depth of caring that went beyond the bonds of mere kinship. They were closer than sisters, for they could depend only on each other. Now Madeline realized she didn't comprehend the depths of Eleanor's mind.

Dimly they could hear the rumpus from the common room. "Who is this Mr. Rumbelow, and why must he hire such ruffians to patrol his party?" Madeline asked.

"I don't know, but perhaps he's respectable." Eleanor spread both of their cloaks before the fire.

"So many gamblers are—until they lose everything and have to flee their debtors." Madeline passed a restless hand over her hair. "I wonder if I shall be among them."

Putting her hands on her hips, Eleanor said, "Lord Campion could help us."

Madeline caught her breath to hear his name spoken aloud. "No."

With a doggedness rare for Eleanor, she said, "I always thought he would come after you."

"He didn't."

"He couldn't. Napoleon's blockade cut us off—"

"You always liked him." That sounded like an accusation.

"Yes, I liked him. He was kind." Eleanor's eyes flashed in a rare temper. "But *you* loved him!"

"Not anymore. Why are we talking about Gabriel?" With an assumption of cheerfulness, Madeline said, "For all I know he's married with three children and another on the way."

"No." Eleanor sounded very sure.

No. Madeline didn't believe so, either, perhaps only because she couldn't stand to imagine such a thing.

With uncharacteristic frankness, Eleanor said, "Every time I walked in on you two, you were kissing and . . . Maddie, I feared for your virtue!"

Madeline winced.

"You wanted him so much, whenever you two were together I could almost smell"—Eleanor waved a hand in vague circles—"passion in the air."

Madeline tried a feeble jest. "What do you know about passion?"

"I know I'm a stick and a prude, but I hated being your companion then. I was your chaperone, and you were always sending me off on some ridiculous errand so you could sneak off into the gardens and . . . kiss." Eleanor raised a defiant chin. "And a great deal of other activities, I fear."

Remorseful, for Eleanor had never expressed such reservations, Madeline said, "I beg your pardon, it was too bad of me to be so careless of you."

"I'm not looking for an apology, I'm telling you why I think you should find Lord Campion and ask his help!"

"No." Eleanor didn't know all the truth, or she wouldn't urge such a course. "I can't ask him for anything. We must wish him well."

"I do."

"And handle the situation ourselves." Thinking of Gabriel would avail her nothing. Leaning her hands on the table, Madeline stared into the fire. "Papa has to ante up ten thousand dollars or its equivalent, and he's retained only one thing."

Eleanor's composure faltered. "The queen's tiara."

"My mother made him vow he would retain that." Madeline placed her hand over her aching heart. "I can't let him wager that away. I can't."

"No. Of course you can't." Eleanor's support

was swift and resolute. She perched on the bench and declared, "We shall do something to prevent him."

"Yes." Madeline's mind skittered from plan to plan. "But Mr. Remington Knight is waiting, and he'll cause a scandal if I don't show up at the proper time."

"Will you be able to convince him of the foolishness of this marriage?"

"I'm very persuasive and it would be craven not to try."

"I . . . I could travel on without you and make your excuses."

Madeline knew how Eleanor hated traveling on her own. Eleanor hated meeting new people. Most of all, she hated tirades, and she comprehended how likely it was that Mr. Knight would stage just such a scene. With sincere admiration, she said, "That's very brave of you, but I may have to . . ." Inspiration blazed suddenly; she straightened so quickly, she almost snapped her corset strings. "No! No, that's not at all what you'll do!"

"I think I must." Eleanor straightened her shoulders. "I promise to do my best by you in this mission. You've done so much for me over the years."

"I'm about to do more." Madeline could scarcely breathe from excitement. "I'm about to make you a duchess."

Chapter Three

Slowly, Eleanor rose. "Wh-what?"

"You shall go to London in my place—as me."

Eleanor stumbled backward and almost fell over the bench. "Claim I'm you—Madeline de Lacy—to the very man who would wed you? That's impossible! What would that accomplish? I couldn't!"

"Yes, you could." Madeline enthusiastically embraced Eleanor. "We look alike, and I haven't been in society for almost four years."

"And I have never been in society, and don't have the pluck to carry off such a masquerade," Eleanor retorted.

"All you'd have to do is hold Mr. Knight off for a few days until I can dissuade Papa from this wild scheme." Madeline could see she wasn't convincing Eleanor, and she *needed* to persuade her cousin. "You would be a wonderful duchess. Your manners are impeccable, much better than mine."

"I'm a dreadful coward," Eleanor countered. "I can't talk to men."

"Nonsense. All you lack is a little practice."

"Practice? When I must speak to a man, I stammer and stutter. And since Mr. Knight thinks you're getting married, he might . . . flirt."

"He might do a great deal more than that." Madeline caught Eleanor's wrist as she tried to get away. "I'm teasing! All you have to do is bat those big blue eyes at him and you can wind him around your little finger."

"Now who's being ridiculous?" Eleanor sighed. "When you come to London, will you announce it was all a jest? Mr. Knight will be insulted and infuriated."

"Not as insulted and infuriated as if I don't show up. It will be good for you to have an adventure."

Eleanor twisted her long fingers. "I wouldn't know what to do."

Bracingly, Madeline said, "Whenever you are in doubt, you think, *What would Madeline do in this situation?* And do it."

"I can't . . . and what if someone from the gambling party met you, left, came to London, and identified me as an imposter?"

"Identified *me* as an imposter, you mean. I'll send you in the coach with Dickie Driscoll and the servants. You'll be splendid!"

"Dickie Driscoll won't do it."

"Dickie Drisoll will do as he's told."

"My clothes aren't appropriate."

In this, at least, Eleanor was right. She wore gowns of modest cut and cloth, in dark, matronly colors. Not because Madeline demanded such humility from her companion, oh, no! But because Eleanor insisted such clothing was "suitable."

Seeing Madeline's hesitation, Eleanor pressed her point. "You must admit such an action is impossible. It would be best if you quietly sneaked into Chalice Hall, dissuaded your father from his mad wager, while I go to London to explain to Mr. Knight why you are late."

"You're right. It is imprudent to take the chance that someone would report me in two places. Mr. Knight will more likely forgive us our deception if he isn't made to look a fool in front of everyone. We're the same size." Both five-foot-seven, both slender and well formed. "You'll take my clothes, I'll take yours. I'll go to Chalice Hall. I'll get myself hired on as a servant of some kind. It's a perfect disguise, for no one ever looks at the servants."

In a tone of patient exasperation, Eleanor said, "I have been your companion of five years, and in those five years, you have involved me in a lot of mad schemes, but this one is the most outrageous. I *cannot* be a duchess, and you most certainly cannot be a servant."

"What?" On her mettle now, Madeline asked, "How hard can it be to be a companion?"

"Not hard at all, if one has the habit of being modest and self-effacing." Eleanor seated herself on the bench. "If one is not prompted to give one's opinion on every subject. If one is not moved to arrange things and people, if one is not given to the habit of command!"

Madeline stood over the top of her. "Are you saying I'm officious?"

"Dear cousin, you understand me at last!"

The worst part was—Eleanor wasn't being mean. She was giving an honest reading of Madeline's character, and she expected Madeline to accept it.

But Madeline would not. "I *can* be a servant."

At once Eleanor realized her mistake. "I wasn't trying to challenge you!"

"But you did! I know I occasionally have an imperious manner—"

Eleanor lowered her head to hide—unsuccessfully—her grin of genuine amusement.

"But I'm not obnoxious."

"I didn't mean that you were! Only . . . for the kindest of reasons, you are sometimes . . . managing."

Madeline stiffened. Gabriel had said that. Said it in a low, dreadful voice. He'd said she needed to have respect for others' opinions, others' abilities. He said she rampaged over the top of people's feelings without consideration. But it wasn't true. It wasn't!

"I suspect, with the right staff, you could organize the world." Catching a glimpse of Madeline's face, Eleanor cried, "What's wrong?"

"Nothing. There's nothing wrong." Except Madeline had thought her heart had healed, and she found being in England, knowing Gabriel was on the same island, accessible with only a day's travel, made her sensitive. Made her remember.

"You look pale and . . ." Eleanor put her palm on Madeline's forehead. "You haven't got a fever. You're tired. We should have rested for one more day."

"Don't fuss, Ellie. I'm fine." They had traveled farther and harder these last three years, but somehow having had such a brief homecoming had thrown them off balance. Yes, that had to be it. For no other reason would Madeline, on her first night home, have had a dream of Gabriel. "So it's settled. I'll be a companion, and you'll be the duchess."

"No," Eleanor said in an agony of denial. "No, please, Madeline!"

From the corridor, they heard the sound of voices. A woman's and Mr. Forsyth's, speaking at once.

Content to cut off the discussion, Madeline stood. "It sounds like other guests too genteel for the taproom. We're going to be asked to share our parlor." She teased, "Will you let me manage this, cousin?"

"Please." Eleanor rose.

Mr. Forsyth flung open the door, and a fashionably dressed, middle-aged female pushed him aside and swept in. In a voice both shrill and demanding, she said, "I am Lady Tabard, wife of the earl of Tabard. I apologize for invading your privacy, but the common room is just *too* common. I trust you don't mind if my daughter and I share your parlor?"

Without hesitation, Madeline curtsied. "This is the marchioness of Sheridan and the future duchess of Magnus."

"Oh . . . my." Lady Tabard's eyes rounded, and her hand fluttered to her chest.

With satisfaction, Madeline noted that Lady Tabard was impressed and would render to Eleanor the proper respect. "Her Ladyship would be pleased to have your company." She turned an excessively innocent gaze on Eleanor. "Wouldn't you, Lady Eleanor?"

Eleanor looked reproachfully at Madeline.

Lady Tabard gestured into the corridor and in that penetrating voice commanded, "Come on, girl, come on, let us get a look at you!"

The daughter stepped in. A diamond of the first water, Lord Magnus would have called her, and he would have been right. She was no more than eighteen, petite, blond, and blessed with a fla-grant beauty that put Eleanor and Madeline in the shade. Yet her shoulders slumped and her com-plexion was gray with weariness.

Eleanor looked again at Madeline, who mouthed, *What would I do?*

While Madeline watched with interest, Eleanor visibly struggled before at last, as always, she gave way to Madeline's stronger will. "Mr. Forsyth is bringing us supper." Eleanor indicated the table. "Join us."

"Mr. Forsyth!" Madeline called.

Stepping inside, Mr. Forsyth bowed stiffly to-ward Madeline. "I apologize, m' lady."

"No apology needed," Madeline said gaily. "Would you set two more places?"

"Aye, as *ye* command." With a single irritated glance at Lady Tabard's back, he hurried off to finish preparing their supper.

"What a vulgar man. And to not wait and help me with my garments!" Tossing her cloak on a chair, Lady Tabard revealed a well-upholstered figure in a gold-sprigged muslin gown with a wrapping front. Her hair was fashionably cropped around her face, and Madeline thought the profoundly black color to be suspicious. *Shoe polish or soot?* Or some dreadful chemical that stank and corroded the skin? Lady Tabard's straight and narrow nose quivered as she considered her surroundings, her nostrils flaring in fine disdain. Her lips were so undersized as to be nonexistent, and the opening of her mouth was tight and small, lending her a smug expression.

Lady Tabard indicated the young lady who was slowly removing her bonnet. "Lady Eleanor—or should I call you Your Grace?"

Madeline quickly intervened. "The duchess is called by both names."

It was true. Because of Madeline's unique position of being a duchess in her own right, members of the *ton* frequently addressed her as Your Grace. Sometimes they did so in flattery, sometimes in respect, and sometimes in sarcasm, although she swore she wouldn't think of Gabriel again today.

"Well, then, Your Grace"—Lady Tabard was

clearly one of the flatterers—"may I introduce my stepdaughter, Lady Thomasin Charlford?"

Eleanor started, then did the honors. "A pleasure to meet you, Lady Thomasin, and I'm pleased to introduce my companion and cousin—"

"Madeline de Lacy." Madeline saw no reason to abandon her first name. She had barely been into her first season when she made such a fool of herself, and the *ton*, of course, had always addressed her by her title. Besides, she would wager not one of them would recognize her now with her modish hairstyle and the tan she'd acquired during travel.

Lady Tabard gave a brief nod that both acknowledged and dismissed her. "It is so hard to get good help these days."

It took Madeline a moment to comprehend Lady Tabard spoke of her, in front of her. What did the woman mean? How dare she discuss Madeline that way? True, Madeline had taken charge, but Lady Tabard didn't comprehend the circumstances.

In blatant imitation of Madeline's voice and manner, Eleanor agreed. "It is impossible, but Madeline is my cousin, so of course I keep her on. I find it lends me consequence to have one of my own family waiting on me."

Madeline bit hard on her lip to refrain from laughing. As if she'd ever needed anyone to lend her consequence. Yes, Eleanor would punish her for putting her in such an awkward position.

Eleanor added, "The de Lacys are incredibly noble, you see."

"Really?" Lady Tabard moved into the room and appropriated the most comfortable chair closest to the fire. "I don't recall the family."

The female had definitely married into her title if she didn't know the de Lacys. Everyone knew the de Lacys—just as everyone knew one didn't sit down before a marchioness and future duchess.

Certainly Lady Thomasin Charlford knew, and winced at her stepmother's *faux pas*.

Going to the fire, Madeline dusted the settee with her handkerchief. In a meek tone quite unlike her own, she asked, "Lady Eleanor, won't you be seated?"

Grandly, Eleanor swept forward and seated herself with a flourish to equal Lady Tabard's. "The de Lacy family came over with the Conqueror."

On her mettle, Lady Tabard answered, "My husband's family served as chancellor to some king or another."

"Horsemaster," Thomasin said. "To King Charles the Second."

Swelling like a toad, Lady Tabard turned on her stepdaughter, who still stood near the door. "Did I ask you, my girl? Lady Eleanor doesn't care what our family did."

Thomasin didn't move. Didn't lift her gaze.

Didn't apologize.

Madeline thought she now had Lady Tabard's measure—and perhaps her daughter's, also.

Madeline also knew how Eleanor hated rudeness, and wasn't surprised when Eleanor hastily said, "Madeline is a wonder with hairdressing."

"Really?" Lady Tabard darted a glance at Eleanor's neat coiffure with its discreet curls around her face and the elegant upsweep of long hair in the back. "Yes, I see."

"Madeline always knows next year's style three months before it's *au courant*."

Lady Tabard sniffed as she openly examined Eleanor's gown. "Are dark colors in, then, for unmarried young ladies?"

"For travel." Getting the bit in her teeth, Eleanor embroidered on the tale. "I'm afraid I am quite a trial for dear Madeline. She wishes to dress me in the newest styles, but I prefer comfortable clothing."

It was a source of dissension between the cousins that Madeline preferred comfort over style, and Eleanor cast her a glance brimful of mischief.

"Lady Tabard cannot be in accord with you," Madeline said, "for she's dressed in the height of fashion."

Her tiny lips upswept in a condescending smile, Lady Tabard smoothed her skirt. "Yes, I am." She examined Madeline as she might a horse she was considering buying. "I select all of Thomasin's gowns, too, but keep them simple. Poor child, she hasn't the panache to carry off true elegance."

That statement was so blatantly untrue both Madeline and Eleanor turned to Thomasin. The girl had the crystal-clear skin and softly rounded cheeks of a baby's. Her mouth was a soft pink bow, her eyes as wide and brown as a woodland creature's. Her blond hair was done in the same style as her stepmother's, but on her the look was ethereal. Madeline could read nothing in her blank stare—Thomasin guarded her thoughts well.

With her heavy hand on the arm of the chair, Lady Tabard shifted uncomfortably. "Well, well, girl, don't stand there gawking. Sit down!"

"Yes, Mother." Thomasin sidled forward and seated herself on the bench.

Lady Tabard confided loud enough for everyone to hear, "I married her father, the earl of Tabard, a mere three years ago, and still she is impertinent." She nodded, obviously pleased with herself for injecting her husband's title into the conversation. "He sent us on ahead to rest before the party starts."

Madeline leaned forward. "The party?" They were going to the party?

Lady Tabard flicked her an ill-favored glance, but spoke to Eleanor. "You're young, Your Grace, so perhaps you'll allow me to give you a piece of advice. Companions, no matter how closely related, should be seen and not heard."

She didn't lower her voice, and Madeline flushed. She began to see why Eleanor said she wouldn't do well as a servant, for she longed to box Lady Tabard's ears.

Eleanor eyed her. "What party is that, Lady Tabard?"

"Why, a party at Mr. Rumbelow's!" Lady Tabard smacked her narrow lips. "He is quite the wealthy gentleman, you know."

"I've been out of the country," Eleanor said.

"He is most generous and most handsome, and very much the bachelor." Lady Tabard's narrow eyes narrowed on her stepdaughter. "He gives the best parties in London, and he has rented Chalice Hall especially to make a splash."

Madeline longed to lead the questioning, and at Eleanor's languid inquiry, she almost twitched with anticipation.

"Where did he come from? He wasn't in society when I left."

"He arrived at the beginning of the year, from South Africa, I think. Or India. I never can keep them apart. But never mind that! Ever since he came, the routs we have had! The parties, the balls!" Lady Tabard clasped her hands over her large bosom. "He has quite singled out my little Thomasin for his attentions, and we are coming to the party to fix his attentions."

Thomasin stared at the door as if hoping some miracle would release her from the purgatory of her stepmother's voice.

Indeed, there was a sharp rap of knuckles.

Thomasin started to her feet.

The door swung open to reveal Mrs. Forsyth and the scullery maid, both weighed down with dinner and its accoutrements. In moments they had set the table, placed the tureen of stew in the middle, the stout loaf of bread, the wheel of Stilton and the mulled wine.

Lady Tabard inspected the table from her seat. "I must protest, this is poor fare for nobility, poor fare indeed."

"But as good as a feast in circumstances such as these," Eleanor interposed. "We thank you, Mrs. Forsyth. We'll call if we need anything more."

Mrs. Forsyth bobbed a grateful curtsy to Madeline, half of a curtsy to Lady Tabard, and as she beat a hasty retreat, she cast a sympathetic glance toward Thomasin.

Lady Tabard heaved herself out of the chair. The cousins cast each other an amused glance as Lady Tabard tried to decide where the head of a round table would be. At last she settled herself at the place closest to the tureen.

Thomasin took the seat at Lady Tabard's left hand, which surprised Madeline. She had thought the girl would sit as far away from her stepmother as possible. But perhaps it was better if they didn't see each other. Madeline remembered to hold Eleanor's chair, and took the seat farthest from the fire.

"Mr. Forsyth gave us to understand the party entertainment was to be a grand piquet game."

"Indeed it is, Lady Eleanor. By invitation only, ten thousand pounds apiece for ante. Only a select few get to play. Oh, it is an honor that we have been selected. An honor, indeed. One we will take advantage of, eh, Thomasin?" Lady Tabard patted

Thomasin's hand, but it looked more like a stricture than a gesture of affection. "We haven't had luck with our companions, but then, they've not been from such a good family as yours, Lady Eleanor."

"I have been fortunate." Eleanor looked meaningfully at Madeline. "Few companions would have stayed with me as I racketed about Europe, being chased by Napoleon's army, sleeping in flea-infested inns, drinking brackish water, almost dying in Italy of a fever."

Madeline watched in awe as Eleanor opened like a flower beneath the demands of conversation.

"Yes," Eleanor continued, "the duchess of Magnus counts herself lucky to have such a wonderful companion."

Later that night, Madeline discovered exactly how persuasive Eleanor had been.

"What do you mean, Lady Tabard hired you to be Thomasin's companion?" Eleanor's tone held sheer, sharp panic—and she was loud.

"Shhh." Madeline glanced around the narrow upstairs corridor, and in a low voice said, "You sold her on my services. You said I did wonderful hair."

Eleanor whispered frantically, "The only time you tried to use a curling iron, you singed your forehead."

"You said I knew everything about fashion."

"You pay no attention to style. You depend totally on my advice."

"I know that. But she doesn't!"

"They brought a lady's maid!"

"But Lady Tabard does not wish to share her lady's maid, not when she can hire a companion from an important family and have the cousin of the duchess of Magnus at her daughter's beck and call." Madeline grinned at Eleanor's dismay. "Imagine how impressed her friends will be!"

"You are doomed to failure!" Eleanor predicted.

"I only have to manage for a day or two, until Papa shows up. I want to retrieve Papa before he can gamble away . . . everything." That, she knew, Eleanor would understand. Madeline steered her down the stairs. "When compelled to perform socially, you acquit yourself admirably. Last night, as I watched your behavior when you had been proclaimed duchess, I realized that perhaps I'd done you a disservice by forcing you to stay always in my shadow."

Eleanor jerked her arm free. "You did not force me, I prefer it!"

Madeline pressed relentlessly on. "This turn of events is nothing less than fate. I'm to be Thomasin's companion. Reading between the lines of Lady Tabard's constant presumption and incredible rudeness, I gathered the tale of Thomasin."

"Poor girl," Eleanor muttered.

"Yes. Thomasin's beautiful, she's wellborn—apparently her real mother was the daughter of the Grevilles of Yorkshire—she comes with an impressive dowry, and she is the season's biggest wallflower. She won't make a push to secure a man's interest."

It was easy to touch Eleanor's soft heart. "Of course not, poor thing! If she secures someone's interest, then they're going to have to deal with Lady Tabard."

"Quite. Lady Tabard's father was in trade."

"That's no excuse."

They stepped outside into the morning fog. There the Magnus equipage waited, footmen in place, coachmen controlling the restive horses, and Dickie climbing down from the groom's box, his mouth puckered and disapproving.

"Thomasin's stepmama is in despair, and that's the real reason they are here for the game. They have great hopes of snagging the biggest prize of all, Mr. Rumbelow."

"I am coming to hate his name."

"I've explained everything to Dickie Driscoll."

Eleanor appealed to Dickie. "Surely you don't approve."

"That I do na', miss, but m' lady is as stubborn as Joann the auld donkey aboot this."

"That's right," Madeline spoke to them both. "Dickie knows if there is any problem with Mr. Knight, he's to whisk you away." Madeline pushed Eleanor up the stairs into the coach. "I'm going to the game as Lady Thomasin's companion. You're going to London to meet Mr. Knight. Don't worry, dear. You'll have a grand adventure! What can possibly go wrong?"

Chapter Four

"Miss de Lacy!"

Madeline realized she was being addressed, and in a tone that indicated disapproval and reprimand.

Lady Tabard stared into the traveling coach, her rabbity nose quivering with indignation. "Miss de Lacy, I do not know what kind of tricks you were apt to play on the duchess in the name of family, but you'll find I'm not as gullible as she. *Thomasin and I* will ride forward."

Madeline gazed around at the luxuriously appointed coach, with its velvet curtains and its leather seats, and said, "Oh." Of course. For the first time in her life, the duchess of Magnus would take the backward seat. "My apologies, Lady Tabard." She moved quickly, tucking in her toes as Lady Tabard shoved her way in.

Thomasin followed, the door was shut, and Madeline jolted forward as the coachman sprang the horses.

Lady Tabard eyed Madeline evilly. "In the future, please remember I am to enter the coach first."

"Of course you should." Madeline felt foolish, and that was a sentiment almost unknown to her.

"And about that gown . . ."

Madeline looked down at the sky-blue muslin skirt. It was Eleanor's, and the plain, modest style she favored, so Madeline couldn't imagine Lady Tabard's objection. "Yes?"

"It makes your eyes look so excessively blue, it's almost vulgar. When you accompany Lady Thomasin, you'll wear something else."

"When I'm with Lady Thomasin, no one will even notice me. She is very beautiful." Without an ounce of vanity, Madeline smiled at Thomasin.

In the watery morning light, framed by a simple straw bonnet, Thomasin's face looked even prettier. Yet she didn't smile back. She turned her head and looked out of the window at the passing woods.

So Thomasin wasn't vain. But she was, obviously, unhappy—and unsociable.

Madeline resolved to make friends.

"Nevertheless, Miss de Lacy, you'll do as I demand."

Madeline returned her attention to Lady Tabard, wondering if Lady Tabard was the root of all Thomasin's discontent, or if some deeper sadness weighed on her. "I'll try, my lady, but my wardrobe is not extensive"—she had sent most of

Eleanor's clothes on with Eleanor—"and I will be forced to rely on this gown occasionally."

"When we return to London, I'll replace it with something more appropriate for a companion." Lady Tabard studied Madeline. "A brown, I think, or rust."

Both colors guaranteed to make Madeline's complexion turn sallow.

"Look!" Lady Tabard pointed. "There's the lake. We must be getting close to Chalice Hall."

The park was extensive, not well tended, but with that ruggedness one expected of an estate close to the Channel, exposed to the winds and storms that battered the coast. To rent such a place took a great deal of money, indeed, and Madeline inquired, "Who *is* Mr. Rumbelow?" When Lady Tabard bent her disapproving gaze on her, she realized that Lady Tabard must think her impertinent, and added, "Her Grace didn't recognize his name."

Apparently, the mention of the duchess made Madeline's inquiry acceptable. "Mr. Rumbelow ..." Lady Tabard clasped her hands at her chest and beamed. "A very wealthy man of unexceptional background."

"Indeed? What background is that?"

"He is from the Lake District, where his family has lived for years. Good stock, the descendants of one of the late king's knights." Lady Tabard nudged Thomasin. "Which king?"

In a toneless voice, Thomasin said, "Henry the Seventh."

Madeline was unconvinced. The Lake District was—had been—a wild place of mountains and rivers, and the families who lived there had been set apart by the natural barriers that made it difficult for them to travel. It would be easy for a man to claim a family background he didn't possess, and if he had wealth, or the appearance of wealth, no one would ever check.

Lady Tabard continued, "Unfortunately, the family fortunes took a downturn, and it was up to Mr. Rumbelow to rescue them. He has done an incomparable job."

As they rounded a bend, Madeline caught a glimpse of the large manor. "So it would appear."

Both Madeline and Thomasin craned their necks to see—and both of them sat back at once.

Chalice Hall looked as if the architect had been intoxicated during the planning, then in a subsequent fit of sobriety tried frantically to fix his mistakes. The three-story house of pale pink stone glowed in the sunlight like a dog's tongue, with a rounded tower on each corner and the occasional random balcony to offset any hint of refinement. A staggering combination of minarets and cupolas capped the edifice. For some reason—pretension, perhaps—gargoyles sneered from every corner and crevice.

Madeline laughed out loud at the absurdity, earning her a sharp glance from Lady Tabard. "It's so ludicrous," Madeline tried to explain. "A monument to bad taste."

Lady Tabard drew herself up. "I hardly think you're in the position to judge your betters."

"Mother, she did just return from four years on the Continent," Thomasin dared to say. "And she's a de Lacy."

So Thomasin did speak without being prodded. And to defend Madeline, too. How lovely. Madeline smiled at her again.

Again Thomasin turned her face to look outside.

"Obviously Her Grace benefited from the experience. She has that air of regality that assures one of her superior taste." Lady Tabard bent a frown on Madeline. "But I doubt if the lesser members of the de Lacy family are blessed with her capacity for culture."

"Her Grace is excessively cultured," Madeline agreed pleasantly and with a fair amount of irony.

"Are you saying I'm not?" Lady Tabard drew herself up.

Madeline blinked at the unexpected attack. "It hadn't occurred to me to say such a thing."

Lady Tabard charged on. "Because I've long been of the opinion that culture in a woman is unseemly. Before you know it, a woman begins to read, to reason, to imagine herself the equal of a man, and there is nothing more unattractive than a female with pretensions toward intelligence."

Madeline stared, trying desperately to gather her composure. At last she managed, "I think you may feel safe in that matter, my lady."

"I would hope so!" Lady Tabard turned at Thomasin's sudden fit of snorting and coughing. "Do *not* get ill, my dear, for you have a party to attend."

Thomasin, her mouth covered by her gloved hand, nodded vigorously, and for the first time met Madeline's eyes with her own brimful of amusement.

So. Thomasin was quick-witted, at least as long as the wit was turned against her stepmother.

When the coughing had subsided, Lady Tabard turned Thomasin's face toward her own and, while Thomasin sat docilely, pinched the girl's cheeks until they glowed. "It looks as if we're the first ones here, Thomasin, so cast off that eternal melancholy and capture Mr. Rumbelow's attention at once!"

As they stepped out of the coach, the rough men from the inn were very much in evidence, holding the horses' heads, removing the luggage from the back, and looking rather more threatening than most servants Madeline had ever seen. She stared at the man who directed the operations, memorizing his features. Dark, greasy hair hung lankly about his narrow face, his nose was blunt and red, as if he'd run into too many walls and smashed the end. He stared back at her, examining her with a freedom that bordered on insolence. But then—he thought her a servant.

As she watched, he spit a long stream of brown tobacco at the ground, splattering two of the other men. Both of the ill-featured fellows cursed, and one raised a threatening fist.

The leader looked at him. Just looked at him.

The fist dropped, and the fellow returned to his duties.

With a harrumph, Lady Tabard said, "I shall speak to Mr. Rumbelow about his hostlers. Such language is unfit for a lady's ears!"

As the baggage coach containing Lady Tabard's lady's maid rumbled up, the wide, heavy red-painted door was flung open, and a well-built gentleman of an unusually handsome, open countenance stepped out. "Lady Tabard! I'm so pleased that you've come."

His blond hair glowed in the sunlight, giving him a golden halo. Dark lashes surrounded his blue eyes, setting off the color like sapphires on black velvet. His teeth were white, and a well-trimmed blond mustache decorated his upper lip.

Taking Lady Tabard's gloved hand in his, he bowed and kissed her knuckles, watching her with all of his attention. Only when she had blushed did he release her and turn to Thomasin. "Dear Lady Thomasin, I had hoped you would be here early. I depend on your graciousness to make the other girls feel at ease."

Thomasin blushed, too, and smiled back. "Of course, I'd be happy to help in any way," she mumbled. As soon as he turned toward Madeline, Thomasin's color faded and she watched him with what Madeline thought was resentment, or perhaps disdain.

But she had no time to ponder Thomasin's reaction, for Mr. Rumbelow took her hand. He wasn't as tall as she had first thought. No taller than she was, really, but stockily built with broad shoulders and beefy arms.

"Please, Lady Tabard, introduce me so that I may greet my unexpected guest." He smiled down at Madeline with such charm, an unanticipated thrill ran up her spine.

"That young lady is Madeline de Lacy of the Suffolk de Lacys. She is Thomasin's companion and lady's maid." Lady Tabard flicked Madeline a glance designed to depress any pretensions she might have.

But Madeline couldn't spare Lady Tabard notice. She was too caught up in the unwavering fascination of Mr. Rumbelow's smile.

"Welcome, Miss de Lacy, I'm sure your presence will greatly add to Lady Thomasin's enjoyment of our little gathering."

He didn't kiss her hand, but he didn't have to. She reveled in his interest, fixed on her as firmly as it had been on Lady Tabard and on Thomasin. A seductive thing, a man's attention. Most women never received more than a fraction of it, yet Mr. Rumbelow lavished attention like an Italian gigolo.

His eyes widened as if he'd seen something in her face that surprised him, and he smiled like a man amused by developments.

She didn't care to amuse him, for what could he have to be amused about?

Returning to Lady Tabard, he offered his arm. "Come into my temporary abode. It is not so fine as you're used to."

Madeline cast a glance up at the hideous dwelling. Not what *she* was used to, anyway. The house did not improve on closer inspection.

"But I trust you'll enjoy your stay here." Mr. Rumbelow led Lady Tabard toward the house. "Is your husband close behind you?"

Thomasin fell in behind Lady Tabard. Madeline fell in behind her, and she watched Mr. Rumbelow with a keen eye.

Under the force of his allure, she had to struggle to remember that a man who was clean and handsome was not necessarily good.

Not that, four years ago, she'd been fooled by such a gentlemanly facade. No, she had been fooled by something much more primal.

Gabriel had been neither handsome nor charming, but rather a dark, scruffy man-beast who cared nothing for appearance and little for courtesy.

Yet he had captured her interest from the first moment she'd laid eyes on him. La! He had captured every woman's interest. He had an air about him that claimed a woman's attention, a scent that made her move closer, changeable green eyes that seized a woman's gaze and held it until he chose to release it. When he walked . . . oh, my. He strolled, hips swaying in a way both sleek and predatory. His hands: broad-palmed, with long, dexterous fingers that bespoke a skill in cards, in fighting . . . in loving. His shoulders, wide and providing the illusion of shelter.

No, he hadn't had to bother with charm. He had only to tilt his chin toward her, and she had followed him like a lapdog.

How the memory of that humiliated her.

She had dreamed about him again last night. In her dream, she hadn't remembered humiliation. In her dream, she had recognized him and her body had grown soft and damp with longing. In her dream, he had done all those things to her he had once done, teasing her, taking her almost to the edge . . . then beyond. She woke only when her body spasmed in orgasm.

Bitterly, she had stared into the dark and wondered if she would ever truly get over him. Since her return to England, his spirit hovered close, waiting to pounce on her, to carry her away to that place of quiet whispers and rich passion.

But not love. He had never loved her, or he wouldn't have betrayed her so decisively.

"Miss de Lacy, you will listen!"

Lady Tabard's shrill voice brought Madeline back to the present. "My lady?"

"Accompany our luggage upstairs and see to it that our things are properly dealt with."

"Yes, my lady." Madeline remembered to curtsy, wondering why couldn't Lady Tabard's maid carry out all necessary functions.

Mr. Rumbelow interfered. "Please! Lady

Tabard! My men will safely convey your luggage to your chambers. Miss de Lacy should be allowed refreshment after her arduous journey."

Lady Tabard didn't like that at all, but Thomasin took Madeline's arm in the first gesture of friendship she had offered, although Madeline felt sure it wasn't so much friendship as defiance of Lady Tabard. "That would be lovely, Mr. Rumbelow," Thomasin said, "and it's so kind of you to think of my companion's well-being."

"Very lovely." Lady Tabard was not pleased at being contradicted. "Of course you may stay, Miss de Lacy."

As they strolled through the great foyer with its suits of armor and its wall-mounted weapons, Lady Tabard said, "I assume we are the first to arrive?"

"No." Mr. Rumbelow looked mildly surprised. "No, actually, there are three parties already here. Lord and Lady Achard and their two lovely daughters arrived at ten this morning."

"Really? So early?" Lady Tabard made her displeasure clear.

With a small smile, Thomasin looked down at her feet.

"Mr. and Mrs. Greene arrived in time for lunch with three of their lovely daughters."

"Gracious! I would have never thought!" Lady Tabard exclaimed. "So many young ladies!"

"Yes, I am the luckiest of gentlemen, for Monsieur and Madame Vavasseur and their four daughters preceded you by half an hour."

The last name captured Madeline's attention. She had met the former French ambassador in Vienna two years ago. He was a small, mustachioed, elegant man with the sharp eyes and impeccable memory of a seasoned diplomat; she would have to avoid him. "Will they be taking refreshments with us?"

Lady Tabard whipped her head around and glared at her.

Mr. Rumbelow answered smoothly, "They're upstairs resting from their extensive journey. They arrived only after much difficulty with Napoleon's army."

"I can imagine." Madeline wondered at the depths of Monsieur Vavasseur's compulsion to game, for he was Napoleon's man and if the government discovered he was on English soil, he and his family would be detained.

Mr. Rumbelow spoke over his shoulder, seemingly to her. "To my own delight and pleasure, my invitation for a friendly game of cards brought in a guest I scarcely dared to hope for."

The duke of Magnus? Was Mr. Rumbelow going to brag about securing her father at the game, when her father had never in his life tried to resist temptation?

Mr. Rumbelow continued, "Although he's been rather reclusive of late, I'm sure you know of him; he is famous in gambling circles as the most coolheaded man ever to win a fortune."

Madeline caught her breath. Not her father, then. Another gambler, one renowned for his luck. Surely Mr. Rumbelow didn't mean . . . no. No, fate couldn't be so cruel.

As they walked into the drawing room, a tall, saturnine gentleman put down a cup and saucer and rose from an easy chair.

With a triumphant flourish, Mr. Rumbelow announced, "May I present Gabriel Ansell, the earl of Campion?"

Chapter Five

Gabriel's gaze skidded over Lady Tabard, over Thomasin, over Madeline . . .

Breathless and horrified, she waited for him to call her by name. The explanations would be impossible, and all the while Gabriel would watch and smile, and wait for his chance to pounce again.

Instead, he looked back to Mr. Rumbelow without a hint of expression. He bowed abruptly, gracelessly. "Rumbelow, introduce me."

He hadn't recognized her. *He hadn't recognized her.* This man who had haunted her dreams, who had driven her from England, who had taken her pride and her virginity . . . didn't remember her.

Madeline tried to decide if she was insulted or relieved.

"Delighted," Rumbelow said. "Campion, this is Lady Tabard, her daughter Thomasin . . . and her companion, Miss de Lacy."

That got Gabriel's attention. Striding up to

Madeline, he stared down at her. "Miss de Lacy, I believe I was betrothed to your cousin once."

Lady Tabard gasped.

"I believe you were," Madeline answered, and she was proud of her insouciance.

"Is she still cowering on the continent to avoid a confrontation with me?"

"She was never cowering. She was traveling." Madeline smiled without humor. "And she has returned."

Without a hint of curiosity, he said again, "Cowering like a child. If you see her, tell her she need not fear. I have no interest in her any longer."

Madeline's temper, usually even, rose to meet the insult. "She never cared, but especially not now, as she is betrothed."

"I heard." His gaze locked with hers. "Her father lost her in a wager."

At that moment, Madeline realized that he *knew.* He did recognize her, and he insulted her to her face, secure in the knowledge she would not—could not—respond.

Gabriel had changed. Before he was smooth, suave, a devil who laughed and teased and made her happy. Now he was rude beyond belief, angry and domineering—and overwhelming in his masculinity. He wore dark brown tweed and white linen, proper, conservative dress for a country party. Standing so close to him, she could smell his unique scent: wind and rain and uninhibited wildness. He had the height Mr. Rumbelow could not boast, towering over a woman in a way that could make her feel protected, or threatened, depending on his mood. He tied his straight brown hair at the base of his neck in a brown ribbon. With his swarthy skin, he was a very *brown* man. Except for his eyes ... they were green, they were gray, they changed with his mood and his garb and the light. Right now they were almost black with scorn, and the lips she had so loved to kiss were pressed into a tight line.

To think she had ever imagined she could call this man to heel. If ever she had needed confirmation that she had been a fool, she had it now.

"Someone always has to win a wager," she answered softly. "Mr. Knight is reputed to be both handsome and rich, so it would appear the duchess has won this wager."

Gabriel smiled, a genuine smile, and at such a break in his unrelieved hostility, she caught her breath. "Then I wish her good fortune," he said.

The smile changed ... or perhaps she now read it correctly, for it seemed more teeth than geniality.

Lady Tabard must have decided the companion had been the center of attention for long enough, for she asked archly, "What about you, Lord Campion? Are you still on the marriage mart?"

Gabriel turned, a slow pivot like a fencer's move, and faced Lady Tabard. "I'm not married, if that's what you mean."

"Really? You've invited so many eligible men, Mr. Rumbelow, I vow Thomasin is all atwitter." Lady Tabard batted her eyes. "Any man who wants my daughter will have to put in his claim early!"

Thomasin cringed at Lady Tabard's heavy-handed matchmaking.

"Married!" Madeline snorted softly. "Married."

She didn't think Gabriel heard her, but he answered softly, "There are men who wish to be married, Miss de Lacy. Then there are men who count themselves lucky to have escaped the trap with only a few teeth marks."

"You being among the latter, I suppose," Madeline said just as softly.

"I would show you my scars, but they cannot be viewed in public." He smiled that savage grin again.

And Madeline remembered how she'd bitten him on his bare, broad shoulder during her ecstasy. Her face flooded with color, and she thought—she wasn't sure, but she thought—Mr. Rumbelow scrutinized the byplay with the attention of a swooping hawk. Blast Gabriel. How dare he taunt her here, in front of everyone?

Once more Lady Tabard demanded Gabriel's attention. "Lord Campion, my husband will be thrilled that you're here."

"Will he indeed?" Gabriel asked.

"He watched you win your fortune, and he speaks of your exploit with awe." Lady Tabard clasped her hands as if about to swoon. "How you bet everything on the turn of a card. How Lord Jourdain was sweating and you were cool. When the hands were laid down, you nodded as if you never harbored a doubt, told Lord Jourdain you would wait on him in the morning for his accounts, and vanished into the night."

Gabriel listened to the recounting as if he had had no stake in it.

Although she didn't want to, Madeline paid close attention. She had never heard the details; she had only screamed with rage and hurt and charged in a fury to Almack's. There she had ended her betrothal in a scene so scandalous she had humiliated Gabriel—and afterward suffered the full weight of his passion and his fury. Although suffered was the wrong word. He had shown her, in infinite detail, just how much her body needed him.

Try though she did, she had never forgotten.

"It was a long time ago," Gabriel said to Lady Tabard.

"Didn't Lord Jourdain try to escape to the continent without paying?" Thomasin asked.

"If I remember correctly." Gabriel seated himself and adjusted the crease of his trousers.

"You know he did," Mr. Rumbelow said. "You stopped him yourself on the docks, relieved him of all his possessions, and sent him on his way."

"To a life of debt and unhappiness," Madeline said.

Eyes glinting, Gabriel inclined his head.

"Miss de Lacy, you don't know what you're talking about." Lady Tabard's penetrating voice grew sharp. "The gentleman deserved no better. I know for a fact he was a wicked man, a man who would commit murder if it suited him."

At her stepmother's tone, at her words, Thomasin stared.

Madeline didn't know why Lady Tabard was so sure of Jourdain's iniquity, but Madeline did know better than to argue. With an assumption of meekness, she looked down at her intertwined fingers. "Yes, my lady." At that time, four years ago, Gabriel had tried to tell her he'd picked his target well, that Lord Jourdain was a brutal blackguard. She hadn't cared; she'd seen only Gabriel's callous betrayal, the proof he was a gambler like her father, and she did not now wish to think any differently. She didn't dare think she'd made a mistake.

Taking a long breath that brought her bosom to quivering prominence, Lady Tabard brought the conversation back to frivolity. "But it's the tale of Lord Campion's win that is renowned in the annals of gambling history."

"I won all," Gabriel admitted, "but I lost my bride. She jilted me, and before I could retrieve her, she left England."

"Of course I heard of that, but my husband, the earl, found only the gaming interesting." Lady Tabard leaned forward, the gleam of curiosity in her eyes. "Why did she jilt you?"

"She didn't approve of gambling, and took it as a personal affront that I dared to win a fortune without her approval."

"Silly girl. Did she think to control you?"

"Oddly enough, she could. Just as I controlled her. It was an engagement of strong wills, battling it out. Probably it's good that we ended the betrothal before we broke each other."

Madeline stared at the floor. She'd thought that, too, in the rare moments when she'd thought of him and sanity prevailed. But beneath the wisdom was an aching awareness that never would she find another man who could see beneath the sensibility to her passion, and feed it . . . and sate it.

"Yet I think Miss de Lacy bears the reputation of resembling her cousin," Mr. Rumbelow said.

Gabriel sat forward in his chair and, starting at her toes, began a long, slow perusal that brought furious color to Madeline's cheeks. By the time his gaze met hers, he had examined the shape of her legs through the thin material of her skirt, the depths of her bosom, the texture of her skin and the details of her countenance.

And Madeline's body came to attention. Heat rushed to her skin . . . everywhere. Deep in her belly an ache formed, grew, spread. His gaze worked on her, reminding her. . . .

"No one else has what we have, Madeline." He held her shoulders, stared into her eyes, while slowly he thrust into her.

The pain made her twist, trying to get away, but he dominated her in a way she hadn't imagined . . . hadn't known was possible.

In a low, savage tone, he said, "This kind of passion happens once in a hundred years, and you want to toss it away." She tried again to escape, but he shook her. "Look at me. Look at me!"

His eyes were stormy gray with fury or . . . or some great, driving passion. She wanted this to stop. The pain, now fading; the pleasure, spiraling to greater heights with each movement. If it didn't stop, if he didn't stop, she'd lose control . . . again. In a temper, she'd betrayed herself once today. This wasn't temper, this was . . . she didn't know what it was, but he owned it, he directed it, and he was relentless.

"The lady who has gone to marry Mr. Knight is much more beautiful than this young woman." He relaxed, smiled at Madeline's chagrin—and allowed his gaze to again slide down to her bosom.

For during his examination, her nipples beaded against the material of her bodice, and she pressed her thighs together to contain the inner melting of her body.

And he leaned back in his chair as if well satisfied with the results of his obnoxious assessment.

"That is exactly what I thought." Lady Tabard nodded. "It's clear by their looks which is the more noble of the two girls. Miss de Lacy has a boldness about her manner and a coarseness about her countenance which bespeaks a lesser nobility."

Madeline thought idly of smacking her with her fist—after first smacking Gabriel, of course.

"I think she is charming." Mr. Rumbelow bowed to Madeline with a smile that could have won her heart, if he were not a gambler and she were not, in truth, the duchess.

"I thank you," she said with an edge of crispness in her voice.

Thomasin stood. "I wish to go to my chamber now. Miss de Lacy, please accompany me."

Gabriel and Mr. Rumbelow stood, and Mr. Rumbelow rang the bell by his hand. "The housekeeper will show you to your room."

Thomasin swept from the drawing room without looking back.

Hurriedly, Madeline put aside her teacup, curtsied toward Mr. Rumbelow and followed.

Thomasin stood stock-still in the middle of her bedchamber, her arms stiff at her sides, her fists clenched. "I hate that man."

So do I. But Madeline knew they weren't speaking of the same fellow. "Mr. Rumbelow?"

"That Woman and Father want me to wed him, and I won't. I won't. I'm going to marry Jeffy, and they can't stop me."

Jeffy? Madeline jerked her attention away from her dismayed contemplation of Thomasin's gowns, laid out on the bed and creased by the packing, and back to Thomasin. "Who's Jeffy?"

Thomasin sighed with queenlike tragedy. "Jeffy is my true love."

Madeline had more to do than she'd realized. She had to iron clothing, and she had to iron out the difficulties of Thomasin's life. And when her father got here, she would have to cope with him. "Tell me all about it."

"I knew I could talk to you." Thomasin's big

eyes fastened on Madeline. "As soon as I saw the way you handled That Woman, I knew you were a force to be reckoned with."

"Indeed I am." A force to be reckoned with, and a woman who had never in her life had to iron a garment. She didn't suppose Thomasin could offer any help, but that snoot of a lady's maid had left the ironing board stretched between two tables, and two irons sat flat on the coal heater. How hard could ironing be?

"Jeffy is the only man I could ever love." Thomasin gazed off into some sweet memory. "He's tall and he's so handsome! He's the most popular gentleman in the county, and he has cast his gaze on me."

"Hm. Is he pleasant? Honest? Kind?"

"Better. He's dashing!"

"Does he like to talk to you?" Madeline draped one of Thomasin's gowns over the board.

"He likes to dance with me."

Madeline had heard nothing of substance about Jeffy, and the adoration that lit Thomasin's face could only be described as infatuation. This did not bode well for her romance. Madeline's eyes narrowed as she stared at the two black irons. She needed a mitt to hold over the cast-iron handles . . . there. She picked up the padded cloth with the scorch marks. "What are his connections?"

Thomasin's glowing face fell. "Well . . ." She picked at imaginary lint on her skirt.

"Not the best, I assume." But if Jeffy were a

good man, what difference would that make? Gabriel was the earl of Campion, of a family even older than hers, and he had been a fortune hunter when he met her. She hadn't minded; after all, few men had a greater fortune than hers. Then he'd become a gambler and a cad, and here he was, plaguing her life once more.

"He's not poor!" Thomasin assured her. "His father is a squire and his mother is the daughter of a baron."

Vaguely, Madeline remembered seeing her own maid test the iron. Licking her finger, she touched the surface. *"Merde!"*

"Those are respectable connections!" Thomasin protested.

"Pardon me. Don't repeat that." For Madeline could tell Thomasin didn't recognize the curse, which Madeline had learned from a French soldier. A curse Eleanor informed her she was never to use.

Putting the iron down, Madeline held her finger over the washbowl and poured water out of the pitcher over the blister forming under the skin. "I wasn't speaking to you, dear. The iron. It's too hot." Too hot to be putting her finger on it, anyway.

Too hot to iron the gown? Madeline didn't know.

With a great deal more caution, she returned to her duties. Carrying the iron to the board, she pressed it to the fine cotton and lifted it up. It looked all right, a little flatter, perhaps, and that was the plan. "Tell me about his circumstances," Madeline invited, and ironed a crease out of the skirt.

Say, this wasn't so difficult!

"He's their only son." Thomasin hugged herself, a dreamy smile on her lips. "They have a lovely estate beside ours, and quite a respectable fortune."

"How old is your Jeffy?"

"Nineteen."

Too young.

"He's good with horses. He helps his father raise them, and looks so handsome in his shirtsleeves as he rides those beautiful, noble beasts." Avoiding the stack of gowns, Thomasin flung herself backward on the bed and stared up at the canopy. "They're famous breeders."

"Really? Would I know them?"

"The Radleys."

"Yes, I do know of them! Eleanor says they're some of the best breeders in the country." Eleanor would know, for she was a horsewoman *par excellence.*

"The duchess says so!" Sitting up, Thomasin struck her fist into her palm. "So I shall tell Father. Until he married That Woman, he liked Jeffy. But That Woman has aspirations."

"You make them sound like a disease." Madeline ironed with increasing confidence. The creases were smoothing out. Like everything, ironing yielded to a little good sense.

"So they are. Because of her, Jeffy and I have

been torn apart and I've been forced to endure a Season."

Thomasin's tone of high tragedy exasperated Madeline. Thomasin demonstrated a lack of good sense. The good sense for which Madeline was justly famous. Or had been, until that awful scene at Almack's.

Oh, why was she thinking of that?

She knew why. Because she'd seen Gabriel, and all the old memories were sabotaging her composure. Taking a deep breath, she resolved to handle this situation with maturity and grace. After all, she had known she would see Gabriel sooner or later. The meeting had just occurred . . . sooner. In a brisk tone, she said, "A Season is not so awful a thing."

"It is when I'm being pushed toward someone as loathsome as Mr. Rumbelow."

"Yes, that connection won't do. I assume the attraction is his grand fortune?"

"Yes, dear Mama has an eye for filthy lucre." Thomasin lounged on the pillows. "But the *ton* very much likes the romantic tale of his background, too. *I* think someone should look into it, but no one listens to me."

"I think you're right."

Thomasin sat up straight. "You do?"

Caution caused Madeline to add, "Although I'd appreciate it if you'd guard that sentiment." She put the first iron back on the stove, and with great pride hung up her first ironed garment. "Not so difficult, indeed," she murmured. She chose another gown off the bed, a silk in spring green. "What does your father say about the match with Jeffy?"

"Father doesn't care."

Madeline lifted an interrogating brow.

"Oh, all right!" Thomasin flung herself backward in an excess of unhappiness. "He says I can wed Jeffy after my Season if I still want to and he still wants to, but I fear Father will knuckle under to That Woman in the end."

Carefully, Madeline arranged the gown on the board, picked up the other iron, waved it around to cool it slightly, then, with a little more caution, dampened her finger and tested it. This time she pulled back in time to avoid a burn, and grinned in triumph. "So all you have to do is prove that you have experienced all the pleasures of the Season, and then you may have your Jeffy. Very sensible."

"I thought you would understand!"

"I do. Your father thinks that if you truly love Jeffy, your love will survive. So . . . what you have to do is be the hit of the Season, dance and smile and flirt, and at the end, tell your father you love Jeffy and wish to wed him." Enthusiastically, Madeline pressed the iron to the silk.

This time, the iron didn't glide as easily, and when Madeline lifted the iron, the silk looked funny. Rather puckered and a little crisp.

As Madeline frowned at the silk, Thomasin said, "But I don't want to be a belle."

"Of course not," Madeline said absently. "To be always admired and courted must be difficult, but to prove to your father you gave this Season a fair chance, I'm afraid you're going to have to put forth the effort." She tried to iron again, and this time the silk turned slightly brown. "It's a sacrifice for your Jeffy."

"Yes. Yes, I suppose. But I've already got a reputation for being . . ."

"Difficult? Don't worry, dear." Madeline nodded reassuringly. "*I* have a reputation for arranging everything to perfection. You do as I tell you and in no time you'll be the hit of the Season."

"Really?" Thomasin eyed her doubtfully. "How?"

"Nothing to it. You will have to flirt with Mr. Rumbelow, but you'll be flirting with all of the gentlemen, so it won't matter." Still Madeline frowned at the silk and ventured an inquiry. "Do you know anything about ironing?"

"What's wrong?" Thomasin hopped off the bed. "Why are you—" Catching a glimpse of the silk, she gasped and sprang back. "My new gown. You've ruined it!"

Thomasin was overreacting. "Just this piece of it."

"It's part of the skirt. It's in the front! What difference does it make if it's only a piece of it?" Thomasin clutched her throat. "That Woman wants me to wear this tonight."

Madeline looked her in the eyes. "If you know

how to iron the rest of the gown without ruining it, I know how to save the costume and make you a fashion leader all at the same time."

Thomasin stared, mouth slightly open, eyes disbelieving.

"Do you have ribbon?" Madeline could duplicate Eleanor's ingenuity from a similar emergency in the past, "A great length of it?"

"Yes. Yes, of course I do."

"Give it to me. Don't worry, dear. By tonight, I will have given you your first lesson about turning lemons into lemonade."

Chapter Six

Madeline strode down the empty corridor in search of something to place in the middle of the rose ribbon she had created for Thomasin's ruined gown. A real flower, or . . . she wondered if one of the footmen would sacrifice a gold button off of his livery. Repairs had taken the entire afternoon, and she wasn't as good with this thing as Eleanor, but she thought she'd done a marvelous job of saving the gown—and convincing Thomasin to take her proper place in society. Not that she expected Lady Tabard to realize it and thank her, but—

A hand shot out of one of the open doors, grasped Madeline by the arm and pulled her into the room.

She allowed it only because she knew it was *him.* Knew by his touch. Knew by his boldness. "Gabriel." She gave him a cool smile. "What an unpleasant surprise."

"For us both." With the slightest of slams, he

shut the door, closing them into—she glanced around at the male accoutrements—what was undoubtedly his bedchamber. The room contained a tall dresser, a vanity, a cheval mirror. The bed was large, wide enough to fit two people should he decide to acquire a mistress. . . . She looked away at once. A door opened onto one of the balconies, and another door into a dressing room. By the size of the room and the amenities, she knew him to be an honored guest.

He shook her slightly. "What in the hell are you doing here?"

She looked at his hand on her arm, and when he didn't remove it, she picked it up and dropped it as if it were a particularly unpleasant insect. "You dragged me in."

He must have been changing for dinner, for he now wore black breeches and stockings, yet his shirt was open at the throat, and his crumpled cravat hung loose around his neck. He stood over her like Dickie Driscoll at his most admonitory. "Don't play games with me, Madeline. Why are you at Chalice Hall?"

"One might ask you the same thing. After all, you've already ruined one man's life by taking his fortune." Although after Lady Tabard's unexpected and spirited defense this morning, Madeline didn't care to pursue that line of reasoning, and she hurried to counterattack. "Have you already spent it all?"

He scrutinized her as he had in the drawing room, but this time the attention he had lavished on her figure he now focused on her face. "You haven't answered my question, so I'll ask another. Why are you posing as that silly twit's companion?"

She looked into his eyes, with difficulty. He'd always had such clarity of vision, but before that clarity had been tempered with affection. Now, stripped of warmth, his gaze saw too much, right down to the wretched uncertainty that so seldom touched her . . . and that plagued her now. Restlessly she moved away from him. "I didn't answer you because I don't have to answer to you."

"So you're bound on some mischief." He observed, eyes narrowed, as she paced toward the balcony and looked out onto the drive where a few last carriages pulled up. "I had hoped your time away would bring you maturity, but I see that's wasted optimism."

His accusation left her almost speechless. "I am very mature. I was born mature."

"You ran away."

An unanswerable accusation. She *had* run away. Stung, she retorted, "But not from my responsibilities. From you." Blast. An unwise admission.

"Why would a mature woman run away from a mere man?"

"Not from the man." She took a breath. Gabriel always sucked up all the air in a room. "From the gossip. I wanted the gossip to die."

"Four years. . . . Yes, it's all quite, quite dead. Dead and picked clean by the crows."

She considered him, trying to read his

thoughts. That was always difficult to do with Gabriel. His words had more than one meaning. With Gabriel, there were layers within layers, and when he looked like that—as if he were two steps ahead of her and planning to stay that way—she could scarcely fathom his subtlety. Did he mean all that flagrant emotion between them was dead?

Well. Good. As it should be. She was conscious of nothing but relief. *Nothing* but relief. "That's the ticket!" she said encouragingly. "I knew we could come to an understanding. I shouldn't have made the scene. It was wrong of me." A huge admission, one she was sure he would appreciate.

He did not. "It *was* wrong of you."

She waited to hear him apologize, also.

He said, "You broke your word to me."

"What?"

"You vowed you would be my wife. The date was set. The notice was in the *Times*. You broke your word."

Her temper rose one notch. Temper all the more easily roused because of her own guilt. A duchess of Magnus never broke her word. It was a family creed—yet she had. "You shouldn't have gambled when you knew how I felt about it."

"This issue was power, darling. If I hadn't won that fortune, you would have run our marriage with a ruthless hand, just as you run everyone else's life."

"Instead, we have no marriage"—the injustice of his accusation cut her—"and I do not run everyone's life! I simply take steps other people are too lazy to take to set matters right."

"Really?" His tone ridiculed her. "Where's Eleanor?"

Madeline started to explain, then clamped her mouth shut.

"Let me guess." Still he watched as she roamed toward the dresser, touched the silver-handled brushes, the shaving cup. "You sent your cousin Eleanor to Mr. Knight to make your excuses because you always told her she was too timid, so you're throwing her into deep water to sink or swim."

"She'll be fine." Eleanor would be fine.

"Unless she drowns. Mr. Knight is not a gentle man in any sense of the word."

For a moment, doubt niggled at Madeline. Then she remembered Eleanor's bravery in the face of fire—French fire—and relaxed. "She'll do. She's just like Jerry. She has hidden depths. She has only to plumb them."

Gabriel's mouth turned down. "Jerry."

"Jerry. Your half-brother." She smiled with remembered affection for the shy, charming lad who had been her age and seemed so much younger. "How is he?"

"He's dead."

"Dead!" She staggered back a step, too astonished by the news to respond with the proper platitudes. "How? Why?"

"He was killed at Trafalgar." Gabriel's lips

barely moved, and his eyes were as green and chilly as the North Sea.

"He died a hero, then." *Stupid* comment, and no comfort to a grieving brother. Despite Gabriel's lack of seeming emotion, she knew he did grieve. Jerry had been the son of a second wife, and he had adored and emulated Gabriel. Gabriel had protected him from the low elements of society. They'd had no other family, only each other.

"A damned waste of a good man," Gabriel said.

Finally she was able to form the words that should have come first. "I'm sorry for your loss. I grieve for him, too." In her first spontaneous move toward Gabriel, she held out her hand.

He stared at it, unmoving.

Dropping her hand, she wondered what else she could say, how she could make matters right. But that was beyond even her powers; before her stood a cynical, angry man, and she would be lucky to escape from his retribution unscathed. "I am sorry," she reiterated. Retreat was the better part of valor, so she walked toward the closed door, toward freedom. "Our little reunion is over."

He sprang forward, moving with that peculiar grace and speed that made women watch him . . . and men hesitate to challenge him. Setting himself between her and the door, he commanded, "Tell me what you're doing here, dressed so modestly and pretending to be a companion."

She would be trapped forever if she didn't yield. And really, what did it matter? Gabriel could do nothing to her. "I'm going to stop my father from playing in this game."

"He's not here."

"He will be. Do you think my father has the will to stay away from a game like this one?"

"It's possible. He gambled but little while you were gone."

Bitterly, she said, "Except to lose me to a stranger."

"He was enticed."

Her temper and her suspicions stirred. "You know a great deal about it. Were you there? Did you help entice him?"

Stepping closer, he pressed her into the corner between the tallboy and the wall. Spacing his words, he said, "I . . . don't . . . gamble."

That was so palpably untrue, she could scarcely speak. "The last time I saw you, you were fresh from a kill. Now you're on the path of another conquest."

"Unlike the rest of your dependents, Your Grace—"

"Don't *you* call me that."

"What?" He pretended surprise. "Your Grace? But others call you that, and you respond courteously. And you *are* the duchess of Magnus."

He had a fine way of irritating her, and he was in top form. "The future duchess, and no one else calls me Your Grace in that tone of voice."

"I will endeavor to please Your Grace with my tone of voice."

She ground her teeth. She wasn't going to win. Not against Gabriel.

"As I was saying, *Your Grace*, unlike the rest of your dependents, I do not live to please you." He stroked his finger along her cheek. "Except in one, very important way."

She jerked her head back. "Don't."

"Don't? Why not? No one knows what we did that night. I told you, the gossip is dead." He stroked her cheek again. "But my claim is not."

This time she smacked his hand away, and hard. "What claim is that?" As if she didn't know.

"My claim on you. Don't you recall, darling?" Leaning in to her, he drew in a breath as if relearning her scent. "I made my claim that night, after your magnificent scene at Almack's."

Of course she remembered. Even now, her heart hurried. "I acknowledge no claim."

Moving ever closer, he said, "Obviously, or you never would have dared to leave me after giving yourself."

"You took!"

"Lying to ourselves, are we? You are such a coward. You were always a coward, and you hide it so well." His voice dropped to a whisper. "You fooled even me."

"I am not a coward!"

"A desperate craven."

"*How* can you say that?"

"How can you say I *took* you? One moment, you were struggling against me. The next, you grabbed me and bit me, right on the lip." He touched the corner of his mouth. "Bit me hard enough to draw blood."

Her chest rose and fell as she gazed blindly into the past.

She had wanted to hurt him. Hurt him as he had hurt her. She called him a blackguard. A gambler. And grabbing his head in both her hands, she had curled her fingers into his hair and bit him. He jerked, and cursed, and tried to take control again. But she held him tighter, and licked the small dribble of blood, and suddenly they were rolling on her bed, ripping at each other's clothes.

She had been insane.

Now her gaze came to rest on Gabriel's throat, brown and smooth, and on the ruff of hair at the top of his chest.

He said, "One of the attributes I admire about you—besides your magnificent figure—is the way you ignore the facts right before your eyes."

She jerked her eyes to his face. Was he laughing at her?

But no. She recognized the signs of his temper. "Did you have my baby?" he demanded.

"No!"

"Don't lie to me, Madeline."

"No. I started my . . . I knew I wasn't expecting before I left England."

He surveyed her grimly. "How nice for you."

Not really. At a time when most women would have been on their knees praying to God for their monthly flow, she had cried at the first signs . . .

and told herself her distress was nothing but typical female emotion. Not love thwarted. Not desperation and grief.

"I wondered for four years," he said. "Like a fool, I thought you were coming home. By the time I realized you were not, it was too late. You were beyond my reach, and I had—" Abruptly he cut himself off, and pressed her further into the corner. "What would you have done if you'd found yourself *enceinte*? Or didn't you think about that? Is that a sign of your vaulted maturity?"

"I would have returned to England and married you." She answered steadily, for of course she had thought of it. What woman would not? And although she hated the idea, she would have come back and married the man . . . and been miserable all her days.

"That's the first right answer you've given me."

"I don't answer to you."

He watched her, one corner of his mouth kicked up, until she wanted to squirm. Instead, she tried to brush past him.

He caught her before she had taken two steps. Holding her shoulders, he propelled her toward the mirror and, standing behind her, made her face herself. "Look at you."

Instead she looked at him.

"Look at *you*," he insisted.

Her eyes met her own in the mirror.

"I'll never forget the first time I saw you. You were so young. Tall, proud, sure of yourself when the other debutantes were only pretending. At that moment, I wanted you."

She remembered. He'd been leaning against the wall at Lady Unwin's ball, surveying the newest crop of debutantes as they fluttered in, all dressed in white and pink and light blue. The whisper had run through the girls: *There he is, the earl of Campion, a notorious fortune hunter. Notorious, wicked, exciting.* Tittle-tattle claimed he had only to crook his finger and ladies ran into his arms. He ruined reputations, and each female he graced with his attention counted herself lucky.

By the time Madeline heard the gossip, it was too late. He had straightened away from the wall, held out his hand, and she had gone to him. She was in love. And she had thought he was in love with her.

Now, in the mirror, she saw herself . . . and she saw him. Them. Together, as if they were in a portrait painted to celebrate their marriage. And some cruel truth made that look right.

His hair grew away from his forehead in a sharp widow's peak, giving him a demonic appearance. His eyes were a mocking green . . . a passionate green. His lips . . . he dipped them toward her neck and paused, just above the skin. His breath caressed her, and she wanted to close her eyes and give herself up to exquisite, almost forgotten sensation.

Instead she lifted her hand to shove his head away.

His voice stopped her. "Have you forgotten? What it was like that night?"

He didn't mean the night they met. He meant the night they made love.

"In your own bed, darling. I took you in your frilly, girlish, virginal bed. Do you remember? You were pacing across your bedchamber like a virago, still furious at me for daring to ruin your dream of Sir Galahad, and furious with yourself for making a scene. And I came through the window."

"I tried to push you back out."

"A two-story drop beneath me, too. Darling, I love it when you're savage. When you bite and scratch. . . . I still have scars on my shoulder where you dug your nails into me." His voice mocked and reminded. "All that ferocity, and you thought it was rage."

"It was rage!"

"It was passion."

She wouldn't win that fight. In the maelstrom of sensation that had possessed her that night, she hadn't recognized any of the emotions. They'd all been new and fresh, harsh like freshly pressed wine and just as heady. She hadn't been herself . . . or else she wasn't the woman she knew herself to be. "You were angry, too."

"Livid. That you thought you could throw away what we had—"

"I didn't throw away anything." Why was he doing this? Saying this? Making so much out of times long past? "We had nothing. Nothing that was real."

"It felt very real when you wrapped your legs around my hips and met my every thrust."

"Stop." She tried to cover her ears.

Grasping her wrists, he pulled her arms down. His breath stroked her ear, his voice was husky and far too deep. "When you came, your body grasped me, caressed me like no other woman ever had."

She strained against his grip. "Don't talk to me of other women!"

"Jealous, darling? You don't have to be."

How she hated that smile on his face!

"You are unsurpassed in your passion." Still clasping her wrists, he wrapped her arms around herself to hold her in his embrace. "I'll never forget those sounds you made—not little, ladylike sounds, but full-bodied screams of delight. I thought your father would blow the lock off and force us to wed at gunpoint."

"Father wasn't home."

"No, of course not. He could never be depended on." With a bitterness that sounded deep as a well, Gabriel said, "As usual, that blackguard ruined everything."

"He hasn't ruined anything. *You* did."

"You're lying to yourself again. Your father separated us. You try to claim I broke us apart, but he's the one who's scarred you."

That shard of truth cut so deeply she caught her breath on the pain. "That's outrageous!"

"Is it?" Like a cat at a mouse hole, he watched her in the mirror.

She tried to wrestle herself away. "I admit it! Because of my father, I don't like gambling. But that's good sense. I've seen the damage gambling can do."

"Only if it's out of control. Have you ever seen me out of control?" Gabriel chuckled, and answered his own question. "That's right. You have . . . once."

Treacherous, starving for caresses, crazed at being in Gabriel's arms once more, her body reacted . . . as she watched. He was too clever. While he held her like this, she saw what he saw, and she couldn't deny the hectic color in her cheeks. Breasts swelling over the neckline of her plain blue gown. A shiver that worked its way down her spine.

He pulled her securely against him. Like the sun of Italy, his heat warmed her. Against her back, she felt each muscle of his chest. Against her bottom, she felt the strength of his desire. And in her heart, she wanted, lusted, beyond good sense and discipline.

"Maddie."

She'd dreamed of his voice, ardent and breathy in her ear, and for a moment she shut her eyes and pretended time had no meaning, and he was her dearest love.

But he said, "Maddie, open your eyes."

When she did, he was watching her with that catlike intensity. Arms around her still, he slid his palms down onto the backs of her hands. He lifted them, guided them . . . and she cupped her own breasts.

Shocked, she struggled to escape from his grasp.

"No. Wait. Watch." That damned seductive voice spoke again, his breath stroking her ear.

And she stilled, her gaze transfixed, her every sense on alert.

Delicately he guided her. With her fingertips, she circled her nipples. With her palms, she rubbed the lower curve. And when he pressed her hands against her own aching flesh, she moaned. Once. Short and sharp.

There was no denying the proof of what she saw. There was no denying that moan. He had his triumph. He could laugh at her if he wanted.

Instead, with narrow-eyed concentration, he placed her arms around her waist. His own hands rose to pleasure her. His palms circled her breasts, enjoying a very masculine pleasure in the shape, the weight . . . her desire. Taking her nipples between thumb and forefinger, he pinched them lightly, driving her against him to escape the yearning, or to quench it. Half mad with desire, she fought to turn in his arms, but he held her still, tasting the shell of her ear with his tongue, then biting lightly on her lobe.

Her head fell back against his shoulder. Each breath she took was redolent with her desire and his wildness.

His hips moved in a slow roll, lascivious and

inviting. "Do you remember how good it was, that first time? You were a virgin, Maddie, and I made you shudder and sigh. Now your body's open to me. Think . . . think what I could do to you tonight."

"No." Thank heavens, she retained some semblance of judgment. "No."

With his hands on her rib cage, he turned her to face him. "No?" He smiled, one of those smiles with too many white teeth and not enough charm. "How long do you think you could tell me *no* if I kissed you?"

"No."

"Like this?"

Caressing her lips with his, he ignited memories of stolen minutes in the sunlit garden, of midnight meetings outside a crowded ballroom. She'd kissed other men while in Europe: Italians, Spaniards, even a stray French soldier. For surely other men could wipe the recollection of Gabriel's kisses from her mind. But no. None of them kissed like he did, as if they enjoyed the act. None of them took the time to learn the shape of her mouth, to whisper love words in ardent tones, to open her lips and—

"Stop thinking about them," he murmured. "Think about this."

He supported her head with his elbow, bent her backward, and with firm pressure possessed her mouth. His lips opened hers. His breath glided down her throat, filling her lungs with his air, his life. Ravenously, she tasted him, and savored the return of a passion that had slipped away, leaving a fire that blazed like a comet's tail. The act reminded her of making love for the first time; he took care not to hurt her, but he brooked no opposition. Instead, with his tongue, he forced her to remember the primeval rhythms that had ensnared them before.

And now ensnared them again. Like the beat of a drum, he thrust, and thrust again. When she tried to remain passive, he sought her out, made her join him in the twisting dance of teeth and tongues and lips.

He took pleasure from her, and he gave pleasure in equal measure, and that good judgment on which she had prided herself only a moment ago vanished in a rush of craving. Her arms crept up around his shoulders, around his neck. She clutched him to her, her heart thumping against his. She pressed her chest against his, seeking to ease the ache in her breasts. She wanted to rub against him like a cat, marking him as her own. Her mind knew he was not her own, but her soul recognized her mate.

She wanted him. She wanted to say *yes*.

Seizing her skirt, he lifted it in a smooth movement.

The air caressed her bare legs. She slid her calf along his.

He chuckled softly, his breath gusting into her mouth.

For one moment, a vast discomfiture held her in its grasp. He was laughing at her. She couldn't bear that.

Then he kissed her again, his lips and tongue intricate and enticing. His hands slid down to bare and cup her bottom, lifting her hips to meet his thrust. Against her belly, she felt the long, hard proof of his desire . . . and how he did want her. It was flattering. It was enticing. It was what she'd dreamed about—the drive of his hips against her body, the promise of fulfillment. She submerged beneath a wave of passion.

Lifting his head, he looked down into her eyes. His fingers touched the skin on her thighs, and she knew, she *knew* he was totally involved in this moment. In her.

And under a stern hand, the door slammed open.

Chapter Seven

Madeline jumped.

Gabriel dropped her skirt and cursed.

Gabriel's valet stood in the doorway and glowered.

Gabriel glowered back, refusing to take his hands off of Madeline, refusing to feel guilty for doing what came as naturally as breathing—making love to Madeline.

Proud and tall, like the duchess she was, Madeline said, "Good afternoon, MacAllister. I hope you've been well."

"Fine, thank ye, Yer Grace." MacAllister's mouth moved as if he had to chew the words, and his face, which always looked like an autumn apple in the spring, grew more wrinkled as he frowned.

Gabriel laughed with grim humor. Short, bandy-legged, and Scottish to his very bones, MacAllister had disapproved of Madeline from the first moment they'd met. He'd predicted disaster.

He'd been right, and never had he allowed Gabriel to forget it.

Gabriel stared at MacAllister, daring him to make a comment.

But before he could, Madeline pulled away. For one moment, Gabriel's arms tightened. Then, reluctantly, he let her go.

Long-limbed and graceful, she strode to the door. MacAllister gave way, the damned old coward. Of course, Madeline was taller than the valet, and that accounted for at least part of MacAllister's deference.

Before Madeline could step into the corridor, Gabriel called, "One question, Your Grace!"

She hesitated. She didn't want to face him. He knew she didn't, but she looked over her shoulder in unconscious coquetry. "What?"

"Does Rumbelow know who you are?"

She blinked. "No."

"You've never seen him before? You're sure of it?"

"I've never seen him before."

Gabriel nodded. "Go on, then."

She bobbed a curtsy, one so patently sarcastic he lowered his head like a charging bull and strode toward her.

She, wise female, hurried down the corridor.

He stared after her, trying to find satisfaction in her flight. Knowing there would be no satisfaction until she was back in his bed. She didn't realize it, but from the moment she had set foot on English soil, her time as an independent woman had come to an end. He did not marvel at the good luck that had brought them here in the same place at the same time. He had known she might be here at Rumbelow's game—and Gabriel always had good luck.

Turning a disgruntled face on Gabriel, MacAllister said, "Ye should have warned me ye were chasing after that skirt again."

Gabriel hadn't adequately prepared for the punch of lust he felt when he first saw her. Nothing could have prepared him for that. "What would you have done?"

Shoving Gabriel back inside, MacAllister shut the door with a slight slam. "Left ye t' go t' work in Bedlam where folks aren't as daft as ye are."

"You hate all women," Gabriel observed. "You've certainly never approved of any of my women, and if you have to be around a woman, you want them meek and silent."

"What's wrong with that?"

"Nothing, except God didn't make them that way."

"Aye, He did, but na' yer duchess."

"No. Not my duchess." MacAllister had yowled like a scalded cat about Madeline's defection, citing it as proof positive that women were no good. Gabriel hadn't agreed—but Gabriel had had other things on his mind. The French had declared war on England. Gabriel had taken part in organizing the defense of the coast. While he was gone, Gabriel's brother had fallen afoul of a scoundrel and in his shame, Jerry had enlisted in the English navy.

By the time Gabriel had gotten wind of Jerry's problems, the lad was at sea, beyond Gabriel's reach. The whole dreadful time had culminated in Jerry's death, and Gabriel's eternal grief. For it had been his responsibility to watch out for his beloved younger brother, and in his obsession with Madeline, he had failed.

Moreover, for all the passion between them, Madeline had refuted his claim, fleeing England rather than face him. His heated fury had chilled into a cold and relentless rage. Because he believed in fate, he had known she would someday come within his grasp again, and he'd sworn vengeance on the woman who had captivated his soul, then left him because . . . oh, not because of the gamble. Because she was afraid. Afraid of any man she didn't direct and control.

Stripping off his cravat, Gabriel threw it in the pile of dirty linens.

"Take off yer shirt, then, and hurry. The first dinner bell will ring soon, and ye want t' be there t' watch the players." MacAllister gathered up the linen and headed for the dressing room, then came back with a crisply ironed shirt. "I should have known ye were going t' let a woman take yer mind off yer vengeance."

"Because I'm so weak, you mean?" Grinning derisively, Gabriel pulled the shirt on.

"Weak as water, if ye allow that one t' sink her claws in ye again."

"I was *trying* to chase her away." Gabriel's grin flattened. "This is no place for a woman."

About that MacAllister agreed. "They're all over! Maids and ladies, traipsing about, their squeaky voices asking where t' go t' get an iron, asking me how t' stir the fire. I dunna know why Rumbelow allowed women t' come t' a game!"

"Insisted they come, you mean."

"I dunna like it." MacAllister slipped the shirt over Gabriel's head.

Gabriel could see MacAllister's scalp through the thin red wisps on the top of his head. "Nor do I." Rumbelow was a blackguard through and through, but neither MacAllister nor Gabriel understood the significance of the families at such an important game. "Is he going to use the confusion created by the party to cheat? Is he going to kidnap one of the girls? . . . I met a Lady Thomasin, quite beautiful, quite innocent. Just the type of girl he likes."

"And she's fool enough t' like him, too, na' doubt."

"Not her. She seemed momentarily dazzled by his charm, but as soon as he turned his attention away, she sneered at him." Gabriel rather enjoyed the size of the chip Thomasin carried on her shoulder. "It's her mother who wants him for Lady Thomasin."

"Women." MacAllister snorted. "Ne'er smart enough t' see the scam."

Grimly, Gabriel said, "Jerry didn't see the scam, either."

MacAllister's voice was gruff as he pinned on Gabriel's collar. "Nay. That he dinna." Never one to belabor a man's foolishness, especially that of Gabriel's beloved younger brother, MacAllister added, "All the more reason for ye t' keep yer head clear of female wiles and on yer mission."

"Are you back to complaining about Madeline?" Gabriel sighed. "First I tried to frighten her with threats, then I tried to make her flee my seduction."

" 'Tis the daftest scheme I ever heard." MacAllister jerked his chin at the bed. "After ye'd pleasured her silly, did ye think she'd run?"

"It worked last time."

MacAllister stared, hands on hips.

"All right," Gabriel admitted. "Today, I lost my head."

"Ye always did with her. What made ye think this time would be different?"

Gabriel stared at MacAllister, but he didn't see him. Instead he looked into the past, seeing that night at Almack's.

He leaned against the wall, his spine an indolent comma of relaxation. He had done what he'd set out to do. He'd won himself a fortune, and in the process made himself independent of his future wife's largesse. It was a matter of pride for him. Fortune hunter he might be . . . but not with Madeline. He would not live as Madeline's toy-husband, to be picked up and discarded at will, patted on the head, never the master of his own home, not even a partner in the marriage.

So now he waited for her. Waited to make the announcement of his triumph. Waited to smooth her ruffled feathers—for they would be ruffled. In the time he'd come to know her, and fall in love with her, he'd assessed her. She lived to direct people's lives. She imagined she would direct his, and she wouldn't be happy about this development.

But his ring was on her finger, the word of the betrothal had been placed in the Times, and the wedding date set. In three weeks, she would be his. Soon, but not soon enough, she would be his.

When she arrived, she swept in with all the dignity and desirability of an Egyptian queen. She wore a magnificent gown of rose silk that clung to her figure like a lover. Her black hair was piled high atop her head and rose-colored feathers bobbed higher yet. Her chin was lifted just a notch too high, her shoulders were almost too squared, her stride was long and slow and . . . off somehow.

He straightened away from the wall.

She knew. She already knew.

She was furious. Livid.

He hadn't anticipated this.

She didn't see him at first, and he concentrated his gaze on her, playing the game he always played—make Madeline look at me.

She did. Her feather-coiffed head swept in a quarter circle, and she spotted him against the wall. She stared at him, unsmiling. Then she turned and spoke to

Eleanor. Poor little Eleanor, who tried to restrain Madeline with a hand on her arm. Madeline shook her off and strode toward Gabriel.

Gabriel's temper rose, too. He braced himself for battle—but he thought that battle would take place in an empty drawing room or in the darkened gardens. He never imagined it would start in the full sight of the ballroom with the palm of Madeline's hand striking his cheek, and end when she rushed away from him, their engagement broken.

Cold, pure, invigorating fury rose at the memory of that scene, and Gabriel said, "I've got a score to settle with her, too."

"One score at a time." MacAllister handed him a crisp, starched cravat.

Without replying, Gabriel tied it into the knot called a waterfall. The first one failed. He tried it with another. He was persistent—in tying his cravats, in taking his revenge. Revenge on Rumbelow. Revenge on Madeline. "Did you find out where the gaming is to take place?"

"In the dowager's house, separate from the main house."

That made sense. Whatever swindle Rumbelow planned, he would want his victims to be far away from any help. Satisfied with the results at last, Gabriel inspected his cravat in the mirror. "You'll go in tonight and look it over."

"I'll try, but I warn ye—Rumbelow has hired an army of mercenaries t' patrol the grounds. Looking in the window almost got me nabbed."

Shrugging into his dark blue waistcoat

trimmed in gold, Gabriel asked, "Expecting trouble, is he?"

"Or making trouble." MacAllister held Gabriel's jacket and helped him into the form-fitting garment. "Just curious—why did ye ask the lass if she knew Rumbelow?"

"I would swear that, when he saw her, he recognized her."

"But he denied knowing her? More tomfoolery. Na' good." MacAllister meditated. "She looks like her cousin. Maybe he knows the other lass."

"Maddie's pretending to be her cousin." Gabriel thoroughly enjoyed the horror on MacAllister's face. "She's pretending to be the companion to Lady Thomasin so she can stop her father from playing in the game."

"Doesn't make a bluidy bit of sense."

"Actually, it does. Lord Magnus has ruined her already with that wager of his against Knight. Now she believes he'll attempt to recoup with more gambling—and he depends on luck, not on the odds."

"So she should arrive as the duchess and tell him . . ." Even MacAllister, belligerent as he was, comprehended Madeline's predicament.

"If she arrived as herself, she would be the object of attention, and if she urged her father not to participate in the game, pride would obligate him to remain. After all, he wouldn't want to suffer the label of petticoat-bound." No man enjoyed that, especially a father who'd been so offhand as to wager his daughter's hand in marriage. Such obedience to her wishes might indicate weakness—as if the gambling didn't already indicate his frailty.

Gabriel hated her devotion to her father. He'd seen the results time and again. Lord Magnus would promise to come to visit her, raise her hopes, and not appear, never even remember to send his regrets. He would promise to take care of some task on their estates, and inevitably disappointment would follow.

Madeline never complained. She had always put on a brave face. But Gabriel knew how deeply her father's neglect wounded her, and he did not forgive. If somebody was going to hurt Madeline, Gabriel wanted it to be him. Like a greedy lad, he wanted all her attention focused on him.

"So what does she think she's going t' do about her father?" MacAllister asked.

"I suspect she plans to sneak up on him, frighten him out of his wits, force him to do what she wishes, and leave without anyone being the wiser. His withdrawal from the game will seem his own eccentricity."

MacAllister didn't wish to admit that Madeline had planned well. "Humph."

Gabriel inspected himself again. He looked handsome and in fashion, like a man who cared more for his clothes than anything else. That was what he wanted Rumbelow to see. Once more Gabriel wondered at the game Rumbelow played. Not a game of chance, he feared, but a scheme to bilk everyone out of their money—and, he feared, perhaps their lives. "I wonder why Lord Magnus has not yet arrived."

"Dunna know." MacAllister brushed at Gabriel's shoulders with a garment brush. "But I do know she'll distract ye."

"Madeline?" Gabriel thought about the scene just past, when he held Madeline in his arms and proved to her she still wanted him. He'd proved that he still wanted her, too, but that he'd always known. "Oh. Yes. I promise you she will. I will enjoy every bit of that distraction."

Stepping back, MacAllister considered him skeptically. "What is it ye want from the lass?"

"Retribution. Retribution for the humiliation. Retribution for the years alone when she should have been at my side." She would be his again. She would give herself totally to him, and when she did . . . Reaching into his valise, he pulled out a lady's glove, yellowed with age and worn from being carried with him everywhere.

MacAllister eyed it, too, recognizing it, knowing well what it meant. "Yer brother—"

Gabriel turned on MacAllister. "Do you really believe I will fail to avenge my brother's death?"

MacAllister coughed. "Nay."

"No. I will have my revenge on Rumbelow. But I will also have Madeline in every way possible." With a smile that would have warned her if she'd seen it, he added, "My life will be all the sweeter for that."

Chapter Eight

Madeline clasped her hands in pride as she surveyed her handiwork.

The candlelight glimmered on Thomasin's teal gown, giving it a richness of texture and color surpassed only by the glimmer of silver ribbon as it passed from the seam under the bosom and beneath the hem, lifting and gathering the skirt just above her knee. Madeline had sewn the silver ribbon flower over the worst of the ruined silk, and in the center she had placed a single rosebud of blazing red. Beneath the gown, Thomasin wore her best white linen petticoat, decorated with white satin and lace and so sheer, every time she moved, her pale skin gleamed through the material.

Thomasin stared into the cheval mirror and fingered the ribbon anxiously. "What do you think?"

"Of the gown? It's perfect. It's so different, no one will ever know it was an emergency repair. The effect is subtle ... most of the girls will be wearing gowns which are see-through or they'll have dampened the skirts. With your beauty and that restrained glimpse of knee, you'll put them all to shame."

"Really?" Thomasin beamed. "Do you think so?"

"I'm very good at predicting social success, and I predict yours quite happily." Quite hopefully, also. Madeline needed something to distract herself from the disaster that faced her. A disaster with the name of Gabriel.

Thomasin had done her own hair, and now she tossed her head, allowing the blond curls to dance around her rounded cheeks. "But . . ."

Madeline could read the transparent emotions that chased across the girl's face. "But what about your true love? Is it fair to go out and enjoy yourself when he isn't here?"

Turning to Madeline, Thomasin grasped her hands. "I knew you would comprehend my feelings. You have a superior understanding."

Yes, Madeline did have a superior understanding—for a woman who was obviously insane. She had to be. After almost four years of exile and adventure, she had succumbed to the very trap she had fled, and with barely a murmur of protest. She had thought she could manage seeing Gabriel, speaking to Gabriel, behaving in a civil and distant manner to Gabriel. After all, she had had four years to distance herself from that madness of passion, that surfeit of love. Instead, instead, she had allowed him to . . . to touch her.

What advice could she really give to Thomasin? Run away from love as quickly as ever you can? Don't let love get its claws in you, else you suffer eternal anguish?

But no. Madeline had to be sensible. Her suffering wouldn't necessarily translate to Thomasin. Not if Madeline had anything to do with it—and Madeline did. "You'll dance every dance, play charades, ride and walk with the other young ladies and young men, but you and I know there's no real satisfaction in such activities. Not in any way that matters. It's the conversations that start from the heart that truly matter, and the long, quiet evenings with one's loved ones." Madeline couldn't believe she was spouting such poppycock.

But she wasn't surprised when Thomasin nodded vigorously. "That is what I think, too."

"Just as a man's wealth and title don't lend him importance. Only a kind heart and a true nature can do that."

"Yes! Exactly!" Thomasin's enthusiasm was infectious.

"Nevertheless, during this house party, I wish you to do everything you can to flirt with gentlemen of money and consequence."

Thomasin's chin developed a surprisingly stubborn jut. "Not Mr. Rumbelow."

"Absolutely not," Madeline said decisively. "But other gentlemen will be here. Proper suitors, *sons* of the gamblers. You know who they are— lords and wealthy gentlemen."

"Yes." Thomasin nodded.

"Pick one. Charm him. See how easy it is. Once you've established that you've changed from surliness to vivaciousness, all will flock around you." Thomasin's expression started to lower again, and Madeline added hastily, "You won't really enjoy yourself, of course, but you'll give such a good imitation no one will realize it!"

Thomasin brightened. "That's true."

"Now put on your gloves, and let's go to your stepmama."

The two young ladies made their way across the corridor to Lord and Lady Tabard's bedchamber, there to find the lady's maid trussing Lady Tabard's stoutness into a gown. The material consisted of overpoweringly large pink cabbage roses that reminded Madeline of the pattern on one of the chairs in Mr. Rumbelow's drawing room. Discreetly, she averted her eyes.

Lady Tabard took one look at Thomasin and squawked like a chicken facing the farmer's ax. "Thomasin Evelyn Mary Charlford, what happened to your new silk costume?"

The pretty color in Thomasin's cheeks faded as she glanced down at her gown. "Don't you like it? Miss de Lacy wanted to add a continental flare."

"A continental flare?" Red suffused Lady Tabard's plump neck and broad cheeks. "Miss de Lacy, I would hardly call this a continental flare!"

Assuming a pleased air, Madeline said, "You were testing me, I think, Lady Tabard, but I realized at once what you wished when I found so much silver ribbon among Lady Thomasin's accoutrements."

Lady Tabard's eyes bulged as she stared at the ribbon flower on Thomasin's knee. "What?"

"You were right, of course. Such an arrangement is all the rage in Europe, yet since I've returned, I haven't seen one young lady wearing the style."

"Zipporah, what do you think?" Lady Tabard blared.

Zipporah cowered. "Lady Tabard, I would never suggest such a thing!"

In a respectful tone, Madeline said, "Of course not. An accomplished lady's maid like yourself knows that such an innovation is only for the newest debutante, not for the lady who has already established her style, as has Lady Tabard. And a very handsome style it is, too." Briefly, Madeline wondered if she would be struck by lightning for lying. "Lady Thomasin will be the newest *ton* leader," Madeline assured Lady Tabard.

Madeline had finally said the right thing, for Lady Tabard stepped back, looked the dress over once more, and made a humming noise. "Yes. Yes, I see what you mean. It is quite dashing."

"It *is*, isn't it?" Thomasin gave her stepmother a tentative smile.

Lady Tabard's eyebrows shot up. Her mouth twitched for a second in what looked like a startled return smile. Then her eyebrows lowered, and she said severely, "Don't get above yourself, my lady daughter. To be a *ton* leader is a big responsibility for such a youngster as yourself."

"Yes, ma'am," Thomasin answered with suitable meekness.

Lady Tabard inspected Madeline's costume, an evening gown of a green so dark to be almost black and trimmed in nothing more than a bit of green braid around the modest neckline. Madeline had scolded Eleanor for having it made. Eleanor had retorted it was suitable for a lady's companion.

Apparently Lady Tabard agreed, for she nodded. "That's more like it. Quite acceptable. I think you'll find, Miss de Lacy, that if you practice maintaining your proper position and dressing appropriately, you shall be with Lady Thomasin for a long, long time."

No force on earth could persuade Madeline to stay any longer than it took her to see her father and persuade him to return home. Not after her own behavior in Gabriel's bedchamber.

Unfortunately, she had to see him this evening. Pray God her father hurried to get here.

But nothing about her properly meek posture gave any indication of her furiously churning thoughts. "I thank you for your generosity, Lady Tabard."

"Now." Lady Tabard picked up her fan. "Let us go down to dinner."

Rumbelow, as he now called himself, could almost taste sweet gratification as he surveyed his drawing room. The chamber was large, candlelit and comfortable. In it, he had assembled nine men so dedicated to the game they were blind to any danger to their families. On Rumbelow's command, they had brought their wives and their children of marriageable age to the "house party" for a bit of country fun.

Rumbelow was constantly amazed by the rich and their gullibility.

The elderly Lord Achard sat in an easy chair, his gouty leg propped up on an ottoman, his walking stick clutched firmly in his knobby fingers. He and Lord Haseltine, good friends indeed, were hotly debating a hand of whist played thirty years ago at Hampton Court. Haseltine's heir, a pimply, unsocial young man of seventeen, sat close, listening intently.

The two daughters of Lord and Lady Achard hung back against the wall, their eyes huge as they watched handsome, well-turned-out Mr. Darnel converse with the eldest Mademoiselle Vavasseur. Apparently the Ladies Achard had developed a longing for Mr. Darnel, a longing fated to be thwarted, for Mr. Darnel was interested only in gambling—and in his dear valet, Norgrove. He was quite in love with Norgrove, which would have been a scandal if anyone else knew of the matter. No one did—except Rumbelow, who made it his business to know everyone's secrets.

The marquess of Margerison and his imperious

wife watched fondly as their only son and heir, Lord Hurth, droned on to one of the bored Mademoiselles Vavasseur about his horses.

Rumbelow's scornful gaze lingered on Hurth's costume. A young man of ever-increasing girth should not be wearing a coat of silver cloth with a nipped-in waist and padded shoulders. That entire family consisted of bores and fools, and none more indulged than Hurth.

Baron Whittard's oldest son, Bernard, was ignoring the wiles of Miss Jennifer Payborn, the only child of Mr. Fred Payborn, a coal merchant known for his bad skill at gambling and his ability to make up his losses in no time at all in his business. Mr. Payborn might have dreadful luck at cards, but he had the Midas touch when it came to making money, and he was very fond of his darling daughter.

He would buy her Bernard if she wished.

He would buy her life when he had to.

As far as Rumbelow was concerned, Mr. and Mrs. Greene were amiable fools, good for nothing except producing daughters and smiling inanely— and gambling. This time, only Mr. Greene was playing—Rumbelow wanted no romantic distractions at the gaming table, so he had invited only men—but Mrs. Greene had been known to bet an estate on the turn of a card.

The younger people were conversing and flirting, doing everything in their power to find a rich and titled mate from among their peers. The older ladies, mothers and matrons, sat together, teacups balanced in hand, assessing their offspring with sharp eyes and discussing their prospects.

Lord Tabard had arrived during dinner and now sat listening to his vulgar, lowborn wife as she berated him for his daughter's ingratitude. It appeared that the insipid blond Lady Thomasin Charlford did not wish to pursue Rumbelow as her stepmama demanded. His gaze lingered on the girl. When he escaped, he would take her if he wished—but he didn't wish. Not when he could have—he smiled—the future duchess of Magnus.

Ah, yes, Her Grace, Madeline de Lacy, sat in the corner, dressed in plain clothes and trying hard to be meek, quiet . . . a proper companion. It was a delicious amusement to see her feeble attempt to fit into the role. A greater amusement to manipulate her to his own delight. He wondered why she was here. Was this a mischief, a dare? Or was she chasing after Lord Campion, her lost love? Lost, from all accounts, through her own fault. Rumbelow would enjoy finding out, and he did not worry that she would recognize him. Why would she? An English duchess in her own right paid no attention to a manservant in a Belgian spa.

And manservant in a Belgian spa had been only one of the many roles Rumbelow had played in his time. It was always best, he found, to slip into a servile role after pulling off a heist, for the very rich ignored servants with a serenity that bordered on foolishness. Often, criminals lived right under their very noses. It was a rare lord who observed what happened under his nose.

Which turned Rumbelow's attention to Lord Campion.

Campion leaned an elbow on the mantel, staring into the fire and sipping a brandy, looking like a man who cared not a whit that his former fiancée sat less than twenty feet from him.

Rumbelow's gaze narrowed on him. When he'd first learned that Campion had accepted his invitation, he'd been jubilant. For the last four years, no one had managed to lure the reclusive gambler into a game, and Campion's presence assured that everyone else who had received an invitation would accept. Now he was here, his ante of ten thousand pounds had been counted and was locked away in the safe—and Rumbelow couldn't shake the niggling feeling he had overlooked something.

But as he'd done with everyone else here, he'd had Campion thoroughly investigated. Campion had no family. His younger half-brother had died at Trafalgar. His fiancée had jilted him. Now he lived alone on his estate, using his fortune to build a yet greater one.

Rumbelow's plan was coming to fruition. His insurances were in place. When this was over, he would take ship to France and present himself to Bonaparte with a few prime secrets he'd managed to obtain during a sojourn as secretary for the

Home Office. It was good to have a myriad of skills to fall back on, skills that would assure him a safe place to live and much honor.

The clock chimed nine. Standing, he clapped his hands. "Attention! Attention, please!"

Immediately everyone quieted and turned to face him, their expressions alive with anticipation. They treated him as one of themselves, and for a man born in the muddy Liverpool slums, their respect was a particular triumph.

"I wish to tell you about the events for our house party." He glanced around the room, touching on each of the females briefly, providing an illusion of interest that later, he flattered himself, they would hotly debate. "Tomorrow, breakfast will be served in the dining chamber, and I would advise you attend by eleven, for you'll not want to miss out on our excursion. Tomorrow afternoon, I've arranged for games and frivolities . . . on the cliffs overlooking the sea!" He paused for the oohs and ahs. "We'll play tennis and croquet. My cook is even now working on a fabulous repast to be packed in baskets and served under the tents. I myself will walk to the events. I invite you all to join me, but I've arranged for carriages for those who wish to ride. I promise a festive afternoon, to be followed by . . . a ball tomorrow night!"

More oohs and ahs.

"A ball in Chalice Hall's magnificent blue ballroom. I dare not show you the chamber yet, but I promise it's decorated in a manner sure to please. I can't wait to see our beautiful ladies clothed in their best."

Mr. Darnel lifted his monocle and examined the young ladies with a faintly ridiculous, bogus interest.

So he didn't want anyone to recognize his predilection.

Too late. Rumbelow knew.

"The next day, we'll prepare"—Rumbelow gestured grandly—"for the Game of the Century."

Everyone broke into applause.

"The gaming shall start at nine o'clock in the evening in the dowager's house not far from Chalice Hall. Those of you who are housed in the South Wing can view it from your windows. I've had bedrooms made up for those who must rest."

"I won't need it," Mr. Darnel said heartily. "I once gambled for three days straight!"

"Not everyone has your stamina, Mr. Darnel. Of course there'll be refreshments available at all times. We'll play until we have our winner. I anticipate that will take more than a day, so"—Rumbelow gestured again, and everyone leaned forward—"while we game, I've hired carriages to take the families to Crinkle Downs. The town is quaint and there's quite a handsome church, as well as a tea room which serves the best cakes I've ever had the pleasure to taste. Indeed, it is the cakes at the Two Friends Tearoom which convinced me to take Chalice Hall for this occasion!"

The ladies nodded, especially stout Lady Tabard, who enjoyed her food with a little more gusto than was decorous.

Rumbelow concentrated on looking boyishly roguish. "It's not proper, but I admit I hope I win."

Everyone laughed, and Monsieur Vavasseur shook his finger at him. "*Non, non,* that is not proper for the host to have such longings!"

"A man must be insane—or a liar—not to wish to win *one hundred thousand pounds.*" Rumbelow observed as the gamblers drew in a collective breath, as their eyes lit up and their fingers twitched. Yes, he was doing the right thing by holding them off, by building the excitement. They'd be so focused on the game, Rumbelow could steal their clothes off their backs and they wouldn't realize it. "Those of you who are here may hold your ante until noon on gaming day. At that time you can personally place it in the safe in the dowager's house, and there your ante will remain until someone wins all at the end of the game."

Campion crossed his legs and looked for all the world as if he were bored.

Rumbelow knew how to catch his interest. "We are yet missing one of our gamblers. As you all know, the rules stated that if you were likely to be late, you could reserve your place by forwarding your ante, and that gentleman has done so. But the game will start in two days from this very hour"—he indicated the tall clock—"and if the gentleman hasn't arrived by noon on gaming day, when everyone places their ten thousand pounds in the safe his ante is forfeit."

A collective sigh went through the crowd.

The duchess of Magnus sat up straighter in her chair, and her paltry illusion of meekness fell away.

"So—if our gambler has not appeared by the appointed time, I declare that at noon on our gaming day, the gamblers shall play a preliminary round for that ante." A babble of excitement and pleasure broke out, one that Rumbelow halted with an upraised finger. "The ante is not ten thousand pounds. It is, instead, an *object* worth *more* than ten thousand pounds. In fact, it has been appraised at over thirteen thousand pounds."

The women gasped. The men murmured greedily.

"So we hope this unknown gambler remains away," Lord Tabard called.

"An uncharitable thought . . . but yes." Rumbelow brushed at his mustache. "May I say . . . the ladies would be happy to own this object."

"Please, Mr. Rumbelow, won't you tell us what it is?" The second oldest Vavasseur daughter batted her luxurious lashes at him.

"I should not."

A chorus of pleading rose from the girls.

Rumbelow held up his hands. "All right, all right! I can't refuse so much feminine pulchritude." He hesitated, building the tension. "It is a tiara." Out of the corner of his eye, he saw Lady Magnus jump. *She* was certainly interested. "A tiara? I misspoke. It is a crown, a crown of unusual beauty and age. Any woman could imagine herself a queen when she wore it."

"Oh, Papa!" Miss Payborn clasped her hands at her bosom. "Won't you win it for me?"

"Of course I will, little missie." Mr. Payborn smiled affectionately at his daughter and assured her he could perform a feat he had no chance of completing.

"I think not!" Lord Achard said crisply. "I will win it for my daughters."

The two shy girls put their heads together and giggled.

Their father smiled benevolently at them.

"Enough. Enough!" Rumbelow laughed indulgently, quite as if these displays of affection charmed him. In fact, these men and their famed devotion to their families had been the impetus to invite them. Love, wielded in the proper hands, could prove a weapon. "I have invited the best gamblers in the world here, and only one of you can have the crown—that is, if the owner hasn't shown up. And only one of you will win the fortune."

Campion spoke up. "The crown is already here, you say. Where, and how is it guarded?"

Interesting. Why would he wish to know that? And what game did he play, that he allowed Rumbelow to see his interest?

But if Campion wished to steal the crown, he should be encouraged to try. It would add to the excitement of the house party, and confuse matters when the time came for the grand finale. "It is already in the safe in the dowager's house. I promise, the crown is perfectly safe. My men are patrolling the grounds."

Campion didn't blink. Didn't say another word.

What was he doing here? Did he have an ulterior motive? Rumbelow's gaze slid to Lady Magnus. Besides her?

Campion bore watching. In fact, Rumbelow would make sure he was watched very closely indeed.

Chapter Nine

※

Madeline's plan had been too simple. She realized it now.

As she walked along the wooded road toward the ocean cliffs the next afternoon, the wind blew. The grass rippled. The sun shone. And she brooded on the difficulties that had complicated her life. When she'd made her plan to retrieve her father, she'd failed to take into account the many unknowns: the myriad of people at the party, the schedule that Mr. Rumbelow had set up . . . her father's inability to do as expected.

Why hadn't he shown up yet? Would he let the tiara go so easily?

Would she always have to fix her father's muddles?

The aristocrats walked in the front of the party, and Madeline was almost glad to be left back with the servants and companions. This left her free to stare at Gabriel resentfully. Gabriel, who strode among the guests, speaking to everyone, settling

with no one. He wore a broad beaver hat, a costume of green cloth threaded with black, and carried a walking cane with a large gold knob. He
appeared to be indifferent to the dust that coated
his polished boots . . . indifferent to her. This
morning, he hadn't glanced at her once. Thank
heavens.

Madeline walked alone, fitting in nowhere.

Even after Gabriel betrayed her, she had still
thought him an intelligent man. Now she knew he
had blithely handed over ten thousand pounds
into another man's keeping. What a fool.

She cared only because his lapse indicated a
lapse in her own good judgment.

A lapse compounded yesterday by her visit to
his bedchamber. In the space of a few moments,
Gabriel had banished her resolve to confront him
with dignity and good sense. Under his whiplash
tongue, all her old resentments had come roaring
back, carrying her like a riptide into deeper wa-
ters. She shuddered to think what would have
happened if MacAllister hadn't arrived when he
did. She had walked away from that room determined not to let Campion near her ever again . . .
until she heard what Mr. Rumbelow had said last
night.

The tiara. She had to retrieve the queen's tiara.
Why, oh, why had she trusted her father when he
said he hadn't yet wagered it?

How could he send a precious tiara, a family
heirloom, presented by Queen Elizabeth the First,
ahead to a gambling party with no guarantee his

host was reliable? Unwarranted trust appeared to be a failing for all of these gamblers.

And why hadn't she checked to make sure the tiara was still securely housed in the safe at home, taken it and concealed it? Instead, if her father didn't appear by tomorrow at noon, she would have to ask—no, beg—Gabriel to win it back for her.

Never had she so heartily wished she could walk away from her duty.

A rough, masculine voice hailed her. "Miss de Lacy! Wait up, miss."

She turned to see the man she'd seen yesterday in Mr. Rumbelow's drive, the man who had stared so rudely at her.

He strode up beside her.

Astonished and a little unsettled at being singled out, she asked, "Yes? What's wrong?"

"Nothin's wrong, miss, just thought ye and I might walk together fer a bit." His broad lips tilted up and his blue eyes crinkled in what he might have hoped was a charming smile.

His teeth were stained brown, and as she watched, he spit a stream of tobacco out of the corner of his mouth onto the grass on the side of the road. Disgusted, she wondered if that was his version of company manners—spit toward your subordinates, spit away from the ladies.

She remembered only too well his sharp glance the day before, and today she'd seen him watching the guests with the weighing gaze of a cutpurse—and she had no doubt he had indulged in that practice at some not-so-distant moment in his past.

"Like wot ye see, miss?" he laughed, and gin-laden breath blasted her face.

It was on the tip of her tongue to tell him to go away, but she glanced up and down the long line of guests strung out in little groups down the road. She could see Thomasin, flirting vivaciously with one of the young men. She could see Gabriel walking, hands clasped behind his back in his habitual pose, listening to Mr. Payborn. Far ahead, she could see Mr. Rumbelow's golden hair glowing in the sun.

But no one was close. There was no one to rescue her. In truth, the fellow presented no real danger, and Madeline de Lacy prided herself on being a woman who recognized opportunity when it was presented to her, and this was an opportunity. The lout was a little drunk. He was walking well. He was talking without a slur. But perhaps he was befuddled by the liquor. Perhaps, if she interrogated him with the correct amount of finesse, she could discover a little of Mr. Rumbelow's background and plans. "You may walk with me if you wish."

The lout's laugh became a grin, one that showed a gap where he'd lost a tooth. "Ye've got an air about ye, ye know that? Like ye're a princess or somethin'. That's why I plucked ye out from among the other girls."

And, she surmised, she was supposed to be

flattered. "Thank you. It's not every day a girl like me attracts a man like you." An understatement. "How did you know my name?"

"I asted around. Some o' the lads 'ad already cast their eyes on ye, but I put them straight in a 'urry." His long black coat flapped as he walked, revealing knee breeches, knee boots and a grimy blue shirt.

"I see." Madeline couldn't wait to tell Eleanor what she'd missed.

"I got t' walk today anyway. I got t' follow that chap." Mr. Rumbelow's man pointed toward . . . it looked as if he'd pointed toward Gabriel.

Startled, Madeline asked, "Why?"

" 'E's a puzzle, 'e is. We got us suspicions about 'im." The fellow nodded as if he owned a tract of mystery.

"Why?" she insisted.

"Ye're a nosy parker, aren't ye?" His red-veined nose crinkled, and he got a mean look in his eyes. " 'Ave ye got an interest in 'im? Because it won't do ye no good. E's a nobleman, 'e is, and all noblemen are good fer t' a girl like ye is t' put a bun in yer oven, then toss ye out on yer ear."

Evidently, it was time to stop asking about Gabriel and start asking about the fellow walking beside her. And how did one talk to a man like this?

Silly question. Just as one talked to a man of the *ton*—with a liberal dose of flattery. "What's your name?"

Sticking his thumb in the waistband of his

pants, he hitched them up, wiggled his eyebrows, and in an artificially deep voice said, "Big Bill."

It took her a few seconds to understand the significance of his moniker, but that did explain his confidence and boldness. "Well, Big Bill . . . do you have a surname?" When his brow crinkled in puzzlement, she said, "A family name. One that is the same as your father's."

"Me father didn't stick around long enough t' give me a name."

"I see." Not that she was a snob—one of her friends had inherited money from three different noblemen, none of whom had married her mother—but she suspected Big Bill's circumstances were much different. "It sounds as if you've had a difficult life, yet you've done well for yourself."

"Aye, that I 'ave." He scowled ferociously. "Some people—I don't want to name names, but it's that blond gent up there charming the bigwigs—think they've done all the work t' get us so far, but that's not the truth. Not a-tall."

He was speaking of Mr. Rumbelow. How fascinating! "I can see you're a clever man."

Big Bill tucked his thumbs into his suspenders and swerved closer. "And ye're a clever girl."

She hoped so. She hoped she could get information out of Big Bill without landing in hot water. Edging away, she said, "So you've been with Mr. Rumbelow for a long time?"

"Rumbelow." Big Bill cackled. "Rumbelow." He laughed again.

"Why do you laugh?"

"Rumbelow kind o' sounds like the name o' a town, don't it?" Big Bill broadly winked at her.

"Oh." Madeline had been suspicious of Mr. Rumbelow, and it appeared her suspicions were correct. "You mean it's not his real name."

"Ye never 'eard me say that."

"No. I didn't." Although she was listening so hard, her ears were burning. "You've been with him for a long time?"

"Aye. Me and 'im go way back. Mind ye, I'm not saying 'e's not a smart one." Big Bill's brow puckered and he stared fixedly at his feet. " 'E is. But if 'e's the brains, I'm the muscle, and what's a brain without yer muscle, eh?"

"You're very wise." She brushed her hair back from her face. Despite her best efforts to fix it, tresses persisted in falling down from beneath her straw bonnet.

"I am."

"How long have you known Mr. Rumbelow?"

"Since we were lads. Forever, I guess ye'd say."

Madeline could scarcely breathe for excitement. This was information indeed! "You grew up together? Where?"

"In Liverpool."

"Liverpool? Not the Lake District?"

" 'Ow'd ye get that idea?"

"It was an impression I got." One Mr. Rumbelow had taken care to foster.

"From Liverpool, we are. We're no country rubes from no Lake District." Another long stream of tobacco juice darkened the grass along the road. Jerking his thumb toward Mr. Rumbelow, whose golden head was clearly visible above the ladies crowded around him, Big Bill said, " 'E was smart even then. Couldn't 'elp but brag on 'im, at least until the magistrate got 'im. Then I barely snatched 'im away in time. Got a rope burn from that, 'e does."

"A rope burn. Where?" Enlightenment dawned, and she whispered, "Do you mean he was hanged?"

Big Bill cast her a crafty glance. "Guess not. 'E's still 'ere, ain't 'e?"

Madeline had had her doubts about Mr. Rumbelow's background, but to know he had run afoul of the law and almost been executed put a different complexion on the whole affair. This was no longer a stupid game from which she had to rescue her father—and the queen's tiara. This game could result in . . . murder.

Despite the warm sunshine, a chill ran over her skin. She would have to tell Gabriel.

No. Wait. She could handle the situation on her own.

With a sigh, she conceded that was nothing but a wistful desire. She needed Gabriel to retrieve the queen's tiara, and she needed him to take action to stop this so-called Game of the Century before something deadly occurred. She didn't question why she thought Gabriel could fix everything; Gabriel had always had an air of capability that made her trust him.

To assist him she would unearth as much information from Big Bill as possible.

Yet she couldn't help a momentary delight when she considered pointing out Gabriel's imprudence in placing his trust, *and* his ante, into a character as shady as Mr. Rumbelow. "Big Bill, you're obviously a man of great resources."

Big Bill grinned again. "Where did ye learn t' talk like that?"

"Like what?" *Like what?*

"Like ye're grander than the grandest doochess." He gazed at her in frank admiration.

"Imperiousness runs in the family." She didn't give him time to comprehend. "Does Mr. Rumbelow often set up games like this one? Games with such stakes?"

" 'E's a good one fer grand stakes, but this is the grandest ever. 'E'll pull it off, though, ye'll see. 'E's spent years perfecting his plan."

His words raised goose bumps again. "His plan?"

"Aye, there'll be blunt when it's over." He snapped his suspenders. "In a few days, I could afford a fancy piece like yerself."

Madeline knew for a fact she'd never before been described as a *fancy piece*. She didn't know whether to be amused or outraged. She did know she should be quashing his pretensions, but he was giving her so very much information, information that might save fortunes. That might save lives. "You know that Mr. Rumbelow is going to win the game? But it's a game of chance."

Big Bill laughed long and loud. "Let me tell ye, we don't leave nothin' t' chance. Nothin'."

Madeline caught her breath.

"Not after that one time in Scoffield when we had a corpse on our 'ands, not that I didn't get rid o' it, but Rumbelow said that made things messy."

A corpse. Did Big Bill mean he'd *killed* someone? Madeline looked at his stained fingers, his wide lips, his greasy hair, and knew she couldn't control a man like this. Like it or not, it was time to retreat.

With a sense of relief, Madeline saw Mr. Rumbelow had extricated himself from the young ladies and was gesturing insistently. "I believe Mr. Rumbelow desires your attendance."

"What does 'e want now?" Big Bill spat the whole wad of tobacco out of his mouth, then fished a flask out of his pocket and took a long swallow. " 'E looks like 'e inhaled a hot poker."

I'll wager he worries about your discretion—and your drinking.

Big Bill offered the flask to Madeline.

She refused with an inner shudder of revulsion. She couldn't smile at him. Not after that comment about the corpse. Stiffly, she said, "I've enjoyed speaking with you."

Big Bill snatched her hand. "So I'll see ye tonight after ye're done fixin' yer mistress?"

His boldness made her skin crawl. "No."

"Feisty. I like that. Look out." He steered her toward the side of the road.

The carriages carrying the baskets of food and those guests too indolent to walk barreled by.

"Oops, there's yer mistress, and she's glaring knife blades at ye. Guess I'd better go afore I get ye in trouble."

"Guess you'd better." Not that Madeline couldn't handle Lady Tabard when the time came, but the time was not yet.

At another gesture from Mr. Rumbelow, Big Bill took off at a trot.

Lady Tabard was indeed glaring, but Madeline waved to her, nodded toward Thomasin and indicated she was doing well.

As indeed she was. The young lady had taken Madeline's instructions to heart and flirted like a woman born to the sport. For the younger men, it had taken nothing more than an inviting glance from her limpid eyes. At once, all her past transgressions were forgotten and they were at her beck and call. The rakes had taken a little more attention, but right now she was walking side by side with Mr. Darnel while Madeline kept her within sight.

Lady Tabard stopped glaring and deigned to relax against the seat, speaking volubly to Lord Tabard and pointing to Thomasin. He nodded with approval, and the carriages drove on.

Scanning the long line of people strung out along the road, Madeline managed to locate Gabriel not far ahead. She had to speak to him. Tell him he had to do something about this nefarious game and—

With a chuckle, Thomasin came back, snatched Madeline's arm and squeezed it. "Madeline, all the gentlemen like me, and I scarcely have to do more than smile and behave as if they were interesting."

"What?" Madeline wrenched her attention from Gabriel. "Oh. Yes. Of course. You're just what they want."

"Pretty, young and blessed with a fortune," Thomasin recited. With a last, flirtatious wave at Mr. Darnel, she observed, "Mr. Darnel's nice, and he said my dress last night was the most stylish thing he's ever seen. I told him you had designed it, and he's most impressed. Perhaps you could catch his interest and marry him!"

"I'm not here to catch a man's interest. I'm here to help you." Madeline knew that Mr. Darnel wasn't interested in females—she'd met his valet this morning and realized the affection between them was more than a mutual affinity for fine clothing.

"But you were talking to that coarse serving man of Mr. Rumbelow's." Thomasin's bowlike mouth turned down in a reproving frown. "You can do better than that."

Madeline couldn't believe the girl's impudence. In her best, superior tone, she said, "I believe *I'm* advising *you* on the propriety of your suitors."

"And I believe *you* need advice on your suitors if you're willing to stoop so low as that rough, disgusting fellow."

Madeline blinked at Thomasin's roundly expressed opinion. She hadn't realized the girl could sound so forceful. "I didn't speak to him with the intention of securing his interest."

"Perhaps not, but whenever a woman speaks to a man, the man always thinks she is fascinated by him."

Startled by this piece of wisdom from one who was little more than a child, Madeline asked, "Who told you that?"

With obvious pride, Thomasin said, "Jeffy. Jeffy is extremely wise."

Madeline had to agree. In this instance, at least, Jeffy was definitely wise. "Jeffy's right—and you're right."

"I am?" Thomasin looked startled. "Yes, I am."

"I won't speak with Big Bill anymore." Unless she needed more information.

"Good. Look." Thomasin waved a hand. "Mr. Rumbelow is scolding him for talking to you."

"I'm sure he is." Big Bill was shuffling along beside Mr. Rumbelow, looking mutinous and disgruntled, but Madeline had plainly heard the admiration Big Bill felt for his cohort. Big Bill wouldn't rebel against Mr. Rumbelow's strictures. Too bad, for Madeline had learned a great deal from Big Bill in a few short minutes. At the same time, her years on the continent had taught her situations existed that required she bring in a specialist. Her gaze shifted to Gabriel. She chafed at every moment that slid by when she couldn't speak with him.

But Thomasin required Madeline's guidance.

"Never mind Big Bill. You're doing very well for someone who has never flirted before. Your parents are ecstatic."

Thomasin smiled smugly. "They'll be so surprised when, after all this, I declare my intention to wed my true love."

"That they will." So would Madeline. It sounded as if Thomasin loved her Jeffy because of his looks and because he thought she was pretty. Without meeting him, Madeline couldn't make up her mind, but she thought Thomasin could do better. Madeline was very good at arranging matches, so she would look around—

Her gaze skidded to Gabriel and, for just a moment, she closed her eyes. Good at making matches? Yes, but not her own. She turned her head, so when she opened her eyes, she wasn't looking at him. "Do you and Jeffy ever disagree?"

Thomasin laughed, a chiming peal of merriment. "Absolutely not. We're perfectly in accord about every subject."

"*Every* subject?"

Thomasin gave a sigh and rolled her eyes. "Well . . . he wants to marry and stay in the neighborhood so he can help his father. I think his mother and That Woman will drive me mad giving me advice, but I want him to be happy, so we'll live there. I'll argue first, and he will yield concessions." With a grin, Thomasin fluttered her lashes at Madeline. "I'm not so fragile as I appear, you know."

"No, you're not." Irresistibly, Madeline's gaze was drawn to Gabriel again. Was that what she should have done? Compromised?

But no. He knew how she felt about gambling. He had betrayed her.

She looked again at Thomasin, her bonnet ribbons fluttering in the strengthening sea breeze. Thomasin's dewy beauty and melting blue eyes hid a mixture of maturity and childishness. She loved a man who was unsuitable, yet prepared intelligent plans to make their marriage work. Her cleverness made Madeline's love seem shallow, her reaction childish.

"I have only a few more men to entrance." Wrapping her arm through Madeline's, Thomasin said, "To please my parents, I should approach the titled lords who have a great deal of money."

"Absolutely."

"I'll feel safer with the older gentlemen." Thomasin gave a little skip and pulled Madeline toward Gabriel. "Come on, Madeline. I'm ready for a challenge. Let's talk to Lord Campion!"

Chapter Ten

"My lord, you look lonely." Lady Thomasin dimpled as she came up beside him, dragging Madeline.

Gabriel raised his eyebrows. He'd noted the young lady's flirtatiousness, but never had he imagined she would try her wiles on him.

Then he observed the expression on Madeline's face. Never had Madeline imagined Lady Thomasin would try her wiles on him, either, and clearly she didn't like this new development. Reason enough for Gabriel to encourage Lady Thomasin.

"I would be delighted with your company, Lady Thomasin." He bowed to the girl. In a conspicuous afterthought, he added, "And of your company, too, Miss de Lacy."

Madeline gave him her tight, close-lipped smile.

Good. Give her a taste of the frustration that he had suffered for so long. He waited until Lady

Thomasin walked at his right hand and Madeline had fallen in behind her. Then he turned swiftly to Madeline. "No, please, Miss de Lacy, walk beside me. I find it makes me nervous to have a woman such as yourself dog my footsteps."

"Yes, Madeline, join us," Thomasin said.

When it looked as if Madeline would refuse, he took her elbow and moved her to walk beside Thomasin. "Please, Miss de Lacy. Don't be shy."

Shy was the one thing Madeline had never been, and she flung him a contemptuous glance as he took his place on the other side of Thomasin.

Oblivious to the undercurrents, Thomasin said, "We'll have a jolly time on our way to the cliffs. Madeline, you can tell us all about your adventures abroad with the duchess of Magnus."

"That would be jolly indeed," Gabriel said with overhardy enthusiasm. "Her Grace is quite high at hand. You can regale us with tales of her headstrong behavior."

He saw Madeline's hand lift in a fist. If they'd been alone, he didn't doubt he'd now be fending off a clout.

Damn, it was good to see Maddie again . . . to come alive again. When she had left him, he'd been lost to anything but duty to his estates and his country—and his brother had paid the price. Then Jerry had died, and Gabriel's heart had shriveled. He had felt nothing: not pleasure, not happiness, not anger, not pain. His soul had been a wasteland, abandoned by love and unbound by duty. He'd been alone as no man should ever be.

Now he was aware of every heartbeat, every breath of air. He wanted nothing so much as to turn the full force of his concentration on the pursuit of Madeline. Instead this business with Rumbelow took precedence. But when it was over, Madeline could count on one hand the days of freedom left to her.

Gabriel gazed at Rumbelow as he moved among the guests. So many guests. So many innocents. Gabriel liked Rumbelow's setup less and less. Last night MacAllister had tried to sneak into the dowager's house, and discovered nothing except that buckshot stung when it met one's posterior.

Tonight Gabriel would do his own investigation.

In the meantime, he had Madeline to entertain him.

Her fist dropped. "Her Grace is all that is kind."

"Yes, sir, when I met her at the inn, I found her delightful. She seemed almost shy, and very gentle, which gave me hope that I might be as kind a lady as she someday." Thomasin clapped her hand over her mouth, and her wide eyes rounded. "But Lord Campion, I forgot! You said you were betrothed to her at one time, and the subject of Her Grace must be painful to you. Pray forgive me."

Faith, but the child was a pleasant creature! "There's nothing to forgive. The subject of the duchess is of only mild interest to me. She broke her word to marry me, and I never expected that. Her family takes pride in always doing as they promise, you see, and I hope she suffers guilt for ending a centuries-long tradition, as well as for backing out of our marriage at the last moment."

"And breaking your heart." Thomasin sounded so sympathetic, and so astonished. "I met the duchess. She seemed so pleasant. I would have never thought she could be so dishonorable, and so callus, too."

Madeline snorted indelicately.

"But Miss de Lacy is not the duchess, and I think it would be delightful to hear about her travels." He looked across the wide-eyed Thomasin to the only woman who could ever stir his blood to madness. "Where did you go when you left England, Miss de Lacy?"

Madeline was blunt to the point of rudeness. "Turkey."

"As far away as possible," he said in a voice of approval sure to chafe. "Good idea."

"Surely your geography is better than that," Madeline said. "Turkey is scarcely on the other side of the world."

"But it is in the far reaches of the Mediterranean— and no place for two ladies traveling alone. I fear the duchess's headstrong flight put you into danger." That truth still had the power to send him into a frenzy of ineffectual worry.

"Not at all. Her Grace is quite resourceful and when we left Turkey, it was under Turkish escort."

Thomasin clapped her hands. "Impressive! They must have greatly admired Her Grace."

Gabriel knew better. "My God, what kind of

trouble did you cause?" He held up a hand. "No, don't tell me now. I would be tempted to do a violence."

Thomasin giggled self-consciously. "Surely not, Lord Campion."

Madeline primmed her mouth like the self-righteous prig she most definitely was not. "Lord Campion is a man given to violent outbursts."

"You have no idea." As if he would ever harm a hair on her head.

The walk was long, and two of Rumbelow's carriages came by to pick up the ladies—and gentlemen—whose boots pinched. The number of walkers thinned. As they neared the coast, the road grew more isolated.

"Where did you go from Turkey?" Thomasin asked.

"Italy." Madeline tucked a strand of hair into her bonnet. "Tuscany, especially, was beautiful. Then Greece. I adored the food there."

"I suspect you adored the food everywhere." Long ago, he had teased Madeline about her appetite and her willingness to try any dish so long as it didn't run away. Now he smiled at the memory, and at the thought of Madeline making her gustatory tour of Europe.

"Not so much in Germany. They haven't the elegance with sauces the Southern Europeans possess. The French, especially—" She stopped guiltily.

"You were in France?" His assumption of amiability ill concealed his exasperation.

"Only briefly." Madeline looked everywhere but at him. "I thought we might be able to reach Marseille, and from there, home."

"Does the duchess of Magnus depend so much on your advice?" Thomasin looked awestruck and dismayed. "The advice you've given me has been marvelous, but entering Napoleon's France where he has ordered all English citizens arrested seems foolhardy."

"So you would think," Gabriel agreed. "What, pray tell, made the duchess believe she could cross hostile territory without arrest?"

Madeline began to resemble a wolf at bay, her head down, her hackles raised, her arms stiff at her side. "All of Europe was hostile territory. Napoleon was marching and capturing every city, and the French fleet was readying itself for battle. We found no safe harbors, no reliable roads."

Thomasin prayerfully clasped her hands. "Madeline, you and Her Grace were so valiant."

"Imprudent, rather," Gabriel said.

"If you felt so strongly about it, you could have come after Her Grace." At that betraying observation, Madeline bit her lip.

So she had noticed his absence, had she? Good. If he had suffered the agony of wondering if she was well, so should she have been looking over her shoulder, wondering if and when he would appear. "I could have."

"That's unfair, Madeline. He had a duty to organize the coastal defense," Thomasin said. "I

heard Papa talking about it. Lord Campion organized all of the north coast, didn't you, my lord?"

Surprised at Thomasin's support, he looked
down at the child. If she was willing to take on the
duty of chiding Madeline, then she wasn't the
fledgling she appeared.

"I did." He'd done more than that. In his yacht,
he'd ferried spies into France and spirited En-
glishmen out of France—but that task was not yet
ended, and he would never speak of it.

Ignoring both Madeline's startled glance and
Thomasin's decisive nod, he looked around. Here
the land shook off the effects of civilization and,
incited by the sea breeze, became wild and untamed. The grasses got coarser, the trees grew
stunted. His boots sank into the sand and gravel
on the road, then the road disappeared. The walkers broke out of the trees into rolling hills covered
with sedge. A series of red and blue tents had been
pitched, providing shelter for the tables and
chairs now occupied by the gamblers and their
wives. Some of the younger generation had seated
themselves on blankets spread on the ground, and
some walked along the cliffs where, just below,
the waves rolled, the horizon became a thin blue
line and the ocean met the sky.

It took Gabriel a minute to realize they'd lost
Madeline. Turning back, he saw her standing
stock-still, her face alive with pleasure. Her eyes
danced as she gazed upward at the soaring birds,
and her arms lifted slightly as if she would fly
with them. The wind plucked her haphazardly

coiffed hair from beneath her bonnet and plastered her sturdy gown of light green against every curve of her figure. The shining black strands blew behind her, and she was more magnificent than any bare-breasted figure on a sailing ship. She gloried in the wildness of nature—and nature gloried in her.

His heart and his mind leaped at the sight of her joy. He wanted to embrace her, to take her down on the rough, sandy ground and cover her with his body. To let the breeze caress them as he caressed her.

He laughed shortly, harshly.

Thomasin wouldn't understand, nor would any of the other women who strolled and sat, parasols raised to protect their fair complexions.

The men would understand, though. A quick glance around proved he wasn't the only man who had noticed Madeline's bliss. If he weren't careful, she would discover how easy it was to escape his influence in the arms of another man. Hurrying back to her, he took her hand. In his pleasantest tone, he said, "Come, Miss de Lacy. I don't intend to lose you."

She looked at him blankly, lost in the exhilaration of standing so close to the edge of eternity.

He saw the moment she recognized him. Her gaze sharpened, her chin lifted. Their pasts, and all the pain and dissension, possessed her mind. "You never had me."

Softly, he said, "I did."

"Not really. Not in the way that matters."

That, he knew, was the truth. But he would not fail again. With his hand on the small of her back, he drew her forward, back to Lady Thomasin, who stood watching their enmity in open bewilderment. "Miss de Lacy," he said, "I have a word of warning for you."

He knew Madeline fell in beside Thomasin for no better reason than she couldn't gracefully back away—and because she realized he'd put her back in place if she dared drop back again. "A word of warning? From you, my lord?" Madeline laughed, but he recognized the undertone of scorn. "What would that be?"

"I find Mr. Rumbelow's servants to be less wholesome than one might hope. I suppose it to be the result of his hosting a bachelor household, and I'm sure when he picks a young lady to wed, the matter will be remedied." He imagined no such thing, but he cast a smile at Lady Thomasin that suggested he had total confidence in their host.

It wouldn't do to alarm Rumbelow's guests. Not yet. "In the meantime, Miss de Lacy, I would suggest you confine your flirting to the *gentlemen* of the party."

At last he had made Madeline truly angry. She stepped out, her long legs eating up the ground. Her bosom rose and fell with fury. He only wished she wore a gown with a less modest neckline— but then, he was a disreputable male beast with lascivious tendencies. Tendencies directed solely at Madeline.

Thomasin trotted to keep up. "I, too, told her that."

Ruthlessly, Madeline interrupted the girl. "Lord Campion, I hardly think a recommendation from you, a notorious gambler, can influence my choice of persons with whom to associate."

"But Madeline, Lord Campion has only your best interests at heart," Lady Thomasin said.

Matching Madeline's stride, Gabriel took another poke at her composure. "While your adjourn abroad might have made you more susceptible to disreputable characters, I think you'll find that here in England, we expect our young ladies to associate with gentlemen of their own class."

Madeline glared over the top of Thomasin's head at Gabriel. "Yet who of the gentlemen here isn't under the curse of undisciplined gambling, resulting in disaster time and again?"

In her soft voice, Thomasin said, "But Madeline, many gentlemen here aren't gambling. They've come with their fathers, at Mr. Rumbelow's invitation, accompanying their mothers or sisters for a social—"

Gabriel interrupted, his gaze never leaving Madeline. "Don't bother with logic, Lady Thomasin. Miss de Lacy is famous—or should I say infamous—for being unreasonable."

"Lord Campion!" Lady Thomasin looked wildly between the two of them as they strode straight for the cliffs. "That was uncalled-for!"

He barely heard her. He saw only Madeline. "My dear Miss de Lacy," he drawled, "not every man who gambles is undisciplined. Some men gamble with a specific goal in mind, and once that goal is reached, they quit."

"Until they are again drawn into the game by their own weakness," Madeline retorted.

"You two are making me uneasy with your accusations," Lady Thomasin protested.

"Perhaps some females should have more sense than to judge a man when they've not seen him for four years and they know nothing about his circumstances or motivations."

"I'll just stop here and let you two go on." Lady Thomasin stumbled to a halt.

Madeline walked on. So did Gabriel.

Breathing fire, Madeline said, "This particular man cared so little for me he used the very methods I despise to win himself a fortune."

"Ah, but that's not what irks you, my darling. It's that when I hold a fortune, I can be more than your dependent, and you have a man you can't control."

"Like my father."

He caught her arm and pulled her to a stop. "I am *not* your father."

They reached the edge of the cliff, both still seething with fury.

"You don't have to tell me that. I *know* who you are."

"No, you don't." He held on to her, stepped

closer, stared into her eyes. "You never gave me a chance to prove the kind of husband I could be. You were too afraid."

"Afraid? Afraid? How dare you? I was never afraid."

"Afraid I would be just like him. Uncaring, superficial, leaving you to make every decision and pay every dun."

She sputtered incoherently.

"My darling, did you really think you could manage me with an allowance? I'm like a wild stallion. I'll allow a woman to put the reins on me, and take her on the ride of her life, but only with my consent." At last he let her draw back. "You never understood that."

Blue eyes wide, she stared at him. He could see the signs. She was wary now. If they were alone, he would give her more reason to fear him.

But people were watching, the two of them had already made a spectacle of themselves and Gabriel didn't care to have Rumbelow know how very much this woman meant to him. Softly, he said, "Run along, Maddie. You have a lady to chaperone."

Madeline glanced around, realized Thomasin was missing, and, with a gasp of dismay, darted back, away from the edge of the cliff.

Too late. Before it was over, he swore to himself she would tumble over—and land in his arms.

Chapter Eleven

Idly, Thomasin ran sand through her fingers and watched as the servants cleared away the remains of the meal and the ladies whipped out their sketch pads. "Do I have to sketch? It's a dead bore."

"Not if you're good at it," Madeline said as she handed the picnic basket to the footman with a murmured thanks. She returned her attention to Thomasin, seated on the blanket beside her. "Which I might guess you're not?"

Thomasin cast her a sideways glance. "For someone who's been a companion all of your life, you're quite pert."

Madeline sat up straight. "Pert? In what way?"

"Well . . . in that way. Your tone isn't comparable with a servant." Thomasin's nose twitched as she thought. "You don't act like a servant."

Oh, dear. What was it Eleanor had said? *One can only be a companion if one is not prompted to give one's opinion on every subject. If one is not moved to arrange things and people, if one is not given to the habit of command.*

"On the walk over here," Thomasin continued, "you spoke very frankly to Lord Campion."

The girl was not as unobservant as Madeline might have wished. "He and I are old acquaintances. The duchess and he—"

"Were betrothed. I know. So you've said. But apparently you feel quite free with him—and he with you."

The back of Madeline's neck prickled. Gabriel had seated himself behind her, and without even looking, she knew he had watched her through luncheon. *Merde!* How he did vex her with his constant, none-too-silent observation.

What did he think to accomplish by this harassment? She frowned.

What *did* he hope to accomplish? "I'll take more care in the future to behave in a proper manner."

"Don't bother on my account," Thomasin answered. "I find it fascinating to hear you two quarrel so robustly."

"We *don't* quarrel, and it was *not* robustly. We simply discuss matters in an emphatic way." And, Madeline realized too late, she shouldn't have corrected Thomasin in such a manner. Such behavior was exactly what Eleanor admonished her about.

Madeline had to put a stop to this conversation else she betray herself completely. In a mannered tone, she said, "If you don't like to sketch, I see that some of the young ladies and gentlemen are practicing archery, and some are playing croquet."

Thomasin collapsed into a fit of giggles. "See? Even when you're trying to sound like a companion, you say the wrong thing. If I wish to question you, you're not supposed to change the subject."

"I knew that." Certainly Eleanor never changed any subject Madeline had chosen to bring up.

With a glance along the cliffs, Thomasin groaned. "Lord Hurth is headed this way."

Never had Madeline been happier to have a conversation interrupted. "Smile! He's going to ask you if you'd like to walk with him or watch him play lawn tennis."

Thomasin did smile, but spoke out of the side of her mouth. "He's handsome, but rather too impressed with his own importance."

"He's excessively eligible. It would make your stepmama ecstatic should he court you."

Thomasin peeked back at her parents, who lolled in the shade of the tent. Her father chatted with the other gamblers, but her stepmother observed her with a gimlet gaze. "I walked with Lord Hurth part of the way here, and he's a pompous bore."

"Those who live at Hurth Manor have that reputation."

"He uses a hundred words when ten will do, and when he's not talking about himself, he's talking about his activities or his clothes or his family, which is apparently the finest, oldest and most respected in all Britain." Thomasin inspected him as he drew near. "And don't you find that costume vulgar?"

Hurth's gold leather short boots matched his gold-striped cut-away jacket, and his royal blue padded waistcoat sported a gold trim of such contrast the sight gave Madeline a headache. His tall collar points were starched so stiffly he could scarcely turn his head, and the way he moved suggested he wore a corset around his waist to give the fashionably nipped-in look. All in all, a dandy with execrable taste. "I think when a man will inherit the title of marquess, a large fortune and some of the finest racehorses in the country, he can make his own style."

"So you *do* think he's vulgar," Thomasin deduced.

"I'm not an arbiter of sophistication."

"I think you are," Thomasin said shrewdly.

Madeline stared out as the terns hovered, then dove into the waves, and pretended she didn't know what Thomasin meant.

"Hurth spoke to me of his horses."

"Really?" That was good news. "You must have impressed him. Hurth's family is horse-mad, and only deigns to discuss their breeding lines with intimates."

"I did what you instructed. I fluttered my eyelashes, I asked questions as if I were interested and once I lightly touched him on the arm."

"Apparently, it all worked. And surely you are interested in horses. Doesn't Jeffy's family breed them?"

Thomasin looked embarrassed. "Yes, but I don't relish hearing about them."

Madeline contrived to appear surprised. "But that will make your married life rather dull."

"Jeffy usually doesn't talk to me of horses. Usually he talks about my hair and my smile."

"How sweet." *How insipid.*

"Yes. Here is Lord Hurth. I shall make you pay for your good advice." Extending her hand, Thomasin dimpled up at the bowing Hurth. "My lord, how good to see you again."

"I was hoping that you and, of course, your companion would care to take a stroll along the cliffs." Hurth combed through his side-whiskers with his fingers. "You were so interested in the evolution of the medieval horse into its modern, more delicate and faster descendant, I thought I could clarify the matter for your edification."

"How marvelous of you to think of me."

Without an ounce of sensitivity, he agreed. "Yes, isn't it?"

Thomasin rolled her eyes at Madeline, allowed him to help her to her feet.

Madeline scrambled up on her own. Hurth was as much of a bore as ever a Hurth could be, with a consequence much exceeding his charm. Yet nothing could ever convince a Hurth he wasn't the grandest of creatures, and if he decided to woo Thomasin, he would be difficult, if not impossible, to shake.

Well. Thomasin might temporarily suffer, but his attentions could be turned to their advantage.

Yet Madeline's compassion for the girl lasted

only until Thomasin led them toward the tree that sheltered the lounging Gabriel.

"Lord Campion, we're going for a stroll, and my companion is without an escort." Thomasin didn't even have to finish her invitation.

Gabriel rose and bowed. "A delightful day for a walk. With your permission, Lady Thomasin, I'll join you."

"Wonderful!" Clapping her hands, Thomasin cast an impish glance at the fuming Madeline.

In a roguish manner that sat ill with him, Hurth wagged his finger. "I've claimed Lady Thomasin, Campion, but if you want the companion, you may have her."

A maddening smile formed on Gabriel's lips. "I'm enchanted to walk with the companion."

Hurth never comprehended his incivility, although Thomasin looked as if she might give him one of her set-downs.

Madeline shook her head at the girl. Madeline could take care of herself, and indeed, someday Hurth would feel her wrath—although he would probably never comprehend what he had done to deserve it. She had known that aristocrats paid servants no heed; she thought, for the purpose of her masquerade, indifference would work in her favor. But such a blatant insult offended her, and the contrast to Gabriel made her grind her teeth. She would *not* be grateful to Gabriel for his consideration. Yet she could not speak her mind or ignore him or snub him, no matter how much she wished to. She needed this opportunity to speak to him about the information Big Bill had given her—and about retrieving the queen's tiara. So she followed Hurth and Thomasin along the winding path overlooking the beach.

Tucking his hands behind his back, Gabriel paced along beside Madeline. "You have quite an interesting expression on your face. Rather as if you were chewing on gristle."

They walked out of sight of the tents, onto a wild patch of ground that slowly descended toward rolling hills. Golden samphire bloomed in small bright patches, blue butterflies fluttered from blossom to blossom and no one could hear what she had to say. No one except the couple ahead of them. The sound of Hurth's monotonous voice drifted back on every breeze, so Madeline dawdled just enough to allow them to walk out of earshot, yet not out of sight. "It's nothing."

Obviously, Gabriel didn't believe her. "Pay no attention to Hurth. He's the kind of man who kicks his grandmother's dog when she's not looking."

Madeline stopped in the path. "Do you know that?"

"Jerry saw him. Later, Jerry beat the stuffing out of Hurth." The faintest of smiles drifted over Gabriel's lips. "Accidentally."

When Madeline had known Jerry, he'd been happy about his brother's engagement and, at the hint of an invitation, tagging along after them. For the most part, she and Gabriel had been careful not to issue invitations. They had wanted to be alone, or as much alone as any two courting people could be, and the presence of an excitable, if beloved, brother had been too much. "I'm glad Jerry took care of Hurth. I just wish . . ." Stupid sentiment, to wish he were still alive. To wish she'd been kinder to him.

Yet Gabriel understood. "So do I. I miss him, too."

There it was again. A past they shared, an empathy that needed no words. She didn't want this, but such rapport wasn't so easily dismissed.

That rapport was exactly the reason why she felt that she must confide Big Bill's conversation to Gabriel. Gabriel wouldn't dismiss her fears, and he had the power to act on the information. In a lowered voice, she said, "I beg your pardon for my comments on our previous walk. I hadn't realized that you'd taken part in organizing the coastal defense. You obviously made good use of your time while I was gone."

"Apologizing for vivisecting my character, Maddie?" He gave the appearance of odious amusement. "You must want something."

She did, of course, and the way he called her on it put her back up. "No! Rather, I have something to tell you. On the way over, Big Bill—"

"Big Bill?"

"Mr. Rumbelow's servant," she explained.

"Ah. The one you were walking with. The one who swaggers and conceals a pistol in his belt."

She paused, one foot in the air. "Really? A pistol?"

"Did you think he was a good man and a humble servant?"

"No, and if you would just be quiet a moment, I'll tell you why."

Gabriel was quiet. Very quiet.

She realized he had once more goaded her into thoughtless speech. How did he do it? Always digging at her, always prodding and examining the results like a boy performing an experiment. She responded only too often—even now her temper stirred her blood—and she had that wretched favor to ask. Reining in her irritation, she said, "Big Bill told me something which I believe is an indication of trouble."

"Trouble follows you, my dear Maddie."

She gritted her teeth. "He told me that Mr. Rumbelow is not from the Lake District, but from Liverpool." She waited for Gabriel to show amazement, but he did no more than watch her loftily. Determined to shake his composure, she added, "He said they'd been raised together, and that Mr. Rumbelow had been almost hanged!"

Gabriel strolled on as if he had not a care in the world. "Have you told anyone else?"

"I just found out myself." Then she realized what his lack of inflection must mean. "You knew about this?"

"Let's say . . . I'm not surprised."

Trying to gather her equanimity, she looked out at the ocean, then back at the man who she had imagined would . . . would rescue Mr. Rumbelow's guests from possible harm. "We have to do something."

"We?"

"These men are very possibly criminals."

"Without a doubt they're criminals, and *we* aren't doing anything."

"Murderous criminals. Big Bill said he disposed of a corpse one time."

Gabriel nodded so calmly, it was clear he still didn't understand.

"We're in danger," she expounded. "*You're* in danger."

"I can handle myself. It's you who are the wild card."

As revelation struck, she tripped over a stone in the path.

Catching her arm, he set her on her feet, then withdrew his touch and once more walked beside her, his hands tucked behind his back like the gentleman he most certainly was not.

He did understand, she realized. He'd always known about Mr. Rumbelow. "That's why you came to the game. You're planning something."

"I thought you said I came to the game because I'm an irrational gamester."

She dismissed that with a wave. "Never mind what I said. That explains why Big Bill's been set to watch you!"

"Yes, and he's not very good at it."

"You knew that, too?"

Gabriel reported, "I can safely say I've been boring him to death."

She started to glance behind them, but Gabriel shook his head at her. "Rumbelow will rein him in now. After all, what could I do when accompanied by two ladies and another nobleman? Big Bill should have been watching MacAllister last night, but I'll not tell him that."

She could scarcely contain her excitement. "MacAllister is helping you? Let me help you, too."

"This requires a keen eye and a knowledge of the game." He smiled mockingly. "In fact, it requires one of those dread creatures, a gambler."

She ignored that. He was simply digging at her. "I could help in another capacity. I'm a good shot."

"That you are. I've seen you shoot. But I hope it won't come to that."

She'd seen that stubborn expression on his face before. He wasn't yielding. So she would have to watch and help surreptitiously, as her chance came. "*What* is your scheme?"

"To thwart Rumbelow's nefarious plan— whatever that might be."

She deduced, "You know he has a nefarious plan, but you don't know what it is."

"Nefarious plans are his specialty." Gabriel crossed his arms over his chest and had the gall to look amused. "Give it up, Maddie, I'm not telling, and you're not going to help."

A thought occurred to her. "I can't see you going about the countryside saving people from their own foolishness."

"Nor can I. It's a good way to get killed."

"So why are you involved?"

"That's none of your concern." His indifference was complete and exasperating.

On the path in front of them, Thomasin looked around as if to check their progress. "Is all well? Isn't this walk lovely?" she called, and threw Madeline an agonized glance.

Hurth glowered as if the interruption displeased him, and at once returned to his droning speech.

Madeline felt no pity. After inviting Gabriel along on this walk, Thomasin deserved every moment of stultifying boredom she suffered.

She didn't, however, deserve to be injured by a dreadful criminal. "We should tell everyone that they're in danger from Mr. Rumbelow."

Gabriel grabbed her elbow and pulled her to a halt on the headland. "No, we shouldn't, and you won't. I forbid it. You won't ruin this setup. I've spent most of the past year putting the idea in Rumbelow's head, and if you rock the boat now, people are going to get killed. Just trust me. And go home."

"Depart?" His brusque command startled her. She hadn't thought that, once Gabriel had her in his power, he would let her go so easily. "How can I leave Thomasin and the others? They're in danger."

"No. I have matters under control."

"What kind of control?"

"Would you just trust me?"

"Of course," she said in surprise. If Gabriel had

a plan, she could be sure it was a good one.

He hesitated. "Then leave."

"Not as long as that tiara is in jeopardy." Hurth and Thomasin were still within sight, so she was still fulfilling her duty as companion. Taking a fortifying breath, she said, "Papa's not here yet."

"He's not coming, so depart."

"Why should I? I shall take care to remain safe from danger, and I'll keep Thomasin safe, too. In addition, I have every reason to believe Papa will show up. He even sent the queen's tiara ahead as ante." She waited for Gabriel to say something, to give her an opening to beg his help.

His eyelashes barely flickered. "Foolish of him, but considering who he is, not surprising."

"You shouldn't speak that way about my father." Not that it wasn't the truth. That was why she didn't dare do the wise thing and abandon Chalice Hall. Even when she was with him, Papa reliably got in trouble, and look at the grand trouble he got her into when she left the country!

"I beg your pardon." Gabriel's brows pulled together in a scowl. "You don't insult my family. I shouldn't insult yours."

"I could never insult Jerry." She smiled in fond remembrance. "He was charming."

"And young. Very young. Very foolish." Gabriel changed the subject with so little finesse, it was obvious he still couldn't speak of his brother without pain. "You wanted to ask my help, I believe."

Hurth and Thomasin walked unhurriedly,

while Hurth educated Thomasin about something that appeared very important—or at least, important to him. Madeline slowed down yet further to lengthen the distance between the couples. "I need you to win that tiara for me."

Gabriel stopped walking. "Ah, is that what all this appearance of affection is about?"

She flashed, "It's not affection, it's merely tolerance." Then she remembered that a little adulation wouldn't come amiss, and added, "I don't want you dead."

"Just knocked about a bit." His hand caressingly slid up her arm to her shoulder, and he leaned close enough to stare into her eyes. "You don't approve of gamblers, yet you need me now. Poor Maddie, it must have choked you to ask."

So he wasn't going to be pleasant about this. A strand of Madeline's hair escaped and fluttered about her face.

Gabriel tucked it beneath her bonnet. "You want your tiara, do you? What are you willing to pay for it?"

His love made her uncomfortable. "Pay for it?"

"You didn't think I would win something as valuable as the queen's tiara and just hand it over, did you? An immoral gambler like me?"

Disappointment pierced her—although surely she should have expected this. She started walking, her arms stiff at her side. "No, I suppose you wouldn't. I can give you my vowels."

"What are your vowels worth? Your very self

has been lost to Mr. Knight. You and all that you own. You have nothing."

She stared at Gabriel in a kind of helpless horror. Of course, it was true. In some logical corner of her mind, she'd known it was true. But she was a duchess in her own right. She had always owned more land, had more wealth than anyone else she knew. Even her father's gambling deprecations hadn't made a dent in the family fortune.

And Papa had tossed it all away in one throw of the cards.

Even then, she'd thought she would go to Mr. Knight, talk some sense into him and all would return to normal. She hadn't thought that before she could take action, she would need resources and need them immediately. Grasping Gabriel's arm, she said, "You must trust me when I assure you—"

He answered tonelessly. "Only a fool trusts at a gaming table."

She shouldn't be surprised at his ruthless rejection. She shouldn't, but she was. Her hand fell away. "So you won't help me?"

"I didn't say that. But I require . . . a promise. A promise you won't break."

"I don't break—"

He held up one finger. "Don't lie, either."

For she did break promises. She'd broken the promise to marry him.

"What I want from you is a night in your bed."

Her breath caught in her chest. He didn't mean it. "What? No!"

"Yes!" He did mean it. His eyes were filled with something that should have been triumph, and instead looked like rage.

Her voice sounded harsh, not like hers at all. "You said it yourself. I've been wagered to Mr. Knight. Surely that makes me unavailable for the kind of bargain you want."

"He shouldn't have waited for you to come to him. Possession is nine-tenths of the law." He glanced around them. Hurth and Thomasin had disappeared over the rise. They were alone in the valley. Pulling Madeline into the grove of trees, he caught her in his arms and lowered his face to hers. "Go home," he whispered. Pushing her bonnet off her head so it dangled on its ribbons beneath her chin, he kissed her.

She shouldn't let him. She'd already suffered a taste of his seduction, and she'd proved herself only too susceptible. But he kissed so well! And life had become so complicated. The issues were no longer clear-cut. She no longer knew what to think on every matter. She no longer knew who to trust and who to fear.

But she knew she never feared Gabriel. He held her firmly against his body, warming her, letting her feel his strength. Her hands rested on his protective shoulders. Her eyes closed, shutting her into a dark world of the senses. The breeze blew over her skin, cool and tinged with the scent of brine. The branches above them creaked, the leaves rustled, and in the distance, the waves crashed on the shore. Sunshine dappled her with heat. His lips rocked on hers as if that light pressure gave him the greatest pleasure in the world, until she herself opened her lips slightly for just a sample of him. Just a quick flick of her tongue.

Catching her tongue between his lips, he sucked on the tip. With a swirl, he lured her into his mouth. Open to each other, they tasted, touched. She descended into a pool of spinning colors, red and black and bursts of gold. Her pulse beat at her temples and wrists, her breath blended with his and the two of them became one with the wind, the trees, the earth. They were the embodiment of wildness, of nature . . . of untamed, glorious passion.

Lifting his mouth, he waited until her eyes fluttered open, and whispered, "Go home like a good girl, and if the tiara is gambled, I'll win it for you."

She stared into his face, seeing the marks of passion—the faint swelling of his lips, the heaviness of his lids. His hips pressed tightly against her; he was aroused and ready, and she wanted to give him everything, anything, that made him happy.

"Promise me, Maddie," he coaxed.

Luckily, with him her instinct was to be mistrustful. Holding her silence, she waited until her brain functioned once more. Functioned, returned to normal and grappled with the fact that he'd kissed her with the express intent of coercing her into doing his bidding. She breathed deeply of the fresh air, trying to catch her balance when, as always, Gabriel made her dizzy.

Reaching behind her, she grasped his wrists and pulled herself free. She stepped out of his embrace. "I can't go home. As you so callously pointed out, I have no home left." Not be Madeline de Lacy of Lacy Manor? It didn't bear thinking of. "Now I need to follow Thomasin before she realizes she's been compromised." Discussion over, she hurried away, her mind tumultuous with all she'd learned today, and all she must do to set matters right.

He easily paced beside her, his hands behind his back once more. "You're in danger here."

She retied her bonnet to frame her face, then lifted her face to the wind, hoping the cool air would clear the signs of passion from her face. "If I leave and my father arrives, there'll be no one to talk him out of this reckless gamble."

Gabriel's teeth audibly snapped together. The color rose in his face as he stared at her, brows down, jaw clenched. "He's not coming."

She stared back. "There's no changing the facts. He'll be here. He loves to gamble. I only wonder why he's so tardy."

In a hoarse, goaded voice, he conceded, "If he appears, I could talk to him."

Her sarcasm bubbled over. "That should achieve the goal. I'm sure he'll listen to you, a confirmed gambler." Exasperation pushed her over the edge. "He'll imagine you want him gone because you wish to avoid a challenge, and be all the more determined to play."

Gabriel muttered as if to himself—although she heard him very well—"I tried. I did try." Raising his voice, he said, "Then you'll pay my price for your tiara."

Chapter Twelve

"Ye told her what?" MacAllister crumpled the freshly laundered, stiffly starched cravat in his hands. "Ye dunna mean it!"

"Of course I do." Gabriel removed the cravat from MacAllister's grip, shook his head over the spoiled cloth and tossed it aside.

"Ye told wee Miss I'm-the-Duchess-and-Don't-Ye-Forget-It that ye'll win the queen's tiara, and just hand it over withoot a kiss on the rump or a . . . Wait a minute." MacAllister squinted at Gabriel. "I'll wager there *is* some rump-kissing involved. Yers."

"You know me too well." Extending his hand, Gabriel waited until MacAllister gave him an unwrinkled cravat.

"So ye're going t' take precious time when ye ought t' be resting up for the game, and spend it romancing a duchess who's already done ye wrong?"

"I wouldn't put it in quite so unflattering a manner, but . . . yes. I believe that covers the matter."

"What I'd like t' know is, what does that lass possess that makes yer guid sense fly away? She's always been trooble. She's always going t' be trooble, and ye don't need any more trooble. Especially na' now, when ye're so close t' locking a wrench around Rumbelow's ballocks!"

Trouble? MacAllister was right about that. Madeline was trouble.

"Get rid of her," MacAllister urged. "Send her away. Do yer romancing later."

Gabriel carefully placed the cravat around his neck and began the intricate process of tying it correctly. "She still won't go."

"Why in the bluidy hell na'?"

"Because her father might yet appear." He met MacAllister's gaze in the mirror.

MacAllister grimaced. He knew very well what Gabriel thought of Madeline's father. Not long after she'd left for the continent, in a fit of drunken rage, Gabriel had expressed his disgust of Magnus eloquently and vehemently.

MacAllister hadn't understood—he wasn't much for human relationships.

"Did ye tell her she could get killed?"

"She figured it out on her own."

MacAllister's jaw dropped. When he managed to close it, he asked, "And she won't leave? I jump every time I see one of those villains with their guns tucked into their waistbands. I'd go."

Gabriel shook his head at this profession of cowardice. MacAllister had never backed away from a fight in his life. "You can't. I'll need you before this is all over."

"Humph." But Gabriel could tell MacAllister was pleased. "Even with her being here under yer very nose, ye dunna have t' pursue her."

"Yes, I do."

"I dunna know why."

Neither did Gabriel. What existed between him and Madeline was like nothing he'd ever experienced or could hope to experience again. Four years ago, when they were first together, she had been without a clue to the extraordinary nature of the bond between them. A bond of the flesh, yes. They were wild for each other, desperate to mate. But more than that, they were friends, with the same imagination, the same sense of humor, the same ideals—although she doubted that now. If he'd been the kind of man to buckle under and be her puppet-husband, they would have had a good marriage. But he wasn't, and they didn't. Instead she'd made that scene at Almack's, and during her upbraiding, all he could think was that she threatened to leave him.

He hadn't said a word. He had taken her invective.

When she'd returned home, he'd done what he'd spent many previous hours imagining—he'd climbed the tree outside her window and come through to take her as his woman.

He'd thought that would fix everything. He'd

thought she would recognize and acknowledge his claim.

Instead, when she was gone and he was alone, he'd been haunted by memories. And those were worse than his former imaginings, for they were real.

He knew what her breasts looked like, heavy and full, with peach-colored nipples that responded to his touch. He knew her golden skin was soft and warm, especially between her thighs . . . especially in the place that he made for himself. He knew she responded to his touch with demands of her own and with slow, deep moans that gave him her blessing even as he hurt her.

And he had hurt her when he entered her. For a woman so tall, so brash and bold, she had been small inside, wrapping his cock in a heat so tight he still woke, dreaming of her, shaking with desire. But no matter how tiny she had been, he had given no quarter because he could not—could not—pull out. She'd paid him in kind, biting him, digging her nails into his back. She'd marked him; he'd marked her.

Then she'd left him.

"Damn!" He threw the ruined cravat to the floor.

MacAllister slapped another in his hand. "Ye're going t' go through all of them if ye'll na' pay heed."

When Gabriel had been inside her, he had owned her. Her inner tissues had caressed him, her hips had curved up to accept him, her legs had clutched his hips. Each of her movements might have been orchestrated to give him pleasure, for each movement had brought him closer to the climax of his life. When he'd come inside her, he'd emptied himself, his seed spurting into her womb with such force, he died from the bliss. And was resurrected even before he pulled out, to do it again.

Dear God, what a night that had been!

MacAllister made a huge fuss as he brushed Gabriel's fine, dark blue jacket.

Gabriel ignored him.

Then he'd seen Madeline at Chalice Hall, proud as ever, tall, beautiful, perhaps a little thinner, and he'd suffered from a cockstand so persistent more than one married lady had noticed, and provided him with an invitation to indulge. He didn't care to indulge with them. He wanted only Madeline, and having Madeline was next to impossible.

Unless—he grinned savagely in the mirror—she gave in to his blackmail.

MacAllister observed that grin, and apparently didn't approve. "Ye canna have the lass permanently. Her father lost her t' that American."

"Mr. Knight shouldn't have waited for her to come to him. I understand the game he's playing. Having her come to him is a way to establish power, yes, but when his prize is wandering about the country, he's taking a chance someone with less principles will make a claim." Gambling ethics be damned. Gabriel had always known he would make his claim on her; no other man was going to swoop in ahead of him.

"When did ye lose yer principles?"

"I haven't lost them. I simply don't choose to utilize them with Mr. Knight. Winning a wife at cards is a damned poor way to go about a courtship."

"Principles are principles. Ye canna discard them at whim, or ye're no better than Rumbelow."

Gabriel winced. "A low blow, MacAllister."

Gabriel had done his research. Rumbelow never pulled the same swindle twice. He seemed to take delight in surprising his victims—and the magistrates. The underworld of London and Liverpool took a kind of pride in his accomplishments—and they despised him, too. The term *honor among thieves* meant nothing to Rumbelow. He had begun his career with a select group of intelligent thieves to swindle the old and helpless. But after a few years, when he had his crew well in place, he pulled a job, a fantastically large fraud, that fleeced nobles and merchants. Rather than split the proceeds, he cheated his team, and when the law closed in, he disappeared, taking the stolen goods and leaving his men to hang or be deported.

MacAllister knew all that. He'd tracked the few who survived, talked to them, learned all there was to know about the man they had called Master.

But nothing MacAllister said could change

Gabriel's mind about Madeline. "Nevertheless, I'll keep her. It's her word she would marry me against the duke's word that she would marry Knight. I have prior claim."

In his doleful voice, MacAllister said, "Ye should be ashamed of yerself, taking advantage of a young woman's desperate bid t' preserve her one remaining family heirloom."

"You'd think I would be ashamed, wouldn't you?" Gabriel wasn't ashamed. He was glad of the opportunity. "Her father's made her life a misery all these years. If she's going to put her life at risk for him, and I have to let her, then she's going to pay for my worry—and my protection."

"That's stupid."

"Probably."

Gabriel had never been a good man. Until he'd met Madeline, he'd been a rakehell, a fortune hunter and a womanizer. Then all his dormant ambitions had coalesced into one—that of being her partner. Since she'd left, he hadn't experienced one moment of the wildness that had so attracted Madeline.

Apparently, all it took was one disdainful glance from her fine eyes, for now the rakehell had returned in full force.

He was going to have her, and he wanted her to know it, to think about it all the time. He wanted the cockstand in his trousers to be matched by a soft melting between her thighs. He wanted to know that if he slid his hand under her skirt and touched the curling hairs, they would be damp

with her desire . . . for him. That afternoon, when he kissed her, when he tasted her, it had been all he could do not to pin her against the tree and take her where they stood. And to hell with everyone else.

He hadn't because it was too soon and too public.

"Ach, that looks guid."

It took Gabriel a moment to realize his valet spoke of his cravat. A moment to examine it in the mirror. "That does look good. Hand me my jacket and the knife for inside my boot." Lifting the yellowed lady's glove from atop the dresser, he held it to his nose, sniffed the faint, lingering scent of leather and Madeline and smiled. "Let me go to the ball."

Chapter Thirteen

Thomasin snatched the hairbrush out of Madeline's hand. "You're awful at this."

Madeline hated to admit it, but it was true. Thomasin made Madeline, in her plain dark muslin, feel tall and inelegant. Thomasin's gown of white sarcenet was overlaid by a short tunic of pale pink crepe, with short sleeves and a low bodice that displayed her bosom admirably. Only the tumbled blond hair detracted from the vision that was Thomasin, and Madeline could do nothing about it. She couldn't get her own tresses to behave in an orderly manner, much less tame Thomasin's board-straight mane. "Your hair just doesn't seem to want to cooperate. Maybe I should try the curling iron. . . ." Madeline cast an uneasy glance at the round metal tongs sitting on the hot stovetop.

"No! I saw what you did to my new silk gown. You're not getting near me with a curling iron." With a deep sigh, Thomasin rose and pointed at the dressing chair placed before the mirror. "Sit down. I'll show you what I want."

With a flounce, Madeline seated herself. "I hate failure." Like the failure of the afternoon, when she unsuccessfully attempted to convince Gabriel to win her back the tiara.

"Yet you seem to have a lot of them."

Madeline bit her lip on her retort. How could it be so difficult to do what Eleanor had always made look so easy? Madeline had spent fifteen minutes this morning trying to light a fire in the grate, and finally Zipporah had had to be called in. Lady Tabard's skinny maid hadn't believed Madeline's tale of damp flint and steel, and proceeded to start the fire the first try. She'd been insolent about it, too.

Comb and brush in hand, Thomasin brushed Madeline's long, dark hair. "I have suspicions about you."

"Suspicions?" Madeline's voice sounded too high, and she brought it down an octave. "What kind of suspicions?"

"I think perhaps you weren't always a companion. Were you a lady before, and your parents died and left you with no means of supporting yourself?"

A likely tale, and one Madeline wished she'd thought of herself. "Yes, indeed! Quite right!"

Thomasin considered Madeline in the mirror with a most odd expression.

"I mean . . . yes. I feel as if I'm still training to be a companion."

"None too successfully." Thomasin tugged at Madeline's tresses. "I saw you. You failed to keep me in sight this afternoon. I was alone with Lord Hurth."

"Did he try anything?" It would sour Madeline's stomach if she had allowed the ruin of such an innocent girl.

Thomasin snorted. "He didn't even notice you were missing. He was too busy expounding on the new chairs his mother is buying for the formal dining room at Hurth. He's a mama's boy."

Madeline grinned. "It could've been worse. It could've been horses."

"We had exhausted the subject of his horses," Thomasin said chillingly.

"When we caught up with you, I did tell Hurth it was time to turn back."

"You should have done that within the first fifteen minutes. But you were too busy talking to Lord Campion." With her hands on Madeline's shoulders, Thomasin made her swivel to face the room and twirled Madeline's curls around her finger. "You two were at each other's throats on the walk to the beach. Is there something you want to tell me?"

"He's a lout?" Madeline offered.

"No, he's not. He has the reputation of being quite a gentleman, but rather distant. With you, he's anything but distant. Indeed, even when the rest of us are present, he looks at no one but you, and in a manner most improper." Thomasin cleared her throat. "Were you the reason why Her Grace broke off her betrothal to him?"

"No! He gambled and won a fortune and his propensity for cards offended Her Grace so much—"

"That's nonsense! A minor offense at most, and not even true. That Woman says he hasn't gambled since."

If that were true, what did it mean? That he deigned to come to this game, not because the longing to gamble had become too much, but because he considered Mr. Rumbelow a threat that needed to be eliminated? That made Gabriel a hero. That would be too much to bear. That would require an . . . apology.

Madeline shuddered.

Picking her words with care, Thomasin said, "So I think perhaps he loved you rather than her."

Madeline was speechless. When one was not in possession of all the facts, the theory made sense.

"From your demeanor with him, I must assume you didn't love him in return."

"No," Madeline said faintly.

"That's good. I would have to have you broken-hearted at the end of this party, for a companion cannot marry an earl." Turning her once more to face the mirror, Thomasin wrapped Madeline's hair around her fist in a series of loops and began pinning it. "But you already knew that."

"Yes," Madeline said even more faintly.

"Of course, Her Grace is more attractive than you are, but from what he said today about her breaking her vow, she's not as beautiful on the inside as on the out." Thomasin shook her head sadly. "I had liked her, too. But one can never judge on first acquaintance, can one?"

Irritated with Gabriel all over again, Madeline snapped, "The duchess had good reason for breaking her vow."

"I didn't know there was ever a good enough reason. That Woman told me to carefully consider before I gave my word, for to break it is a grave wrongdoing."

Madeline wanted to snap again, but . . . she couldn't. She'd been taught the same thing, and no matter how she tried to justify her own actions, she still suffered a vast disquiet and, yes, guilt. If Gabriel knew, he would be very happy.

"But don't worry about the comparison to the duchess," Thomasin was saying. "You're quite attractive, especially with this coiffure. I would simply advise that you maintain a little more distance when speaking to Lord Campion."

"If I had my way, I would never speak to him again." If Madeline had her way, she wouldn't pay his price for the tiara.

"See? There you go again. I offer a little disinterested advice, and you snap out an antagonistic response. If you wish that people not notice and, more important, not gossip about you and Lord Campion, you'll have to learn how to present a facade of indifference."

Not even Eleanor dared lecture Madeline like this.

Thomasin twisted and pinned some more. "I can't be the only one who'll be able to guess you were the cause of the duchess's scene at Almack's."

Madeline didn't know whether to deny or ignore. After all, if her father hadn't appeared by the time the game started—and she was getting anxious that he hadn't appeared—she would be gone from here and what Thomasin thought wouldn't matter.

But she would run into Thomasin in society, and Lord and Lady Tabard, too. They'd recognize her. They'd realize she had made fools of them, and they—especially Thomasin—would be hurt. Madeline frowned at her own reflection. Eleanor had warned her about this, but she hadn't listened.

Very well. Before the next time they met, she would seek out Thomasin and explain everything. No—first she would confirm that Jeffy was not an appropriate husband. She would arrange that Thomasin receive an offer from Hurth—that shouldn't be difficult, he was as infatuated as ever a Hurth could be. The girl would refuse, which would set the stage for more offers and more refusals. Then Madeline would find Thomasin the proper mate and urge them toward matrimony, Thomasin would forget any lingering animosity toward Madeline and all would be well. Yes, Madeline had Thomasin's life well in hand.

If only she had her own life so well in hand. She had . . . before she joined this party. Now she desperately needed a different plan for acquiring the tiara other than giving herself in sin to Gabriel. Again.

"Are you cold?" Thomasin asked. "You've got goose bumps."

"Someone must have walked on my grave." Madeline answered with the old bromide, and thought more desperately that she needed a plan. Yet what with returning to the house, bringing Thomasin her bathwater, tentatively ironing her ball gown, and helping her to dress, Madeline hadn't had a moment to herself. When did companions ever rest? Eleanor was not as sturdy as Madeline, nor as outspoken. Madeline frowned harder. When next she spoke to Eleanor, she was going to give her a stern lecture about the importance of never overextending herself in Madeline's service.

"Will you stop frowning?" Thomasin snapped. "It's impossible to finish this when you're tugging your face every which way, and we want to finish before—"

From the doorway, Lady Tabard said in awful tones, "Thomasin Evelyn Mary Charlford, what are you doing?"

For one moment, Madeline closed her eyes against the blazing gold feathered turban and matching gown, which gave Lady Tabard the appearance of a large, round pat of butter. Yet Madeline discovered if she squinted, Lady Tabard's appearance was bearable. Sinking back into the well-known role as duchess, she waved her in. "Lady Tabard, please come and see what Thomasin has just shown me. The most marvelous— Ouch!" Madeline rubbed the spot in her scalp where a pin had been placed with rather more force than she thought necessary. "That hurt!" Catching Thomasin's narrowed gaze in the mirror, Madeline abruptly realized Lady Tabard might not view Thomasin's service to her favorably.

Briskly, Thomasin finished and gestured Madeline up. "Now you may show *me* the style *you* favor." As Madeline slid out of the chair, Thomasin slid in, explaining, "My pardon, Mama, for dawdling, but I had a style I wished to show Miss de Lacy, and she has a style she wishes to show me."

"Dawdling?" Lady Tabard's voice hit an ear-piercing note. "You are indeed dawdling. Indeed you are." Bustling forward, she snatched the brush from Madeline's hand. "Miss de Lacy has no hairstyles to show us. She is unable to do even her own." Vigorously, she brushed at Thomasin's hair, then pulled it so tight that Thomasin's eyes slanted.

"Miss de Lacy wears her hair in the Italian style, disheveled and windblown."

Madeline couldn't believe Thomasin could invent such tales.

"Italian style?" Right before Madeline's astonished eyes, Lady Tabard performed miracles with hairpins and a ribbon. "That's a polite way of saying ineptly done."

"I think it's attractive," Thomasin said.

Snatching up the curling iron, Lady Tabard curled the hair around Thomasin's face with amazing efficiency. "Today, if not for her bonnet, Miss de Lacy's hair would have been falling about her shoulders."

Madeline silently admitted the justice in that, but deemed it right she keep her silence.

"There." Lady Tabard pinched Thomasin's cheeks, then hauled her to her feet. Dragging her toward the door, she said, "Hurry, girl, get your gloves and your fan. We're already late!"

"No!" Both Lady Tabard and Thomasin stopped in astonishment at Madeline's boldness, but about this matter Madeline was quite confident, and she spoke with authority. "You shall be the last one to the ball, Lady Thomasin, and you shall make an entrance."

"But . . . but . . ." Lady Tabard sputtered, "the other young ladies have already gotten Mr. Rumbelow's attention!"

"Exactly. They've rushed down there as if they have nothing better to do than to fawn on him. A man doesn't value a woman unless she's difficult to obtain." Madeline observed Lady Tabard's openmouthed wonder. "Don't tell me you didn't play hard to catch with Lord Tabard."

Lady Tabard's mouth snapped shut. "Oh. Well." She fussed with the gathers in her skirt. "There is that."

Satisfied she had squelched any more objections, Madeline turned to Lady Thomasin. "You shall pause in the doorway until people notice you, then you shall smile—you have a marvelous smile—and glide in."

"But I can't glide in," Thomasin said. "If I pause in the doorway until people notice me, I'll be nervous."

"You'll pretend to be calm." Madeline created a rippling motion with her hand. "Think of a swan, who glides serenely along the surface of a pond, while beneath the water, its feet are paddling furiously."

Brow puckered, Thomasin thought about it, then nodded. "I can do that."

"Of course you can. As you make your entrance, you'll wave to the other ladies, just a friendly little flutter of the fingers, and glance coyly at the gentlemen."

Thomasin practiced the flutter and the glance.

"Very good," Madeline approved. "You'll at once be inundated with invitations to dance, and you'll have to make wise choices."

"She's never been inundated with invitations before," Lady Tabard said sourly.

"She's never before had me advising her." With crushing certainty, Madeline answered, "I may not know hairstyles, Lady Tabard, but I do know society."

Chapter Fourteen

"My dear Miss de Lacy, you were right!" Lady Tabard paused beside Madeline's chair, set behind the wallflowers, behind the matrons and against the far wall of the ballroom. "Thomasin is the belle of the ball."

Madeline didn't underestimate the concession Lady Tabard made. She would be willing to wager that Lady Tabard said *You were right!* very infrequently. With what Madeline hoped was proper humility, she replied, "Thank you, my lady. I was happy to help."

Lady Tabard gestured toward the dance floor, where couples curtsied and circled in a country dance. "Mr. Rumbelow is looking on her very favorably, I believe. That is his second dance with my dear daughter."

"Lord Hurth is looking on her favorably, too, and he comes from an ancient and well-respected family." The lively music made Madeline's toe tap beneath her skirt. "Lady Thomasin professes dedication to a young man . . . I can't recall his name . . ." She feigned ignorance.

"Mr. Jeff Radley," Lady Tabard said in tones of doom. "A young Lothario."

"Thomasin sings his praises."

"Of course." Lady Tabard lowered her voice. "He's handsome and dances well. He also flirts with any young lady who crosses his path and has professed his love for three different girls in the past year. That's why we brought Thomasin away. The connection will not do."

Just as Madeline had suspected. Generously, she returned the compliment to Lady Tabard. "If that's the case, then you're right, of course."

"Generous of you to say so," Lady Tabard said acerbically.

Madeline had to stop slipping into the role of duchess. She was giving Lady Tabard heartburn.

"On the other hand, Mr. Rumbelow is immensely wealthy." With obvious relish, Lady Tabard indicated the emphatically blue ballroom, filled with flowers and alive with the chatter of thirty-five guests and melodies played by cello, violin and recorder. "It's rumored he has twenty thousand a year!"

Madeline pursed her mouth. "Really?" She drew out the word, drew out her doubt, until Lady Tabard had no choice but to notice.

"You don't believe it?"

"I've never heard of him before, and *I'm* a de Lacy."

"Well . . . yes, but . . ." Lady Tabard plumped

her bosom like an old biddy plumping its breast feathers. "He puts on a show of amiable wealth, and he is hosting this game!"

"A show, indeed, but how many men do we know who made such a show and who are now done up?" Before Lady Tabard could retort, Madeline held up her hand. "I could be wrong. But I do wish I knew who his people were."

"Well . . . yes, that would be good. However, I'm sure he's a pink of the *ton*." But Lady Tabard had a frown line between her brows as she watched Thomasin circle the room in Mr. Rumbelow's arms. "Lord Hurth, you say?" She hurried off, her gaze fixed purposefully on her husband.

Madeline relaxed and watched the dancers. Lady Tabard was not quite the dreadful woman she'd first thought. Her vulgarity was undiminished, but she had a shrewd eye for a prospect and perhaps a lurking fondness for Thomasin. That was good. Madeline would hate to try and offset the effect of a wicked stepmother. What with establishing Lady Tabard on the right track, Madeline had fulfilled her responsibility to Thomasin.

Now she could worry about herself. Gloomily she watched as Gabriel made his way across the ballroom toward her, plate in hand. She hadn't yet been able to think of another way to win the tiara than to have Gabriel do it for her, nor had she been able to think of another thing to offer him that would satisfy him the way—she took a deep breath—she could.

"Miss de Lacy, I thought you might like a few of the delicacies our host has so thoughtfully provided us." With a bow, Gabriel presented a napkin and the plate, filled with a selection of foods selected specifically to tempt her appetite. It would appear he remembered all of her preferences, and with devilish good timing, he appeared when hunger clawed at her belly.

A matter of indifference to the members of society, for she, as companion, wouldn't be allowed to go in to dinner later, nor to obtain a glass of punch, or even to visit the ladies' retiring room, although she had already disobliged Lady Tabard in that manner. Her job was to sit quietly and observe Thomasin, to be available if Thomasin needed help with her gown, to make sure no rampaging male tried to make unwanted advances. The task bored and tired her, especially since the gathering was small and Thomasin was on her best behavior.

So it was Madeline's great misfortune to have Gabriel appear, looking so handsome and enticing her with provisions. Ignoring the scandalized glances of the matrons, she accepted the plate. Projecting both her voice and great formality, she said, "I thank you, Lord Campion."

His response was sardonically ceremonial. "You're very welcome, Miss de Lacy. May I have the pleasure of your company while you dine?" He indicated the chair next to hers.

She saw the matrons crane their heads around to stare, and her manners disintegrated. Lowering her voice, she hissed, "Yes, yes, seat yourself and stop hovering. You're attracting attention."

A slight smile twitched at his lips as he performed as ordered. "When you're hungry, you're always grouchy."

"I am not." She bit into a tea cake. Her breath caught at the flavorful twist of lemon, and she gave a sigh of pleasure.

"Obviously, I was wrong." He watched her lick the frosting off of her finger with a dark intensity that made her spread her napkin in her lap and utilize it daintily.

There was a reason why women didn't lick anything while a man was present; she just hadn't realized it before. "It's your infamous proposition which has made me unhappy."

Lifting an eyebrow, he tipped his head toward the curious ladies in front of them. "Do you want to talk about it *now*?"

She hated when he was right almost as much as she hated having to be discreet. Taking a restraining breath, she asked, "Are you enjoying the ball?"

"It's a blasted bore."

Madeline grinned. She'd seen him trot every young lady in the room onto the floor for the obligatory promenade. He danced with the two young Lady Achards, with the three Misses Greene and with all four of the Vavasseur daughters. The list had seemed endless, stocked as this party was with young ladies dressed in pale gowns that fluttered and clung. Madeline was glad he hadn't enjoyed himself. Yet if he fell in love with someone else, he wouldn't be interested in her.

She didn't question her own irrationality.

He watched her chew a macaroon with as much intensity as he had the tea cake. "You ought to know: Monsieur Vavasseur has claimed he recognizes you, and identifies you as the duchess."

Madeline swallowed, choked and coughed into her napkin. When she had recovered, she said, "I thought I had sufficiently avoided him."

"Apparently he took note of you this afternoon while you were scolding me to hell and back on the walk to the beach."

"I was not scolding you to hell and back!" Nor should she be using such language, and his accusation had distracted her from the main point, which was, "How widespread is the tale?"

"I heard him making the claim when I returned his fair daughter after our dance."

With wicked delight, she asked, "Which fair daughter is that?"

"What?" He seemed honestly discombobulated.

"He has four fair daughters. Which one are you talking about?"

"I don't have any idea," he said impatiently. "I'm not interested in those silly twits, I'm only interested in you."

"Oh." Her lips formed the word, but she had

no breath to speak. She had thought to tease him. He had cut away the claptrap with his usual single-mindedness.

Satisfied he had silenced her, he continued, "I believe I squelched the rumors about you. I assured Monsieur Vavasseur I had been betrothed to the duchess and I certainly would recognize her." He brought up his quizzing glass and appeared to be scrutinizing the dancers, but Madeline knew very well he had fixed his attention on her. "Of course, I didn't say you weren't the duchess, I only said I would recognize the duchess. It is to be hoped he doesn't realize the disparity."

"Because we can't have you lying," she said sarcastically.

He brought his quizzing glass around and trained in on her. "No. We can't."

And she remembered again that she wished him to do her a favor. Regardless of the provocation, she had to be gracious.

Apparently he read her mind, for without missing a beat, he asked, "While you were abroad, how many men did you kiss?"

"Sh!" She glanced around at the matrons and wallflowers seated before them and whispered furiously, "Are you trying to ruin me?"

"Not at all. It's a reasonable question."

Indignation overcame good sense, and she asked, "What makes you think I kissed any?"

"I *know* you." He dangled his quizzing glass by

its silver chain. "How many men did you kiss trying to get the taste of me off your lips?"

He was so conceited. "Lots. I had a man in every town."

"Oh, *Madeline*."

His disbelief made her huff. "Really. I did. You're not the only man who likes to kiss me."

"Most men are too frightened by you to dare try." He swung the quizzing glass back and forth, back and forth. "How many men did you kiss?"

She stared, hypnotized, at the swaying motion. "Dozens."

He shook a reproving finger at her nose.

So she had overreached the bounds of his belief. "A dozen."

"Better."

She didn't know why she was bothering to lie, except that . . . well, she despised that confidence of his. She needed to end this conversation, and like a bulldog, he wouldn't let go until he had the truth. She ate an apple tart, dusted the crumbs from her fingers and lifted her chin at him. "Five."

"Five men? That's the whole truth?"

For a moment, his teasing tone returned her to the time when they'd been helplessly in love— and like a ninny, she wanted to be back there. "Four and a half."

With a laugh that sounded rusty with disuse, he asked, "You kissed a dwarf?"

"It was only half a kiss. I made him stop. I

didn't like it. I didn't like him. He had bad teeth and smoked cigars."

"Poor darling," Gabriel crooned.

Not that he meant it. His broad, smooth lips smiled, his eyes were as green as the trees and the way he watched her made her feel dizzy and faint. How did he do it? How had he managed to distract her from good sense?

In a tone of breathtaking cheek, he asked, "How many men did you sleep with?"

"Insolent!"

"How many?"

With just a few words, Gabriel administered a slap of passion that made the color rise in her face. She put the plate on the floor and, when she came up, pretended that her blush resulted from that. "The matrons are watching us and gossiping."

"Answer, and I'll leave you alone."

How could she ever have thought she was in love with such an obnoxious man? A frantic glance at the ladies confirmed that their scandalized gazes were fixed on her. "None. Eleanor wouldn't let me." Madeline didn't want any other men, but she wouldn't tell Gabriel *that*.

Apparently she didn't have to. "Your own fastidiousness wouldn't let you."

She had to discover another way to get her hands on that tiara. An audacious plan seized her. Perhaps she could . . . but no. That would be dangerous.

She looked again at Gabriel. *He* was dangerous. Turned in his chair to face her, one foot crossed over his knee, the rich, dark fabric of his coat impressively showcasing those broad shoulders, that narrow waist. Handsome, daring and vividly, fabulously desirable.

Yes, she had to get that tiara without Gabriel's help, and if the only way she could do it was by stealing it, then steal it she would. "After my experience with you, I am indeed fastidious."

Gabriel appeared airily unimpressed by her crushing reply. "So, you kissed four and a half men and didn't like it, and you wouldn't sleep with any of them. One might suppose you're still infatuated with me."

"One might suppose that, because of you, I've had enough of men to last a lifetime," she retorted. "Childish, impulsive, irresponsible—"

His lips flattened into a thin, grim line. "That's your father you're talking about, not me."

"Is there any difference between you?"

"Yes."

His flat reply made her wonder, as she always had. Why did he dislike her father so much? Men usually liked Papa. He was a jolly fellow who gambled, drank and drove with the best of them. So what was it about Lord Magnus that made Gabriel turn curt?

Gabriel watched her as her concentration, which he had focused so thoroughly on himself, turned to her father. The man who had cared so little for her he had gambled her away to a scoundrel, an American.

"He's still not here," she murmured, and

glanced around the ballroom, as if expecting to see the red-faced, bullish older man burst in, clap the men on the shoulder, kiss the ladies on the cheek and finally notice his only offspring, his only relative.

With a lack of inflection, Gabriel said, "The one thing you can depend on is his lack of reliability."

"His gambling instincts would never fail him. In everything else, he is . . ."

"As I said, unreliable." When Madeline had disappeared, Gabriel had sworn he would have her again. He'd thought long and hard about what he'd done wrong, and he'd come to the conclusion he'd been too free with his declarations of devotion. If he was to manage her correctly, he needed to keep her uncertain of his affection and never knowing what he would do next.

After all, her father did that and she was devoted to him.

It was a measure of her worry that she now agreed with Gabriel about Lord Magnus. "I know. I remember . . . the letters he had failed to send to our steward, instructing him to provide me with an allowance so I could run the estates. The times he promised to be home for Christmas and failed to appear." Abruptly, she stopped, covered her mouth for a moment, then gazed about the ballroom as if interested in Madame Vavasseur's flirtation with Lord Whittard.

For the first time, she had admitted to the distress her father brought her. Gabriel didn't underestimate the importance of her revelations—or the fact that she'd turned to him to retrieve the queen's tiara.

Matters were progressing nicely.

In a voice of studied airiness, she said, "Papa's absentmindedness seemed excessively tragic at the time, until I realized I simply had to arrange matters so he could not fail in his responsibilities to me and our dependents."

"Resourceful of you." Gabriel wanted badly to touch her hand, to reassure her that she'd done an excellent job. But he needed her to be off balance. He wanted her to think about, imagine, dread and anticipate her fate before it overcame her. "You've been gone four years. How did Lord Magnus manage without you?"

"I had hired a good steward. He proved to be quite adequate, and honest, too. I am a good judge of character." She snapped her mouth shut, as if realizing she had either not been a good judge of character with him, or she'd made a mistake when she rejected him.

He didn't pound the point home. She was a bright girl. She knew.

"Some companion!" Lady Margerison's shrill voice carried back to them. "Improper and forward. She should be watched!"

Gabriel scowled at her.

"Gabriel, you must go, but first . . ." Madeline's eyes were large and solemn as she inquired, "Earlier. When you were talking about kissing . . . and . . . and . . ."

"Intercourse?" he filled in helpfully.

"Why did you ask me such insolent questions?"

Standing, he bowed and prepared, for now, to retreat. "I want to know if you are equal to the value of the tiara."

Rumbelow took a moment from the dancing, the conversation and the fawning girls to survey the ballroom. Everything was going as planned. The guests had relaxed in the familiar milieu of a house party. The young ladies were flirting, selling their goods to the nearest, richest gentlemen, just like the whores he'd known on the streets.

All except that little Lady Thomasin, who fled Lord Hurth from one corner of the ballroom to the next.

Rumbelow would go rescue her. She didn't like him, either; it would be amusing to see how Lady Thomasin would react when caught between a rock and a hard place.

The gamblers were relaxed, too, giving attention to their beloved wives and dear children to make up for the fact that tomorrow they'd be locked away in the dowager's house, playing as if their souls depended on the turn of a card. When in fact, only their wallets did. Their souls were long lost.

Ten thousand pounds apiece, ten gamblers—that was one hundred thousand pounds. The expenses were twenty thousand pounds, but the tradesmen couldn't dun someone who had fled the country. He would never have to pull a job again. He might, though, just to keep his hand in.

He smiled as he looked around at the baaing sheep waiting to be fleeced. Yes, he might have to, just to prove he could.

Thomasin's "companion" was sitting against the wall wearing an expression that could only be called defiant. Well, of course. Campion had been after her like a hound after a bitch. She was planning something; Rumbelow would give his eyeteeth to know what was hiding beneath that demure facade.

Perhaps she thought of nothing more than the news Monsieur Vavasseur had spread about the ballroom. That she was the duchess, not the companion. Rumbelow grinned toothily. Just as he had foreseen, things were getting interesting.

Of course, he would give a lot to know what Big Bill had said to Her Grace today, too. Big Bill denied doing anything but courting her. Big Bill had always been a fool, and a drunken fool at that, but he never caviled at robbery or murder. So Rumbelow kept him close and utilized him frequently. Rumbelow had never before thought him a *dangerous* fool, but if he had told "Miss de Lacy" anything that had shaken her confidence in the party or in Rumbelow, she gave no indication. So perhaps they were all right.

And perhaps Big Bill would have to be eliminated when this job was wrapped up.

Rumbelow sighed. It was hard to say good-bye to old friends, but money would soothe the sting.

The tall, elegant, preternaturally calm Lord Campion stood chatting with Monsieur Vavasseur.

Campion had a reputation for ruthlessness, and was hand-in-glove with the English Home Office, setting up coastal defenses and doing God knows what in defense of his country—Rumbelow admired himself in the mirror as he sneered—but the Home Office wouldn't be interested in a mere swindler. So what was Campion's game, *really*?

Whatever it was, the duchess had effectively distracted him. Campion knew the truth about Lady Madeline. Would he betray her to the crowd? Rumbelow thought not. Not until he had achieved his goal of bedding her. Then, Rumbelow was sure, Campion would take a pleasurable bit of revenge. Certainly that was what Rumbelow would do.

Rumbelow's gaze lingered on her lush figure. Bedding her would be enjoyable, and if rumors were true, she had experience. There would be no whining about the pain from her—although he occasionally enjoyed that, too.

Instead there would be the pleasure of knowing he was swiving a duchess.

It was a thought that bore attention.

Chapter Fifteen

When Madeline's eyes sprang open, the night candle had burned low. She remembered immediately what she must do.

Steal the tiara.

Rising quietly, she checked Thomasin. The girl slept soundly, worn out from her triumph at the ball, where she had been feted and fought over by the gentlemen, and envied by the other young ladies.

Going to the window, Madeline parted the heavy curtains. The darkness outside was almost total, lightened only by faint starlight. Clouds whipped by, shredded by the wind, and everything below appeared empty and silent.

Madeline took a satisfied breath. She could see the outline of the dowager's house from here, a two-story box of a house looming behind and to the right of Chalice Hall. Not a light shone from its windows. The house waited for tomorrow night's game—and for her tonight.

From the inside corner of her trunk, she removed her pistol and carefully loaded it with powder and ball. She slipped it into the special holster she'd had made of black velvet, and belted it around her waist. She didn't plan on shooting it, but when one intended to steal back one's own treasure, a treasure no doubt protected by some blackguard or another, one had to be prepared for every eventuality.

With a small piece of paper, she made a cone, filled it with gunpowder and folded the top down. One of the French soldiers she'd met had taught her the trick of blowing a lock. She'd always thought it would come in handy someday. She suspected that day had come.

Finally, she tucked the flint in her pocket with the stub of a candle, donned Eleanor's darkest bonnet, one with a wide rim that placed her face in shadow, and slipped from the room.

As she crept down the corridor, she heard the clock strike three, and counted herself lucky that she saw not a single gentleman tiptoeing along toward adultery.

She took extra care in passing Gabriel's bedchamber. The man had always seemed to have a sixth sense about her intentions, and she doubted he would approve of them now. Nor would he care that he'd left her no choice. He would rail at her, demand she stop and probably, right then, insist on payment for a job he hadn't completed.

Her steps faltered. Then she hurried on, fleeing temptation on leather-slippered feet. She had been outraged by his demand that she pay him for his services with her body. She still was. Moreover, that faint sensation of elation she had experienced when he made his claim mortified her. She denied it, and would until the day she died. She might admit, in the secret recesses of her soul, to wanting Gabriel, but she would not be helpless. Bitter experience had taught her the misery of vulnerability, and time had taught her wisdom.

Therefore, when she retrieved the tiara, she wouldn't waste precious time gloating to Gabriel about her coup. Instead she, for once, would do as Eleanor would advise if she were here, and make good her flight, prize in hand. With luck, Madeline would be gone by sunrise.

She departed the main house via the side door, left conveniently open by, no doubt, one of the footmen as he slipped out on a tryst. Eleanor's gown of dark blue might not please Lady Tabard, but it worked admirably well to conceal Madeline as she slinked across an unknown landscape, keeping to the shadows of the trees and the tall trellises.

The wind smelled clean and fresh. It plucked at her skirts with playful fingers, got behind her and pushed her toward her goal. Branches groaned. Leaves flapped. She could distinguish the black shapes against the thinner darkness. A tree, a gazebo, the dowager's house rising before her.

She experienced an unruly exhilaration. If she could just pull off this one heist, she would have control of her life again.

Her sense of omnipotence faded when she rounded the corner and caught a whiff of tobacco. She froze, then stared into the darkness. There. A cigar glowed as one of Mr. Rumbelow's men took a puff. On her guard, she backed away and considered.

Mr. Rumbelow stored the tiara in the dowager's house in the safe. He would have guards, but perhaps the guards were all outside.

She grinned ruefully. And perhaps not.

Staying in the deepest shadows, she moved along the side wall, stopping every few feet to listen.

In her experience, people perceived trouble that didn't exist and refused to try, while she tried and overcame trouble as it occurred. Most of the time difficulties could be defeated with a little daring and determination, and of those qualities, Madeline had plenty. That, and a pistol in her pocket.

But first she had to get in. Blowing the lock or breaking a window would be too noisy, so . . . she found the side door and turned the doorknob.

The door opened easily and without a squeak.

She frowned. The door from Chalice Hall was open. This door was open. It was almost as if someone had already come from Chalice Hall to the dowager's house. And why? For the same reason she had? Or for some other, darker reason?

Well, whoever it was, was in for a surprise, because the duchess of Magnus was a formidable opponent, and that tiara was *hers*.

Quietly, she tiptoed inside, expecting at any

moment to be grabbed. There was no one. By the sounds of her soft footsteps, she knew the room was large and tall, a study perhaps, but drapes covered the windows—and it was *dark*.

Shutting the door, Madeline crept inside, hoping desperately not to bang her shins on the furniture. Taking her time, she crossed hardwood and carpet and, as her eyes adjusted to a yet denser darkness, she spotted the way out of here. She moved toward the inner house, and wondered if she would have to use her stub of a candle to find the safe. Surely it had to be in the gaming room, but where would the gaming room be?

In the library or the drawing room, someplace roomy and luxurious where men could wager away huge sums of money while suffering from the illusion of invulnerability.

She moved into the next room, large enough but bereft of furniture, and made her way through easily. She realized she had reached her goal at the next room. The smell of tobacco permeated the air. She found five small tables, straight-backed chairs and larger, cushioned seats. She searched for the safe. She banged her shins on the ottoman. "*Merde!*" she whispered, and even that seemed too loud in the silence of the dowager's house. At last her hands touched the large, cold metal box— the safe. It stood as tall as her thigh and was solid, heavy steel. She slid her fingers down the front, following the outline of the door until she found the locking mechanism. Groping in her pocket, she found the stub of her candle—

From somewhere behind her, a door slammed.

She dropped the candle, quickly searched the floor, found and pocketed it. She heard men's voices, lifted in argument, and reassured herself with the touch of her hand on her pistol. Light shone through the door, getting closer. She ducked down beside the table. She held her breath, and hoped no one heard the pounding of her heart.

"I'm telling ye, all day yer guests 'ave been sneakin' around, lookin' in the windows, tryin' the doors, an' I saw someone come in the house."

Big Bill. Madeline recognized that voice, although his tone had changed from cocksure to fawning.

"The door was locked. Everything's secure." Mr. Rumbelow sounded sharp and cold.

Madeline's eyebrows rose. The door was locked? She hadn't locked it behind her. How had that happened?

"I'm tellin' ye—"

"I believe you." They moved closer, and by his tone it was clear Mr. Rumbelow was displeased. "But why don't you know who it is? It's your job to watch the safe."

"I 'ave been! Me men are out 'ere night an' day, but we're not supposed t' make ourselves known t' yer fancy lordly guests."

"So you would rather mingle with them." Mr. Rumbelow didn't contain his impatience. "They'd abandon the house and the game if they knew who you are, and demand their ante back, too."

"Stupid cows," Big Bill muttered.

The men entered the room. The light of Mr. Rumbelow's single candle seemed far too bright, and Madeline lowered her head.

"I'm not interested in excuses. If you expect your part of the take, you'll do better than this. Take a guess. Who was it?" In the dark, Mr. Rumbelow sounded less aristocratic and more like . . . Big Bill.

Big Bill sounded surly. "It's a man."

A man? Was there a man in here, too? Which in light of the open doors made sense, but he also added an element of yet more danger.

Mr. Rumbelow must have made a face, for Big Bill snapped, "I couldn't see nothin' else. In case ye 'aven't noticed, mate, it's darker than 'ades out there."

"We'll have to search the house. Get the men out around the perimeter. I'll sweep upstairs and move down. Have someone watch the doors and catch him as he runs out."

"Shoot 'im?" Big Bill asked.

"Let me talk to him first. He might just be one of those idiotic noblemen trying to fix the game."

Big Bill gave a hoarse laugh. "Like that'll matter."

Mr. Rumbelow chuckled, and said in a genial tone, "Yeah." Then Madeline heard a thump, a choking sound, and Mr. Rumbelow snarled, "Or he might be making real mischief."

Madeline peeked up over the edge of the table. Mr. Rumbelow held Big Bill by the throat, up against the wall, his arm like a bar over Big Bill's throat. The candlelight gave Mr. Rumbelow's handsome face a demonic twist . . . or was it his expression, his intention? "Don't ever underestimate these bastards. Some of them are smart. Some of them are honorable. Some are even both, but most of them would rob me and brag about it from a safe distance."

Big Bill gagged.

Mr. Rumbelow let him go, and Big Bill slid down the wall.

Mr. Rumbelow hadn't dropped his pistol. He pointed it at Big Bill's nose. "Never forget who's in charge here."

"Nay," Big Bill gasped. "Won't." Though he still held a rifle tucked in his arm, he looked like nothing more than a thug.

Madeline had dealt with plenty of those on her travels. They were risky, but they could be handled. It was the men of intelligence, vicious men like Mr. Rumbelow, who proved treacherous.

Who was Mr. Rumbelow? What did he have planned? The questions had never seemed more important.

As they moved into the corridor and the light from Mr. Rumbelow's candle faded, she slowly stood up. She needed to discover what was happening here. But first she needed to get out of here, and with men watching the doors, that would be—

Someone grabbed her by the arm. She gasped,

but before the sound escaped a man's hand covered her mouth.

She swung hard with her elbow, catching the fellow in the ribs.

He grunted. Then, in a fierce whisper, Gabriel demanded, "What in the hell are you doing here?"

Chapter Sixteen

As Madeline caught her breath, the thought flashed through her mind—she almost preferred Mr. Rumbelow and his pistol. Prying Gabriel's hand away from her mouth, she whispered, "I came to . . . um . . ." Then it occurred to her—she didn't owe Gabriel an explanation. "What are *you* doing here?"

Still holding her arm, he pulled her across the corridor into another room, darker yet than the gaming room. She heard the faint clicking of his flint, saw the sparks and at last a candle sprang to light.

He did it more easily than she did, but she had time for only a moment of faint resentment before seeing his furious face.

And he *was* furious. He wore a black shirt, black trousers and black boots. His lips were a thin hard line, his eyes were narrowed and shiny hard.

She experienced a faint spasm of pity for Mr.

Rumbelow; if he thought he could win against Gabriel, he was in for a sad surprise.

"What are you doing here?" Gabriel demanded again.

She should stop pitying Mr. Rumbelow and start worrying about herself. She'd seen Gabriel look like this only once before, and that was during her disgraceful scene at Almack's—and the results had been disastrous. For her body, which had learned so much so quickly. For her mind, which had known scarcely a moment's peace since that night.

She toyed with the thought of lying, but no. She was the future duchess of Magnus. Yes, she had broken her word. She would not add another lie. "I've come to steal the tiara, and do you think it's a good idea to light a candle with Mr. Rumbelow searching the house and his men outside?"

"Damn it, woman!" Gabriel took the candle and with it lit three different candelabras with four candles each.

After the unrelieved darkness, so much light left Madeline feeling exposed and nervy.

She and Gabriel stood in a bedchamber, small but luxurious—probably the dowager's, whoever she might have been. For all the gaudiness of the rest of the estate, this room was well appointed, with rich, old-fashioned, airy furniture. The walls were painted gold, and heavy emerald-colored drapes covered the windows. A few cut-glass bottles cluttered the polished surfaces, and the four-poster bed was made and ready for an occupant.

Gabriel nodded as if well satisfied, then caught Madeline and whirled her so her back was against one of the foot posts. He gathered her close.

"What are you doing?" She pushed at his arms.

"There's no way out of it. We're going to get caught. The trick is to make them think they caught us doing something that we want to hide. Something they'll be in the position to blackmail us about."

She knew very well what he meant. She wasn't the kind of female to pretend she didn't. She even knew that it didn't matter who Mr. Rumbelow's men had seen or whose fault it was she and Gabriel were in this position. What mattered was escaping without being caught, without having to explain to everyone who she was and why she had taken on this disguise—to escape without becoming one of Big Bill's victims. With brisk motions, she removed her bonnet and cast it toward a chair. "Very well. Kiss me, and make it look real."

He stared down at her, and he smiled. Not that slashing grin of amusement and derision, but a smile that looked almost fond, almost admiring. "I will. But not yet. Rumbelow isn't close yet."

Meaning Gabriel wouldn't kiss her until he had to?

He murmured, "Did you get close to the safe?"

"I had just touched the lock when I saw Mr. Rumbelow's light." She was willing to answer Gabriel's questions, but she would demand he answer hers. "Did you follow me?"

"No. Has anyone seen you?"

"No, but apparently they saw you!"

"Bad luck all around." He lifted his head as if listening. Feet tromped overhead, but nothing else moved. Looking back down at her, he asked, "Do you remember that night we met? You gave me two dances in a row and your audacity caused a horrible ruckus, but by the time the evening was over, everyone knew we were destined to wed."

Why was he speaking to her like that? That tone, low and sexy, made her edgy—and she didn't want to be edgy. Not when he could feel every breath and every tremor of her body. "Obviously, they were wrong."

His grip around her waist was gentle, yet so firm she knew she could never move away. And where would she go? Her spine rested against the bedpost, the door was miles away, Gabriel moved with that deceptive swiftness and a man with a gun prowled the corridors. She was, she assured herself, helpless. But . . . "If we're not going to kiss now, why do we have to stand so close?"

"Because I want to." Gabriel's voice sounded as warm and comforting as a crackling fire on a winter's day—and just as treacherous. For fires burn as well as give warmth, and in this mood, Gabriel possessed a wildness that boded ill for their pursuers . . . and for her. "Maddie, do you remember when we sneaked into the garden at Lady Crest's party?"

"Reminiscing, Gabriel?" She mocked, but she did remember. "I thought you disdained memories of me."

"Disdained? Not a man breathing would disdain the memory of you. You came alive in my arms." That smile still played around his mouth, sending uneasy chills up her spine. "For all that you were young, you were brash and beautiful, so sure of yourself, I expected to discover another man had taught you how to love."

She moved restlessly. "No!" And cursed herself for admitting the truth when she never had before.

"I knew."

So it didn't matter.

"I knew when I kissed you. You were so eager and so awkward."

She remembered that, too. She had wanted to show him, at once, that she was his, but she didn't comprehend even the basics. She kissed with her lips puckered and tight, and she'd been quaking in her leather slippers.

Now she knew—he recognized her ineptitude. "What a fool I was."

"No. Just very young. Youth is always cured by time. Nothing cures foolishness." Pressing her head onto his shoulder, he offered a moment of comfort. "When I think back, I remember that great, arrogant sense of triumph that I would be the first."

She pushed back from him, rejecting solace. Rejecting him. "What an ass you were. Are."

"Yes." He admitted it without a bit of shame.

Two could play that game. In a mocking tone, she asked, "Who was your first, Gabriel?"

"It doesn't matter." Stroking the back of his fingers up his cheek, he twisted them into her hair and brought her face up to his. "You were my last."

Her heart leaped at his declaration.

Then he kissed her, and she didn't have time to consider pride or dignity. Gabriel took possession of her mind as he took possession of her lips— hungrily, tasting eagerly, biting lightly, treating her mouth like a feast laid particularly for him.

For a moment. When she didn't respond, he withdrew.

Maybe he didn't really want to kiss her. Maybe all this reminiscing was his way of working himself up to a distasteful deed.

She laughed softly. No, he still wanted her. Wanted her off balance, wanted her enough that he hung over her like a great wolf savagely wooing its mate. His eyes glittered, but his voice was soft as he asked, "Do you remember that time in Lord Newcastle's library when we were kissing and you pushed me down on his desk?"

Yes, she did, and now beneath her hands he felt different, yet the same—firm, strong, with a heat that simmered beneath his skin. Her fingers slid along the breadth of his shoulders, seeking out the contour of muscle and bone . . . seeking out the man she'd known with such intimacy. He was here, but different, bigger, tougher, with an edge of cruelty not sensed before. Right now—perhaps never—that cruelty wasn't directed at her. But sometimes, with a glance, with a sneer, this man frightened her.

At one time she would have said nothing had frightened her. She wasn't so foolish now. Men with guns, men with violent pasts, men inured to death and suffering—Mr. Rumbelow and Big Bill—frightened her. She didn't underestimate the danger of her current situation. Only Gabriel, the man she'd jilted, stood between her and death.

Gabriel would save her. But Gabriel had reason to want revenge on her. She stared into his face, lit by soft candlelight but still angular and tough. "Will they shoot us?"

His arms tightened. "I wish you'd thought about that sooner and stayed in your bedchamber."

"I would have if you'd promised to win the tiara without demanding such an iniquitous payment."

"Iniquitous? To demand that you lie with me in return for the queen's tiara?" His hands unhurriedly smoothed down her spine. "Not at all. A laborer is worthy of his hire."

"You're not a laborer. You're a—" She hesitated for a crucial moment.

"A gambler, you mean to say." Leaning close enough to speak into her ear, he said, "Or perhaps . . . an earl from an ancient and well-respected family. Or perhaps . . . your former fiancé." With each word, his voice deepened. "Or even . . . your lover."

She shoved at his chest. "Only once."

"Only one night," he corrected. "I did offer to win you the tiara if you would leave here, but you refused. Now it's too late." Then, as his hands wandered, his expression grew astonished. "My

God, Maddie, what's this?" He lifted the weight of her pistol from her waist.

"A gun."

"I know that," he said testily. "What are you doing with it?"

"I brought it for my protection."

"One pistol? One shot? Against these men?"

"If I carried ten pistols, my reticule would be too heavy to carry." Absurd man. "Besides, what do you have for your own defense?"

"A knife in my boot and my sleeve." He examined the quilting that gave the holster richness and strength, the way the inside was shaped to hold the gun securely and the outside was shaped to conceal the contents. "Very elegant. Very practical."

She didn't like to, but she basked in his admiration. "Thank you."

"No one would ever know you were carrying a pistol."

"No one expects a lady to, anyway." She allowed him to remove the pistol and the holster.

"Why not in your reticule? Or in your muff?" He placed them under the bed.

"I've used both, but sometimes I want both my hands free, as I did tonight."

Mr. Rumbelow was right over their heads now. They gazed up at the ceiling as if they could see him—or he could see them. They were in trouble. They knew it; they just didn't know how grave the trouble would prove to be.

Gabriel gathered her into his arms again.

Her pulse speeded up—probably the sound of

Mr. Rumbelow's footsteps frightened her. "Do you always carry the knives?" she asked Gabriel.

"Always at least one."

Fascinated by this new side of him, she asked, "Did you before, in London?"

"Always. In case of trouble."

"What kind of trouble?"

"Footpads. And now . . . the French. Do you keep your gun with you all of the time?"

"If I feel the need, and if it's possible to carry it without anyone noticing."

"It would be good if you carried it with you, as much as possible, for the rest of the house party."

When she would have asked more questions, he put his finger over her lips. "We need to concentrate on our dilemma. We'll have to convince Rumbelow and his cohorts that we're lovers."

Her heart hurried and tripped. "I can't do that."

He smiled again, but this time she saw that smile she'd become so familiar with these last two days. That toothy smile, that savage smile. "Not even if the alternative is death?"

"You have a way with words." He had a way with fear.

"We'll fool them. Remember the scandals we almost caused? I feared poor Eleanor was going to collapse, trying to keep up with us."

"For good reason." Madeline wiggled, trying to loosen his grip.

"Be still." In a low, intense voice, he asked, "Do you remember what I said when I left you that morning?"

Remember. She hated that word. She did remember, and he carried her away on a wave of memories.

Leaning over the bed, he gazed into her eyes. "Next time, you'll come to me."

As daylight crept into her bedchamber, a sense of defeat choked her. "No, I won't."

His low voice vibrated with intensity. "You'll come because you've got no choice. Because I'm part of your body and your soul, and you need me just as you need the air you breathe and the wind in your hair."

He frightened her, not because she thought he would hurt her, but because she feared he was right. "No!"

"Believe what you like. You'll come to me."

So she had put herself out of temptation's way, fleeing to the continent in an unprecedented act of spinelessness—or wisdom.

He lifted his head and listened, then bent himself over her like a male trying to protect his female. Like a lover trying to protect his mate. "Rumbelow's at the top of the stairs." Gabriel had the oddest expression on his face—not that shark-bright smile nor the affectionate smirk, but an anticipatory smile that made her try to take a step backward. "Tonight, I'll protect you. But about the bargain—you need to make a choice."

She couldn't move away. She was against the bedpost. "What?"

"Make a choice. Pay the price I want, right now, and tomorrow I'll win the tiara and give it back to you. Refuse me, and the tiara is forever beyond your reach."

Chapter Seventeen

"Have you lost your mind?" Madeline thrust at Gabriel's shoulders. "My father might arrive tomorrow."

"He might," Gabriel readily acknowledged. "Then he'll use the tiara as ante, and your family heirloom will be gone."

"Unless I can talk him out of it." Which she *would* do.

"Unless you can." Clearly, Gabriel didn't have faith in her persuasive powers.

"When I do talk him out of playing, I still will have had *you*. An infamous bargain, Gabriel. Infamous!"

"Yes." He stroked his thumb around her nipple in a slow, gentle circle.

Shoving his hand aside, she said, "Don't." But that familiar thrill raced up her spine. That reckless weakness attacked her knees. This was Gabriel, and as always, just being in his vicinity made her want more than was proper. Made her need . . . too much.

He massaged the tense muscle above her collarbone. "Like any good gambler, you must weigh the odds and make your move."

Her chest rose and fell as she stared at him, considered him . . . weighed the odds. Would her father arrive in time? Perhaps. Probably. But if he didn't . . . she could save the queen's tiara with one simple act. "Infamous," she muttered again. She could hear Mr. Rumbelow's boots descending the stairs, and she almost hoped he would appear and rescue her . . . by shooting Gabriel. But that wouldn't be a rescue. She wasn't so far gone as to believe that. And they needed to get this settled before Rumbelow appeared. "Are we going to kiss? If we are, we need to proceed."

Gabriel leaned his body against hers, apparently at ease. "First you need to make a choice."

The man was insane! "We're *going* to get caught."

"Choose."

She kept her voice low, but indignation vibrated from her very being. "You might not win."

"Even the best of gamblers have bad luck," he conceded.

But not Gabriel. He had more than luck. She was well acquainted with his wiliness and his razor-sharp brain.

She tried to be sensible. In more ways than one, he had backed her into a corner.

What did it matter, really? She'd slept with

Gabriel before. She'd already seen his naked body, already taken him and been taken by him. It wasn't as if she were a virgin. Just . . . almost a virgin.

She turned her head away from him and stared at the partially opened door. A door that seemed miles and years away from her.

But to sleep with . . . no, call it what it was, to *fornicate* with Gabriel, after she'd spent four long years getting over him. Four long years remembering the way he had grabbed her, kissed her, ignored her protestations. Remembering how she'd lost her temper with him. That temper had turned to passion. That passion had become a feral demand for satisfaction, and he had been happy to provide it. The pain of his penetration had been intense, but quickly over. The pleasure he forced her to experience had branded her, haunted her, revisited her time and again.

And now he wanted her to experience that pleasure again? Would it be another four years before she forgot this night?

"Choose." He demanded an answer, unyielding in expression and stance.

She had a choice . . . but not really. Because Gabriel was right. The only reliable characteristic her father exhibited was unreliability.

"All right," she snapped.

"All right what?"

Down the corridor, she could hear Rumbelow open the first door. "Gabriel, he's coming!"

With a lamentable lack of concern, he insisted, "Tell me what you're agreeing to."

Show that she understood all the ramifications of her decision, he meant. In a disgruntled whisper, she said, "I'll sleep with you, and if you have the chance—if my father doesn't arrive—you will win back that tiara by fair means or foul."

"You'll sleep with me for as long as I require? You'll come to my bed of your own free will now, before I've won you the tiara, and after, for as long as I wish to hold you?"

She straightened so fast, she almost smacked his chin with her head. "That wasn't the bargain."

"It wasn't the bargain I originally demanded, my darling." His hands traveled up her back. "But you didn't accept those terms."

She wanted to stomp her foot, but that would be immature—and Rumbelow stalked toward their door. "This isn't fair!"

"Life isn't fair, and the man who holds the trump makes the conditions." Kindly, Gabriel explained, "That would be me."

"I know who holds the trump! But what about my position in society? What about Mr. Knight? If I agree to this, I can never marry for fear you'll invoke your wretched condition!" She pointed toward the door and reminded, "And that man has a gun."

"I promise to be discreet and safeguard your position in society. I promise that, if you don't take care of Mr. Knight, I will. And I promise, when you have said your wedding vows, our bargain is ended."

He hid a trap among his promises, but look though she did, she couldn't see it. She weighed the odds, she decided this was the right thing to do, so why should she cavil now because he wanted more than she expected? Ways existed to avoid him.

Of course, she'd already fled to the continent once, and he would be on the alert for a trick. She looked at him, brown, strong, grim and watchful. He had a score to settle with her, and he wanted her. A fatal combination. So she would just have to think of another ploy to escape him. "All shall be as you command."

He failed to note her sarcasm. "Do you *promise* that all shall be as I command?"

"You doubt my word—"

"For good reason."

"—so what is the point of extracting my promise?"

"I want to see what four years in exile has taught you. I want to know who you are."

That sounded more like a threat than anything else he had said. "You know who I am."

"I know who you were—a woman of passion and fire, too frightened by experience to give yourself to me. Is that still who you are, Madeline? Or have you grown into the woman you can be?"

"That's stupid." *That's frightening.* "I could say the same thing about you."

"It would be true. I didn't win myself that fortune out of love for you. I won it to salvage my pride, so I wouldn't be your dependent. What a couple of cowards we were!"

She didn't like this. He seemed to have looked beyond the events of four years ago into the reasons behind them.

To carry a grudge was easier. To cherish her anger kept her strong. She wouldn't make another mistake so long as she concentrated on Gabriel's sins and never, ever tried to look at matters from his perspective.

She wanted this conversation to stop. Now. "For God's sake, Gabriel, Rumbelow's almost here!"

"So he is."

Finally, she gave Gabriel what he wanted. "I promise to do all that you command—in bed."

"In bed is not the correct term." He watched her, his eyes heavy-lidded. "Sexually. You promise to do all that I command . . . sexually."

She nodded.

"Say it."

She recognized what he was doing, making her say words that no lady should even know.

And that was only the start. She would get through this ordeal with her dignity intact. She wouldn't betray herself. Surely her uncertainties were buried deeply enough to remain undiscovered. "I promise to do all that you command . . . sexually."

Her gown fell forward around her shoulders. He'd been unbuttoning long before she'd agreed to his terms.

Before she could do more than gasp and grab for the neckline, he'd wrapped his arm around her waist, lifted her skirt with one hand and kissed her with the passion of a lover long denied. For all its suddenness, his ardor was real, and as he plunged his tongue into her mouth, she grappled with the overwhelming sense of intrusion. Grabbing at his hair, she tugged hard.

He growled and, with his hand on her thigh, brought her leg up around his waist.

From the door, she heard a triumphant chuckle. Mr. Rumbelow laughed at them! Mortified, she tried to push Gabriel away.

His hunched shoulders blocked her face from Mr. Rumbelow's gaze. His eyes burned as he turned his head toward the door. "Get out of here." His voice was guttural, menacing—and, apparently convinced, Mr. Rumbelow laughed again. Then Madeline heard the rapid retreat of his footsteps.

Gabriel leaned her back against the bedpost.

She caught her gown as it tried to slither to her feet.

Striding to the door, he slammed it so hard the wall shook.

"Gabriel," she choked.

"They know we're here." As he turned to face her, his chest rose and fell. His mouth was slightly opened as he breathed powerfully. His hands flexed at his sides. He gave off an indefinable sense of menace and of arousal. "The blackguards might as well know I don't give a damn about them and their guns and their threats."

She could almost see the shimmer of heat around him, and she would have sworn he was ready to attack. Them . . . or her.

Well, not *her*. Not if she could help it. Without an ounce of inflection, she asked, "How do you want me?"

His burst of reckless aggression faded . . . but not his arousal. Still breathing deeply, he crossed his arms over his chest and tilted his chin up. "You mean . . . tell you how long, how hard, how fast . . . how many times?"

"Yes." So she could arm herself with indifference and resignation.

With a slow smile that expressed a very masculine contentment, he started at her toes and ran his gaze up to meet hers. "I want you in every way possible."

Her heart gave a thump. How did he do that? Turn his antagonism toward Mr. Rumbelow into an ardor that made her think of deep, dark, impetuous kisses that lasted all night and traveled to every part of her body? She should be braced, prepared to do her duty and think of England. Instead, between her legs, she grew damp, and she found herself clutching her bodice in a chemise-baring grip.

Turning back to the door, he twisted the key, dragged a chair under the handle and stuffed his handkerchief into the keyhole. "We're trapped in here. If I know Rumbelow, he has men patrolling the corridor with guns. We can't leave."

Snared, and by more than a man and a promise. Snared by bad luck, by fate, by a host with no morals and a criminal past.

Gabriel prowled toward her with a stride that seemed nothing less than pagan. "So the truth about what happens tonight is private, between you and me. I'll never tell a soul." His eyes glowed vividly, gloriously green with anticipation. "You have the utter freedom to do and say and be anything you want."

"I want to be gone."

He chuckled, low and deep in his chest. "No, you don't."

He was right. She couldn't have walked out of here if the door was wide open and the way spread with a red carpet. Her body felt heavy, weighted with desire so heavy it dragged at her every movement. She lifted her hand to her head, and the movement was slow, sensuous, too aware and yet uncontrolled by sense or wisdom. "Why are you doing this? Do you think I'll like you for it?"

"I don't care whether you like me or not. I'm doing this for me. For my satisfaction." His smile was a dark slash of amusement. "All you have to do is lie there."

"Yes." Her whisper was uncertain.

"But will you?" He towered over her, crowding her against the bedpost. "Can you? Lie there and let me have my way with you, then rise and go about your business as if the act meant nothing to you?"

She took a long, shuddering breath. She hated him so much.

This was the man she had dreamed about, longed for, cried over. Now he was here, forcing her to do his bidding, and she wanted to be glad. Glad because later, she could lie to herself about how she had suffered his touch for the good of her family honor.

But he knew her too well. Knew exactly how to undermine her defenses and make her face the truth.

With a single finger, he stroked the line of her neck from her chin, over her pulse point, to the tip of her breast. "You're more exquisite than I remembered. The satin glow of your skin. Your magnificent figure." He slid his fingers through a lock of her hair. "The way you watch me so warily. I shall enjoy vanquishing that wariness. I shall enjoy you."

Chapter Eighteen

"I am not a dish served for your delectation." Brave words meaning nothing.

"You are, and of your own free will, you've placed yourself on my serving plate."

Madeline didn't want to look at Gabriel, to acknowledge him in any way, but somehow her gaze got tangled in his. He touched her mind as surely as he touched her body, and she knew perfectly well he was testing her, waiting to hear her deny him. She wanted to: to protect herself, her hard-won serenity and her moral position.

But that was her mind speaking. Her body had no morals and no sense. Without a care to her future peace of mind or her position in society, her body wanted him.

Right now, she could hear only her body.

Gabriel withdrew his finger. "So silent. You usually have plenty to say."

"I'm a lady. I don't use that kind of language, even to a scoundrel who so soundly deserves it."

"You have." Walking to the dresser, he picked up the glass bottles and one by one sniffed them. "Used unladylike language on me. So it's a little late to be taking the high road. Say what you like. I can bear it." He poured a little of the contents of one bottle into his hand, then nodded as if satisfied and placed the glittering green bottle on the table beside the bed. He turned down the bedclothes, revealing the sheets, clean, ironed and tucked tightly around the mattress.

"I couldn't have found a better place for seduction if I tried. But even you have to acquit me of premeditation in this situation." His already low voice dropped to a whisper. "Not even I imagined you would attempt such a piece of madness as stealing the tiara from professional thieves."

"If I hadn't, you'd have been caught out here alone. What would have happened then?"

Matter-of-factly, he said, "They would have killed me."

She hated him—but she wanted him alive so she could continue hating him. To think of all his gleaming virility still and cold sent a chill through her.

He saw her horror. "You should have left this afternoon while you had the chance. These men are cheaters, blackmailers, thieves who have killed and will kill again to protect their scam. Rumbelow won't let you go now. Now that he's seen you with me. He now knows—or thinks he knows—that we're desperately in love."

"Or in lust," she said in a cold, clear voice.

"Definitely in lust." Gabriel removed a narrow, shiny blade from his sleeve and the longer, handled knife from his boot and placed them carefully on the table beside the bed. They were long and wickedly bright, and he handled them as if he knew how to use them.

Sitting down on the chair, he pulled off his boots.

She didn't know what she was supposed to do. Undress? Watch him? Contemplate her life and wonder how she had come to this moment?

Heavens no, not that last. That would be too dreadful and lead to self-recrimination, an activity she always sought to avoid.

But the last time they'd been alone in a bedchamber hadn't been like this. Then the action had been frenzied, and she hadn't had to worry about what to say. Words had spilled from her mouth at a rate and volume that still stunned her when she thought about it. He was right. Then she had used stable language on him. Now she had time to think, to get embarrassed, to grow uncomfortable.

Not that Gabriel appeared uncomfortable. He stripped off his black shirt with an insouciance that made her blush.

Yet she didn't stop staring.

She'd seen his chest all those years ago, and now she noted the changes. Where before he'd had a whipcord strength, he sported heavier muscles, muscles more sharply delineated on his chest and muscles that bulged in his upper arms. He

looked as if he'd worked in the fields or construct-
ing shelters . . . perhaps the time he'd spent organizing the coastal defense had required hard,
physical labor, and knowing him as she did, he
would have thrown himself into it.

The last vestiges of boyhood had vanished, and
now he was . . . too much. Too strong, too masculine, too hairy . . . the mat of brown hair covered
his upper chest, then thinned and slid in a line
down toward his trousers.

There her gaze lingered, waiting in a sort of
nervous anticipation as he unbuttoned his
trousers. He appeared so carefree and at ease; obviously, it bothered him not a whit if they indulged in lovemaking. He gave the appearance of
a man inured to passion.

Then he lowered his trousers, and she saw she
was wrong. He might behave coolly, but his manhood strained and pointed. Although she'd not
seen his male parts for four years, and hadn't
taken the time to truly examine them then, she
thought the size of his tumescence must indicate a
great deal of interest in her—and in their mating.

His thighs bulged in much the same manner as
his arms; the muscles there made her think he
would ride her ruthlessly, tirelessly . . . oh, God,
she wanted him so much her fingers were shaking. She wanted the past to be forgotten, so she
could go to him and . . . and lick him, bite him, demand from him like a woman who had a right to.
Like his wife.

Ridding himself of the last of his garments, he

seated himself on the chair and gestured toward her. "Undress for me." He looked into her eyes again. "It shouldn't be too difficult. I've done most of the work for you."

That was true. All the buttons were unbuttoned, all the ties untied. She had only to lower her arms, loosen her grip and everything would fall away.

"Go on," he coaxed. He gestured broadly, mockingly. "Unless you've changed your mind."

She thought of her mother, in her formal portrait, dressed in a magnificent gold gown and wearing the queen's tiara. She thought about her own daughter, the daughter she hoped to have one day, and how the child would have nothing if Madeline didn't take action now.

Gabriel knew what she was thinking, and mocked her. "The sacrifices one makes for family honor."

"You're a jackass."

That hard, mocking smile faded from his face. "At the least."

She could trap him in her gaze, too, and make him acknowledge what he was doing and with whom. Coquettishly, she lowered first one of her arms, then the other. The gown slipped down, caught briefly on her hips, then slithered all the way around her ankles atop of her petticoats. She didn't wear the new pantalettes that had caused so much stir among the beau monde, so except for the stockings and garters that tied at her knees, she was bare.

She didn't know why he was doing this. Forcing her hand. Taking his pleasure. Perhaps he sought revenge for her jilting of him. Perhaps some other, deeper reason motivated him. But right now she knew he had no thought in his head but her, and that was her revenge, for making her want him.

His face was set, strong and determined. His lips barely moved as he spoke, and his tone was guttural with demand. "Your hair."

In a languorous upward arc, she lifted her arms, revealing all of her body to him. Slowly she slid the hairpins out of her coiffeur. She scattered them on the floor, indifferent to their fate, and when the last one was gone, she shook the long dark tresses free. They swept her shoulders. One strand fell onto her chest, the length of it circling her breast like a lover's hand.

Gabriel rose as if he couldn't resist her any longer. His gaze lingered on her thighs, ravished the patch of black hair over her pubic area, stroked her soft belly. He looked at her breasts with glorious appreciation, admired her shoulders, then once again looked into her eyes.

He walked to her.

Her heart beat with a drummer's rhythm as he came near, big and naked and everything she'd ever dreamed.

Taking her hand, he pulled her toward the bed. "Sit down." Still he looked at her, deep in her eyes, never relenting in his vigilance. His hands grasped her shoulders and pressed her down on the bed. She perched on the edge of the mattress, watching him and wondering what madness had brought her to this place. She was nude—well, almost. He was nude—completely. The candles blazed, the sheets were cool beneath her rear, and she had a debt to pay. A debt she had not yet incurred.

He rubbed her neck and smiled at her as if he sympathized with her plight, when in fact he was the cause of it.

"On your stomach," he said.

"What?"

"I want you to lie on your stomach."

She stared at him, her mouth unattractively askew. "But . . . I thought you were going to . . ."

"Even on your stomach, it's possible."

Her mind raced as she mentally tried to fit body parts together.

Picking up the bottle he'd placed beside the bed, Gabriel poured a thin stream of clear liquid into the palm of his hand.

Madeline observed with a kind of dreadful fascination, not understanding anything about him, or his plans, or the night. Worse, he seemed to understand everything about her. Where was the justice in that?

He wafted his hands under her nose. "Do you like that?"

The sweet scent of gardenia. The comforting odor of rosemary. "Very much."

"Lie down," he repeated. "On your stomach."

Whether she obeyed or not made no difference . . . did it? She would do her best to separate herself from the act, to be indifferent and blasé.

But she moved carefully, trying not to show too much of her body as she stretched sideways and face down across the mattress.

"Perfect," he murmured, his voice a warm bath of appreciation.

She didn't know what to expect, but certainly not his hands gently fastening around her shoulders in a gentle grip and his fingers pressing into her muscles, easing them into relaxation. The scent of rosemary and gardenia captured in the oil on his hands. He massaged her neck. She struggled up on her elbows. "Shouldn't we get on with it?"

His voice was rich with laughter as he said, "In such a hurry for my possession, my darling?" He pushed her down again. "This time, we'll do it my way."

"Humph." All right, but she wouldn't like it.

Yet she did. His fingers gently, then more firmly massaged her, easing the tension from her shoulders. She struggled to remain rigid, but he was in no hurry as he rubbed her arms, working his way down to her hands and there massaging her wrist, her palm, her fingers. When her hand was limp in his, he kissed each fingertip, then gently returned her arm to the mattress and went to work on the other side.

Madeline didn't know what to think . . . or even if her brain remembered how to think. Each breath she took was deep, relaxed, redolent with the scent of herbs and flowers. He treated each delicate bone and sinew with care. He found the knot of tension under her skull; she moaned as he worked his hands in miracle motions, teaching her to forget everything but the moment and the pleasure.

He leaned over her, so close his lips brushed her ear. "Do you like that?"

"Mm." She tried to pry her eyelids open, to be alert, but his hands kept moving on her.

Down her spine, seeking each vertebra, finding each muscle, easing each strife. When he slung his leg over the top of her, she should have been indignant, but he'd eased her into such a state of relaxation she could only sigh.

As he moved down her body, his oil-slickened hands slipped across the fine hairs on her skin. His knee slid between her legs, separating them, as his fingers encircled her waist and his thumbs worked the muscles in the small of her back.

Turning her head away from the pillows, she took a deep breath . . . and froze as his thumb slid down the crease between her buttocks. The oil eased the way, but nothing could ease the shock of being touched so intimately, so deliberately. That exquisite relaxation became a struggle to remain calm. Unthreatened.

"Beautiful," he murmured. He cupped each buttock, then pressed them together. Once. Twice. In a slow rhythm, over and over.

She didn't understand why or how, but the sensation made her want to press her hips forward, to rub against something . . . against him. Her lips opened; she heard herself panting as her excitement blossomed and grew.

With one hand, he kept the rhythm going. With the other hand, he found the opening to her body, and circled it with one finger.

Her eyes opened wide and with an incoherent cry, she rose off the bed.

He pressed her back down again. Again he circled the small opening, teasing the nerve endings, creating desire in every corner of her body. Desire where she'd never thought desire could thrive.

Just when she was gathering herself, quivering, reaching for climax . . . his hands slid away, and massaged the muscles in her thighs.

She could scarcely breathe, couldn't move. The frustration was so acute, she was almost in pain. Yet what could she say? Pride wouldn't allow her to admit how close he'd brought her to the edge. He probably knew . . . well, of course he knew. But if she demanded he bring her to completion, it would be a victory for him.

Never. Never.

Meanwhile, his hands rubbed the muscles of her thighs. He stripped off her stockings and massaged her calves. Despite the trick he'd played on her, she once again relaxed. Foolishly, for the room blazed with light, and in some corner of her mind she realized he could see between her legs. She ought to be more modest. She ought to be . . . but he had grasped her foot and he manipulated it between his hands. At first it tickled, but slowly he eased the weariness of the long walk from her bones, and by the time he finished the second foot, she was completely indifferent to modesty.

So indifferent that when he eased her over onto her back, she rolled over without a thought to the view she was offering.

He said again, "Beautiful."

She experienced a glow from the warmth of his tone . . . and from his touch.

He massaged the muscles of her legs with the same amount of exquisite detail to attention.

But although the relaxation permeated her body, she experienced an additional sensation as he worked his way up her body.

Anticipation.

He'd touched her between the legs before. Would he do it again? She shouldn't want it, of course. She would complain vociferously if he tried to give her the same pleasure, then withdrew.

But she couldn't. That would be a betrayal of self.

She peeked from under her eyelids and watched him as he again filled his palm with oil.

Never had he looked so handsome to her—the light catching in his dark brown hair, his eyes intent as he warmed the oil with his heat. He knelt with a knee on each side of her body, all sculpted muscle bathed in the golden glow of the candles.

When she looked at him, she didn't see the threat and the danger. She saw only the promise of pleasure. How foolish, much like looking at a wolf and seeing not the shiny teeth or the sharp claws, but only the sleek, glorious hunter—and imagining she could tame him.

She was in so much trouble.

He glanced up.

Immediately, she shut her eyes and pretended she hadn't been looking.

Reaching for her hips, he smoothed the oil over her belly, her waist.

She quivered with mingled relief and damning disappointment.

Then his palm slid nearer to the place she wanted him to touch.

Her heart beat faster.

His fingers combed through the triangular patch of curly hair.

Eagerness sizzled along her nerves.

Tenderly, he opened the cleft and stroked down the edges with two fingers.

She clutched at the sheets and tried not to beg. To plead for him to . . . to move more quickly. To touch her more intimately.

To leave her alone.

Dear heavens, not that. She tried to erase the thought from her mind, fearing he would some-how sense it and obey.

But he didn't—sense it, or obey. Instead he did as he'd done before, circling the entrance to her body as if preparing to enter.

Deep inside, in her womb, she could feel a pool-ing, a tension, as her body prepared to yield. Yet she wanted more, wanted something different.

She struggled with herself, willing herself not to show him exactly where to touch . . . and then he touched the right place.

She moaned, a sharp, plaintive sound that divulged so much. Her hips rose and fell. She wanted . . . my God, how she wanted!

And he gave her what she wanted . . . almost. He stroked her in long, slow motion, smoothing the skin but not touching her feminine tip. Not yet.

She twisted on the sheets, trying to get away . . . trying to get closer. Yet he rested on one of her thighs and controlled her movements with his weight. With his hand.

All her resentments bubbled to the surface, and she reached for his cock, jutting out from the thatch of brown hair at his groin. "Blast you. Let me . . ."

"No. Let me." Catching her hands, he placed them beside her head and leaned over her. His nose was only inches from hers. His eyes gazed right into her eyes. "This is for me, remember? We're doing what I want. You're only doing this to pay for my winning back the tiara."

The fog of pleasure skittered away. Her skin prickled, her breath caught.

She heard what he said, and knew what he meant. She hated him. Hated him. Hated those green eyes, now gray and intent. Hated the way he used his body, stretched over hers, to intimidate her. Hated the strength that held her motionless when she would stand and leave, face the thugs and guns rather than this man.

He had been seducing her. Even when they'd been engaged, he hadn't seduced her. Their passion had been frantic—and mutual.

Now Gabriel concentrated on getting her to admit she wanted him. And she did. Desperately.

But she had her pride. She would not give herself to a gambler.

She knew the pain that would follow.

Eyes locked with his, she stated emphatically, "I'm doing this for the tiara."

Chapter Nineteen

Gabriel commanded, "Then lie still and let me do what I want."

Madeline inhaled, trying to get enough oxygen into her lungs to agree. She couldn't. So she nodded abruptly.

He nodded back, and lifted his hands away from her body.

She wouldn't shut her eyes again. She wouldn't relax again. She would not aid in her own seduction . . . again.

The faintest smile curved his lips as he looked at her, spread beneath him like a pagan offering. It wasn't fair, and it wasn't right, but her body tightened as he gazed at her breasts with open appreciation. He reached for one. His hand hovered over her nipple.

She noted his hands, square and solid, with long, blunt fingers and flat, clean nails cut short. She noted his arms and his chest, the muscles long and heavy, sculpted by the light. She wanted to be furious with him.

She wanted him to touch her, so badly.

Why was it so difficult to be furious?

He shook his head. He reached for the bottle of oil and filled his palm once more. Lifting his hand, he let a thin stream fall into the other hand. Again and again he repeated the motion, and finally she realized he was building her anticipation.

Slowly, torturously, he spilled the oil up the center of her body and between her breasts. His heat had warmed the oil. As it trickled in both directions, she waited for him to catch it.

Instead he watched it, that enigmatic smile making her feel as if she'd challenged the wrong opponent.

But she hadn't challenged him. At least . . . not recently. But Gabriel never forgot, and this was revenge. It had to be revenge.

At last, just when it seemed the oil would trickle onto the sheets, he placed his palms flat on her hips and scooped it up . . . and slid his hands toward her breasts, catching each drip, smearing oil all over her, forcing pleasure on her.

He wasn't doing anything, really, just touching her lightly, firmly, pressing his hands into her muscles over her rib cage, smoothing the skin over her belly, caressing . . . caressing the underside of her breasts.

She pressed her thighs together, trying to ease the throbbing between them, but that didn't help.

She thought it made it worse, but perhaps what tried her patience was simply the stroke of his oil-softened fingers around and around her nipple. Her breasts were swelling into his hand, telling him the truth when she'd rather he knew nothing.

But a woman, stretched on a bed sans clothing, could hide little of her body's reactions. Only her defiance mattered—or so Madeline told herself.

Taking her nipple between his thumb and fore-finger, Gabriel rolled it lightly, sending a thrill through her that made her wish he'd spent more time between her legs, touching her there.

But no. She'd insisted on making a scene, and he'd insisted on confronting her—and winning. If she'd kept her mouth shut, she might now be lolling here in a glaze of satisfaction. Or perhaps she'd be thrashing beneath him. And right now, either sounded better than . . . "Dear heavens." Lifting an arm, she tucked it behind her head and gazed off the bed toward the corner of the room.

That didn't help. Not seeing him didn't dimin-ish the effect of his fingers stroking her nipples, nor the weight and heat of him atop her, nor the knowledge that soon he would be inside her.

His touch on her changed, became firm, sweep-ing strokes. "You have a lovely body, and it's the body I love, but it's just a body. It's your mind that fascinates me, my darling. Your thoughts, your feelings . . . your soul."

She didn't want to fascinate him . . . in any way. But certainly not with her soul.

His hands swept up her chest, up her neck and grasped her chin. He brought her head back so she had to look at him.

Never taking his gaze from hers, he leaned close, rubbing his chest across hers, his skin sliding on the oil. His chest hair created a delightful friction that brought her nipples to full attention. She whimpered as he moved in a circle. Lowering his belly onto hers, he did the same thing. But this . . . this was better. More intimate. Closer to the place where she wanted him to be.

His cock was so hard she winced from the thought of the discomfort she would suffer, and longed to be impaled. He was hot, like a stove aglow with fire, and he brought a fire to her. She wanted to wrap her leg around his leg, to rub herself against him until she found the satisfaction he denied her.

She didn't. She had her pride. She clung to her pride.

With his mouth close to her ear, he asked, "Are you ready to pay the price?"

She hated the question, the way he reduced this act of passion to a bargain.

But he didn't wait for the answer. Instead, he positioned himself. She felt the hot probe between her legs.

She watched him.

He watched her.

Slowly he entered her, the oil easing his way. But not enough. Four years ago, she'd been a virgin. Each inch he pressed into her made her aware of her inexperience, and her abstinence. She trembled as the intrusion became almost a pain, not quite a pleasure. The sensation was rich, intimate. She wanted to weep, but he observed her with an intensity that challenged and frightened her. Instead she stared up at him, and in his face she saw vibrancy, pleasure, possession. Her hands clutched his arms as if holding on to him would help her—when he was the cause of her discomfort.

The silence between them was profound, a moment when acrimony vanished and all that existed in the world was Gabriel and Madeline. At last he filled her completely, and the taking became a joining. She slid one foot up the sheets, lifting her knee, trying to find ease. She tilted her hips; he moved deeper, when she had thought there was no deeper.

With a brilliant slash of a smile, he withdrew a few inches. Then slid back in. Her flesh pulled and burned, but only a little, and she didn't really notice that. She did notice the way he made her feel as he looked at her, as he wrapped her in his arms. As if he loved her. The movements between them became coordinated, a dance to music only they could hear. She lifted her hips to meet each of his thrusts. She wrapped one foot around his hips. The other she rested on the sheet.

It felt . . . good. He felt good. The massage he had given her had gentled her, made her once again familiar with his touch. He had taunted her with illicit passion until she could think of nothing else. Now they were moving together, panting together, joined as closely as man and woman should be.

She wanted to moan and whimper. But no. Some distant, sensible piece of her mind told her no. When he heard the sounds, he would know she was out of control. It was a triumph she couldn't bear to hand him.

As if he realized she still resisted him, he reached between their bodies. He adjusted her, opened her so that with each thrust, he rubbed intimately against her.

At his first thrust, a groan broke from her.

She had lost that battle. The last battle, surely.

"That's right," he said, his voice gloriously warm and completely sexual. "Tell me, my darling. Tell me how you like it."

A flush rose from her breasts to her face. Deep within her, the passion changed, becoming deeper than desire. An undercurrent of wildness ran through her body.

She moved more rapidly, met him more eagerly. Her eyes half closed. Her fingernails dug into his skin. She concentrated on the way his thrusts increased, grew stronger, shook her body and forced her toward release . . . almost . . . she could almost . . .

Inexplicably, he slowed.

She tried to urge him onward.

He stopped. He stopped!

Stunned, incredulous, she groaned. "No. Don't halt now!"

He remained stubbornly still. "You don't have to do this."

"What?" She could scarcely see him, hardly hear him. The pursuit of fulfillment chained her— a fulfillment that hovered just out of reach. If he would just move . . . She made an enticing circle with her hips.

He repeated, "You don't have to do this." His face was close to hers. His eyes stared into hers. His voice was deep and serious. "I'll win the tiara for you no matter what you decide. If you want me to stop, I will."

In her state of arousal, it took a moment to realize what he was saying. How he had manipulated her.

He would stop? Now? He would win the tiara for her whether she gave him the gift of her body or not?

This wasn't about the tiara. Not anymore. This was about her. What she wanted. She needed. "You bastard." Her voice vibrated with rage.

He didn't care what she called him, he only cared about winning. "Tell me what to do. Shall I stop . . . or shall I keep on?"

How could he even ask? Wasn't he as involved as she was?

Then, as she watched, a bead of sweat started on his brow and trickled down the side of his face, down to his jaw.

Oh, yes, he was involved. He wanted her—but he wanted her on his terms. He wanted her not as a purchase, not as a deal, but knowing full well she lusted as he lusted.

If she didn't admit to the passion that gnawed at her, he would withdraw. She didn't have a doubt that he had the strength of will to deny his own desire—and he would live to torment her another day.

Gabriel would never admit defeat.

"Maddie?" Slowly, he pulled himself back from her.

The sense of fullness faded, and she wanted, needed it back. *Now.*

Completely, unconditionally, she surrendered. Catching his hips, she pulled at him. "I want you. Please, Gabriel, I want you."

This time, when he lifted her chin, he was a little rough. A little hurried. But what he saw there must have satisfied him, for he chuckled an odious chuckle, and thrust himself inside her, all the way to the hilt.

It shook her, the forcefulness, the claim, but she didn't care. She lifted her hips, embraced him with her legs and whispered, "Please. Please!"

"I've got you, Maddie. Come with me." His deep voice stroked inside her mind. His manhood stroked inside her body. He moved with swift, brilliant precision, holding her down on the mattress, piercing her with himself.

The search for passion became a race. They moved together, the rhythm glorious, exhilarating. Her heart pounded as she answered each thrust. Each time, he touched the deepest place in her, and her control came that much closer to splintering. She moaned, over and over, beyond caring about anything but satisfaction.

But the satisfaction, when it arrived, silenced her. Intense, pounding fever gripped all her senses, then wiped them clean. For a long, glorious moment there was no past, no future, only her body spasming in glorious climax. Only her body, captured and pleasured by Gabriel.

When she subsided, he was there, moving on her still . . . observing her with a kind of awful triumph.

Then he threw his head back, the muscles in his neck corded and as he reached his own orgasm, his hips pounded her into the mattress.

His frenzy dragged her along, back into ecstasy. The waves of pleasure washed over them, around them and finally, gradually, they subsided onto the bed.

He crushed her beneath him as he relaxed.

They stared at each other still, lust, spent passion, simmering anger, old betrayals in their gazes . . . and like a candle extinguished, she went to sleep.

Chapter Twenty

Gabriel's chest heaved as he looked at Madeline sprawled beneath him. They were still joined. She still cradled him inside her body. And she was asleep.

How did she do that? Slip away every time he got close to her?

But this time she hadn't gone far, and if he were being fair—which he wished to be right now—he would admit she'd had little sleep and that he'd worn her out.

He'd worked hard to wear her out. To wear her down. To make her surrender.

Because it had been surrender.

Unfortunately, he now knew a complete surrender from Maddie equaled nothing but the beginning of the war. For her own safety, he wanted her gone from this place, but she insisted on staying. And tonight—what a piece of bad luck to be caught with her. Rumbelow could just as easily have decided to kill them both. Instead he'd laughed, imagining how he would discomfit them when he revealed the truth about his hapless guests.

So Gabriel had turned bad luck to good. He had taken advantage of their forced proximity to prove to her he still owned her body. That was why, tonight, he'd massaged her, gentled her to his touch, and brought her close to orgasm again and again. That was why he'd gritted his teeth and made the offer to get her the tiara without fully possessing her—and he'd been prepared to leave her body if she'd agreed. She needed to realize he was the only man for her. He would make her realize he was the only man for her.

As he withdrew from her body, his cock sliding from the tender tissues, she moaned in her sleep.

He wanted to moan, too. She held heaven between her legs, a heaven he'd made his own. Would she remember his claim tomorrow?

No. Of course not. With her flight to the continent, his darling had demonstrated how frequently and ruthlessly she needed to be reminded that she was his. And tonight—my God, when he'd seen her sneaking across the lawn toward the dowager's house, he'd been enraged with her—and with himself. It had never occurred to him she would try to circumvent him by stealing the tiara.

But it should have. He should have known she wouldn't tamely submit to his blackmail. Madeline never tamely submitted to anything in her life—blast her.

Rising from the bed, he smoothed the covers over her and went to the door. It was still locked, the chair tucked under the handle, the handkerchief he'd stuffed in the lock in place.

Drawing on his trousers, he contemplated their situation. Here they would remain until Rumbelow chose to let them escape. Gabriel hoped that would be before the other guests were stirring, but with Rumbelow, the timing would have to fit into his plans.

Tomorrow, the Game of the Century would start.

Today, Rumbelow had gone out of his way to make sure his guests were relaxed, convivial, unsuspicious. He'd showed the gamblers the gaming room, the safe and the wooden box that held the crown. He'd taken the key from his pocket, turned the ornate lock and showed them the crown nestled within. Gabriel had held the queen's tiara and felt the weight of the gold and the jewels. Seductive things, gold and jewels. They distracted a man from crucial matters. Matters of life and death.

Rumbelow had invited the gamblers to examine the tables, to make sure they were made for honest gaming. After a few laughing protestations, everyone had done so, and no one with more interest than Gabriel. Everything appeared to be on the up and up, and Rumbelow had assured them they would be required to look again before sitting down for each hand.

Tomorrow, at noon, everyone would take their ante and put it in the safe. They would play for the tiara. And after a meal with the families, the game would start at nine in the evening.

So what was Rumbelow's plan this time?

Gabriel examined the dowager's bedchamber more closely than he had in his first, hurried survey. Rumbelow had gone through a great deal of trouble to make this room appealing. Surely he harbored more than a desire to give his gamblers a place to rest should it become necessary. What could it be?

Perhaps he had hidden something in this furniture. Something that would help him win the game. One by one, Gabriel examined each piece. The bed, the clothes cupboard, the desk, the bedside table . . . all were fine pieces of furniture, with no unusual marks or hidden cubbyholes. Nothing was under the bed except Madeline's pistol in its custom-made black velvet holster, and he grinned at that as he placed it beside his knives on the bedside table.

Again he looked at the room, trying to think with the mind of a cheater, a swindler. He lifted the rugs, scrutinizing the backing and the floors beneath. Nothing.

He walked the perimeter. The walls looked freshly painted, with a marbling effect that bedazzled the eye. Rumbelow had hired an expert, and all for a room that wasn't his in a house that wasn't the main house. Only a lady, and perhaps Mr. Darnel, would appreciate this kind of workmanship, and no ladies would be viewing these walls. Unless Rumbelow planned a seduction, too? Perhaps he, too, wished to win a wife in the manner of Mr. Knight. . . .

Gabriel shook his head. No. Rumbelow took pride in his originality. And Gabriel had hopes that Rumbelow's ever-increasing sense of invulnerability would help lead to his downfall.

Again Gabriel walked the perimeter, looking at the walls, trying to see . . . There. He moved closer to the wall that separated this room from the next. Or . . . should separate this room from the next. Here the marbling took on a uniform swirl unmatched anywhere else in the chamber, and the desk had been placed before that spot. Lifting a candelabra, he held it close. A slight bulge lifted the wall in a long, thin crease. It had been papered over, the marbling had been created over that, but—Gabriel pressed his hand to the line—there was a door under here. A door that led . . . where?

How old was this house? Two hundred years, give or take? Cromwell's time had led to the construction of a great many priest's holes, so perhaps this was nothing more than a hiding place. Or . . . perhaps it led to a secret passage. A secret passage that led far away from the house. Toward the stables. Or the coast. Toward escape.

No wonder Rumbelow had rented this monstrosity of a house. It was perfect for his plan, which was to . . . By damn, Rumbelow wasn't going to pull a swindle and stay in society. Not this time. He was going to make it easy for himself. He was going to steal. Steal all of their antes, walk the hidden passage, board a ship and make his escape with a guaranteed one hundred thousand pounds.

The audacity of it took Gabriel's breath away.

Of course. Gabriel had been assuming he wished to remain in England, to set up more games like this one, reveling in his triumphs until he'd worn out his welcome. But Rumbelow didn't care if he stayed in England. With one hundred thousand pounds, he could go anywhere in the world and live like a king for years. Forever, if he was careful.

So why hadn't he already done it? Why hadn't he taken the money by force and disappeared?

Because he wanted to gloat, to polish his legend as the Master.

Satisfied with his explanation of Rumbelow and his motivations, Gabriel walked back to the bed and stared down at Madeline. He could do nothing to get them out of here. His hands were tied.

So . . . he discarded his trousers and climbed into bed beside her.

Before this was over between them, he would make her fall so deeply in love with him she would have to have him—no matter how much he challenged her. No matter how much she hated what he did.

No matter what.

Just before dawn, Gabriel woke Madeline with a whisper in her ear. "One more time."

She was cuddled into his naked body, her back against his front. He was warm and strong and, in her sleepy state, irresistible. His manhood pressed against her bottom, and she reached behind her and caressed the shaft.

He caught her hand. "Not like that. Face-to-face." Rolling her onto her back, he leaned over her.

In the candlelight, with his hair rumpled and his eyes heavy-lidded with slumber and passion, he made her mouth water.

Just before he kissed her, he said, "I want you to know who you're giving yourself to. I want you to see my face."

Tying the bow of Madeline's bonnet beneath her chin, Gabriel said, "It's dawn. We'll sneak back into the main house and no one will ever know what happened."

Resentfully, she ran her gaze over him, fully dressed and confident. "Except Mr. Rumbelow."

"Not even in his wildest imaginings can he know what really happened." Gabriel slid his thumb along her lower lip. "Don't frown, Maddie. I'll never tell what you gave me last night."

"Mr. Rumbelow will know." Taking the black velvet holster, she tied the long ribbons into shorter lengths and made it look like a reticule.

"Rumbelow's not going to be a problem. There's no one in the corridor. We can go."

"But you'll know." And she was wretched with knowing that.

"That I will." As always, Gabriel stepped too close and stared right into her eyes, engaging her when she wanted nothing so much as to be away from him. "I'm not some inveterate gambler, trapped by the game. I only play for a cause I believe in, and I always play to win."

She was desolate and limp with exhaustion. With too little sleep and too much upheaval. "What are you trying to say?"

"You decide." From the pocket of his jacket, he pulled a lady's glove. "Do you recognize this?"

With a shock, she did recognize it. Limp, yellowed with age, a symbol of one exquisite moment in time.

"It's your glove. You gave it to me. You said that until you could give me your hand, I should keep your glove as a token of your love." He weighed the glove in his palm. "I have kept it ever since."

She gave a silent whimper of anguish. Gabriel reminded her of a perfidy she would prefer to pretend had never happened. A vow she had broken.

"That night, when I took your virginity, I told you I wouldn't come to you again, that you would come to me."

What was he saying? What did he mean?

"Tonight was . . . tonight was serendipity. It doesn't count for us or against us. But from this moment on, I'll be waiting for you to come to me."

"To pay my debt?"

"Don't pretend you didn't hear me last night. There is no debt." Pressing his finger to her chin, he said, "I want you to come to me. Because you want to. Because you need to. Because you love me." With a slow stroke of his hand on her cheek, he stepped away from her. "Come to me."

Chapter Twenty-one

The next afternoon, tray in hand, MacAllister paused and observed Madeline. "I see why ye're na' a gambler."

She stopped her pacing. "I don't know what you mean." Unable to remain still, she started again. Up and down the sitting room, wearing a path in the carpet, her mind swerving between what was happening in the gaming room of the dowager's house right now—and what had happened in the bedroom there last night.

"Ye've na' got what we call a player face," MacAllister said.

Muttering to herself, desperate and uncertain . . . Glancing at the tray, she realized the plates were dirty and the silverware used. She looked out the window where the dowager's house was clearly visible. "You were in there, weren't you? Is *he* winning?"

"I dunna know. *He* dinna talk t' me."

She strode up to MacAllister, taking large steps.

He scurried backward like a crab, but he was shorter and older, and she easily trapped him against the wall. "You know how piquet is played. Did matters appear hopeful?"

He squinted up at her. "Aye, they did."

Hand on her heart, she breathed, "Thank heavens." Of course Gabriel would be successful. For what had he said? *I only play for a cause I believe in, and I always play to win.* He hadn't been talking about cards, though. He'd been talking about her.

Come to me.

Resentfully, MacAllister added, "Although why he's wasting his luck on ye and yer tiara when he needs it for the real game, I dunna know."

It occurred to her MacAllister would know all about Gabriel's plan to discredit Mr. Rumbelow. With guile or force, she could pry the information from him. In a lowered voice, she asked, "If he loses the real game, what will happen?"

His gaze shifted toward the corner of the room. "I dunna know."

Convinced he was lying, she moved close enough to make him break a sweat. "Yes, you do. Why did Gabriel come here? I don't understand what motivates him."

Apparently, she'd hit a nerve, for MacAllister straightened, his dread of her falling away. Placing the tray on an end table, he glowered at her. "Dunna ye? Nay, of course na'. Ye dunna understand anything. Ye never did."

She knew he didn't like her, but he'd never made it so clear. "Tell me."

"Tell ye what? How his lordship's going t' get his revenge? Nay, Yer Grace, na' likely. I wouldna' trust a female to keep her trap shut ever."

Madeline pounced. "Revenge? Revenge for what?"

Stroking his stubbled chin, MacAllister considered her. "Aye, mayhap I'll tell ye *that*. Not the plans, ye know, but ye deserve t' know what ye've done t' Gabriel's family."

"What *I've* done?"

"Was it na' love of ye that caused his lordship t' go out and win a fortune?"

"I don't know, was it?"

MacAllister ignored her snippiness. "Was it na' ye who abandoned him and left him t' work and mourn, and na' see that his brother was needing some guidance?"

She wanted to object about that, too, but after a moment's consideration, she shut her mouth. MacAllister was spare with information. Let him talk.

"Was it na' ye who was gone when Jerry fell int' despair and joined the navy, there to be killed?"

That snapped her to attention. "Fell into despair? *Jerry?*" He had been happy-go-lucky, the exact opposite of his forceful brother.

"Aye, fell int' despair," MacAllister said in salubrious tones.

"What happened to make Jerry fall into despair?"

MacAllister seemed scarcely to hear her, so wound up was he in umbrage. "His lordship's been blaming himself ever since, and seeking out the culprit, and setting him up t' do wrong, and planning t' catch him, but I know who t' blame." He glared balefully at her.

She wanted to grab MacAllister's shirtfront and shake the truth from him. "What did Jerry do?"

MacAllister pointed his finger right in her face. "It's ye, Yer Great and Righteous Grace, and ye should be ashamed of yerself."

Catching his finger, she bent it back. When MacAllister danced with the pain, she demanded, *"What did Jerry do?"* When she knew she had MacAllister's attention, she let go, but hovered close enough to be threatening.

To her surprise, MacAllister must have felt threatened, for he stopped censuring her. "Puir lad. Ye ken, Jerry worshiped his lordship."

"He did." Jerry had worshiped her, too, and now, after hearing of his untimely end, Madeline suffered a guilt similar to Gabriel's—and MacAllister clearly felt that she had reason.

"Jerry wanted t' be like his brother, and when his lordship went off and won a fortune, he saw the respect his lordship won with it." MacAllister observed her expression and said brutally, "Aye, despite ye and yer jilting and yer spiteful scene, he had won the respect of every gentleman with his coolness and intelligence."

Stiff with resentment, she said, "I wasn't spiteful!"

"Weren't ye? Ye could have broke yer betrothal with a note. Ye could have told him in private. Ye didn't have t' shriek like a fishwife in front of the whole *ton*. If ye've got any justice in yer pitiful female body, ye'll admit that."

She took a breath to defend herself, and let it out. She wouldn't admit it to MacAllister—but it was true. The memory of that scene had haunted her, not just because of the embarrassment, not just because of the results, but because of her shame. She'd done her best to ruin Gabriel. There was no excuse—except a rampaging temper—for that. She knew better than to let that temper go. She knew nothing good ever came of such excess.

Moving restlessly from foot to foot, she recalled that night—and last night, and all the haunted, lonely nights in between.

Come to me.

MacAllister judged her sufficiently browbeaten. "Aye, na' even ye can claim ye were justified. To treat a man like that—a man ye said ye loved!"

She *had* loved him. Did she still? "All right. All right!" With a slash of her hand, she said, "Get on with Jerry's story."

Her tense little snap must have satisfied MacAllister, for after a searching look, he continued, "Jerry went out t' win a fortune like his brother. Get all that respect, maybe even make his lordship feel better about losing ye. His lordship dinna know about his brother's plans. He was too busy with the coast defenses."

"Surely not so strenuous a task."

"Not so strenuous . . ." MacAllister puffed with indignation. "Worked night and day, he did, setting up watches, and when he was done with that"—he lowered his voice as if someone could overhear them, when in fact the other guests were playing charades in the library—"he also ferried men and women across the Channel in his yacht, coming and going, if ye know what I mean."

"You mean . . . he helped emigrants escape, and sent spies back to France?" That explained the muscles Gabriel had developed—voyages where he raised sail and hauled anchor. Such labor would build a man's strength to impressive proportions.

"Shh." MacAllister glanced around. "I shouldn't have told ye that. Damn, but ye're an aggravating woman!"

"Thank you. I try."

He glared at her. "As easy as breathing t' ye, it is."

She knew people like that. People who couldn't ever be pleased. But she never thought she was one of them. She had worked hard to be the kind of duchess who was approachable by the lesser members of society and beloved by her servants. Her eyes narrowed on MacAllister. "You're a misogynist."

"I am na'!" He thumped his chest with his fist. "I'm a Presbyterian."

"No. I mean . . . a misogynist is a man who doesn't care for women."

"Oh." He chewed on that, his wrinkled mouth moving silently. "Weel, I do like women. Flat on their backs with their mouths shut."

"Excuse me. I see my mistake now." Sarcasm dripped from every word. "Now, what about Jerry . . . and Gabriel?"

MacAllister settled back into his story. "Gabriel did all that work on the coast, and he worried about ye, being abroad at such a dangerous time."

She folded her arms over her chest. "Go on."

"So a wretched scoundrel got his claws int' Jerry. Gambled with him. Played him like a fish. Took everything."

Madeline felt faintly queasy. "His mother's fortune?"

"Which his lordship had been at pains to keep intact for him. The puir lad couldn't face his brother. Joined Nelson's crew. They buried him at sea after Trafalgar. God rest his soul."

That bright, smiling young man had died without ever seeing Gabriel again. Covering her mouth, she tried, unsuccessfully, to fight back the tears.

Fists on hips, MacAllister stood on tiptoe to look right in her face. "Aye, ye should weep. They told his lordship Jerry died a hero's death. His lordship has nightmares still."

She wiped at her wet cheeks. "The scoundrel was Mr. Rumbelow."

"Ye've guessed! How clever of ye." MacAllister

observed her distress with morbid approval, and handed her a large white handkerchief. "So now ye know. Get away from here. Ye're distracting his lordship from his duty. He owes his brother vengeance against Rumbelow. Jerry might rest in peace without it, but his lordship will never be content until Rumbelow has been brought low."

"I know. I see."

Come to me.

"Yer father's not turning up here. As long as ye're here, his lordship will be more worried about yer safety than aboot uncovering whatever mischief Rumbelow has cooked up. I'll bring yer tiara t' yer bedchamber as soon as he gives it t' me. Then, fast as ye can—go home." MacAllister picked up the tray and stared at the dishes all in disarray. Then he put it back down and looked into her eyes. For the first time, he spoke to her with an awful sincerity. "Rumbelow's a bad piece, Yer Grace, and this is a dastardly scam."

"I could help Gabriel." She wouldn't leave Gabriel to face the danger alone.

"Nay!"

"I know you don't like me, but I'm sensible, I think on my feet, and I'm a good shot."

"It's na' that. Or na' so much that. I've got a powerful intuition aboot this." MacAllister touched her lightly, once, on the arm. "Someone's going t' die."

By the time the game was over, all of the ladies in Chalice Hall were watching the dowager's house, waiting to see which of the men had fulfilled his promise to win the tiara. They stood on the terrace, at the windows, even in the garden. Lady Tabard said nothing to Madeline as Madeline continued to pace in the sitting room. She stared at the house as if she could see through the walls, as if her concentration could help Gabriel win the match.

Finally, at four o'clock, the door of the dowager's house opened and Madeline beheld the men as they staggered out, coats off, cravats askew. Gabriel exited last, with Mr. Rumbelow at his side, and Gabriel looked as cool as when he walked in.

In his hand, he held a polished wooden box. Not the plain box that the queen's tiara used to reside in, but a richly carved box with an elegant silver pattern and a silver lock.

The ladies around the house groaned.

Madeline groped her way to a chair and collapsed. Bowing her head, she said a prayer of thanksgiving. The queen's tiara was safe. Her mother would approve. And Gabriel . . .

Come to me.

At the window, Lady Tabard pronounced, "At least it was Lord Campion who won the crown. We all know how lucky he is."

"Yes, heaven forbid Lord Achard should ever win anything," Lady Achard said peevishly. "With his execrable luck, he should stop playing altogether."

"Mother says we'll be up the River Tick soon if

he doesn't stop," one of the younger Lady Achards confided.

Her mother hushed her, then smiled nervously at the assemblage. "You know how it is. The creditors are dunning us. We may have to repair to the country for a time."

The other ladies nodded. Their husbands were gamblers. They did know how it was to repair to the country, to borrow money to go on, to dodge creditors.

"But it does bode ill for the big game if Lord Campion is basking in luck," Mrs. Greene said.

Lifting her head, Madeline prepared to rise— and found Thomasin observing her. For the first time, Madeline realized Thomasin had been monitoring her quite intently and for quite a while. Why? What did she see that made her curious? What did she *know*?

Madeline should talk to her, but . . . not now. Not when she needed to go, to hold the queen's tiara in her hands. To look into Gabriel's eyes, thank him and say . . . say what? She didn't know. She felt off balance, uneasy with herself. She had accused Gabriel of coming here to feed a frivolous, destructive obsession. Instead, he had come out of pain, out of the dark need to avenge his brother.

She had to say something, do something. There had to be a way to make matters right for Gabriel. She would find a way.

Come to me.

Chapter Twenty-two

Madeline clutched the wooden jewel box. She couldn't open the lock, she didn't have the key, but she knew what the tiara looked like—dainty, golden and glittering. Her mother had worn it on her presentation to court, and again in the formal portrait in the gallery. The tiara was Madeline's only link to her mother—and Gabriel had won it for her.

Now, she thought . . . she thought she must have lost her mind. She had paid Gabriel for her tiara with the present of her body. Of course, he'd stopped and made her choose him for himself and her need alone, so really, she owed him nothing. Nothing.

But he'd given her as much enjoyment as she'd given him. More, for he'd bent his mind on seduction, and he knew how to pleasure a woman.

She had been nothing more than a woman faced with the fierce unleashing of a passion she had hoped long vanquished. And now she felt . . . grateful?

No.

Amazed?

Absolutely.

Uncertain?

She was the future duchess of Magnus, and she was *never* uncertain.

She lifted her head and looked out the window. No. She was not uncertain. For the first time in days, she knew exactly what she wanted. Slipping the tiara under the bed, she prepared herself to go to him.

Silent and grim, Gabriel pulled the thin, handleless blade from under his sleeve and laid it on the table by the washbasin. He kicked off his shoes, peeled off his stockings. He stripped off his jacket, his cravat and his shirt.

Just as silent, just as grim, MacAllister filled the basin with water and placed a rag, a bar of lemon soap and towel beside him.

Splashing water on his face, Gabriel reflected on the action about to begin. The game for the tiara had given him a chance to decipher the other men's playing strategies. Lord Achard was impulsive, hoping for luck against all odds. Mr. Greene was precise, picking through his cards, arranging them from left to right, high to low. Mr. Payborn was a good player with consistently bad luck, but luck could always change. Mr. Payborn was someone to watch out for.

And Rumbelow . . . Rumbelow was good. Rumbelow was the best of them all. Perhaps that was because he didn't care whether he won or lost. He would have the money anyway.

Dipping the rag in the water, Gabriel soaped it up and washed his neck, his face, his armpits and scrubbed lightly across his chest.

One hundred thousand pounds. Gabriel's yearly income was a tenth of that, and he was a wealthy man.

Gabriel rinsed the cloth and wiped off the soap. The cool water felt good, soothing on his hot skin, and inevitably his mind returned to Madeline. "MacAllister, did you give Maddie the tiara?"

"Aye. I delivered it t' the bedchamber she shares with that young girl."

"Was the girl there?"

MacAllister took the basin of dirty water, tossed it out the window and refilled it with clean. As he placed it in front of Gabriel once more, he said, "Only Her Grace. Will ye be wanting a shave?"

Gabriel ran his fingers over his rough chin. "I probably should. It'll be a long time until the next shave."

"I suppose ye'll be wanting hot water?"

He did, of course, but MacAllister could never get it back from the kitchen in time. "Never mind the water. When you gave her the tiara, what did she say?"

"She thanks ye."

Gabriel nodded, and wondered briefly if he could find the key and lock Madeline in that room and keep her safe. But no. She was smart. She'd figure a way to escape.

As MacAllister placed the razor beside Gabriel, MacAllister announced, "She's matured a wee bit since the first time ye pursued her."

Stunned at such a concession from his valet, Gabriel turned on him. "You approve of her?"

MacAllister screwed his face into his most annoyed expression. "I ne'er said that. But for a woman, she's brave. Na' sensible, but brave."

"Hm." Gabriel had given her an ultimatum last night. Would she come to him, or would she try to run as she'd done before?

He wouldn't permit that cowardice again. He'd go after her and drag her back by her hair, he swore it—although that invalidated his demand that she come to him. He smiled savagely. That was a bluff, of course. He was going to reel her in any way he could, but if she discarded false pride and blasted independence to come to him, then he would be assured she would stay.

MacAllister laid out Gabriel's garments and placed the knife where Gabriel couldn't overlook it. "With training and firm discipline, Her Grace could be an acceptable wife."

Gabriel laughed, and the laughter felt odd, as if he never laughed anymore. "You'd be the expert on that, you old bachelor."

"As much as ye, ye young fool." But MacAllister sounded cheerful, or as cheerful as the dour Scotsman ever sounded.

Turning back to the basin, Gabriel splashed

himself again. Looking into the small mirror above the table, he soaped his chin and picked up the razor. "If Rumbelow locks us in the dowager's house, and I suspect that's the plan, I'll signal with the mirror when it's time."

MacAllister's brief fling at good spirits faded. "I'll watch."

"Take my horse." Pulling his skin tight, Gabriel slid the razor across his cheek and over his jaw. Swishing the soap and hair off in the water, he said, "It's a long twenty miles to Renatehead where the king's men are lodged."

"I'll bring them, and yer men, too."

Gabriel met MacAllister's gaze in the mirror. "It's almost over, my friend. We almost have him."

Gloomily, MacAllister said, "*Almost* is the most fearsome word in the English language."

A tentative knock sounded on the door.

The two men looked at each other, caution in their gazes. Holding the razor like a weapon, Gabriel waved MacAllister toward the door.

MacAllister opened it slightly. "Oh. It's ye." He opened it wider. "'Tis the lass," he said with patent disgust.

Madeline stepped in.

Gabriel placed the razor on the table. It was as if his thoughts had summoned her.

"I'll go fetch hot water." MacAllister slipped out and shut the door with a slam.

Gabriel scarcely noticed he was gone.

Damn, Madeline was a fine-looking woman. Tall, curvaceous, with strong, bare arms and skin tanned to the color of cream-laden coffee. Her hair was orderly today, but he'd seen it falling down around her shoulders often these last two days, and last night it had dusted the white sheets with strands of midnight. Her eyes, big and blue, were fringed with the same midnight.

Her strong, angular face could never be called beautiful; she was too lively, too direct. But her lips made a man think of many things, wicked and exuberant activities. She wore a dark blue gown that formed to her bare legs as she walked, caressing her like a lover's fingers. He could see the junction of her thighs and the shape of her mound beneath the thin silk. Her white elbow-length gloves shimmered in rich satin, but their creaminess was nothing compared to the skin above them. As her gaze skittered over his bare chest, he experienced a weakness in his knees, and a stiffening in his groin. Two quite pleasurable sensations he suffered only in Madeline's presence.

What had she come for? To thank him in person? He could think of a simple way for her to do that. To insist he allow her to help ruin Rumbelow? She was out of luck. She looked around the room as if trying to avoid his gaze, and he couldn't resist that challenge. "Welcome," he said. "I never thought you'd come to me so soon."

Her gaze flew to him and she looked vaguely guilty.

Nothing was easy with Madeline. "Perhaps you've come to tell me you're taking my advice and leaving?"

"No! Why would I do that after you've been so good as to win me the queen's tiara?"

"So you'll be safe when the bullets start flying?" His voice was heavy with logic, and he turned back to the mirror to avoid shaking her until she saw reason.

Her eyebrows rose in surprise, then puckered in a frown. "Will it come to that?"

Soaping the other side of his face, he applied the razor. "I doubt that Rumbelow is going to go meekly to prison and to court, there to be sentenced to hang by his neck until he's dead."

"Then I certainly can't leave you."

Why had she come? "I have the situation well in hand," he said.

"Then it doesn't matter if I stay, does it?"

Ah. She had her own brand of logic. Before he could reply sharply, he heard the scrape of the key in the lock. Swinging about, he saw her remove the key and place it on the dressing table. Astonishment held him still. "Did you just lock us in?"

"How astute of you." She stepped closer. "You're shaving."

"Very astute of *you*." Turning back, he watched her in the mirror and again wondered what she was doing here. She'd locked them in. Why would she lock them in together? There were only a few choices. She was either going to kill him, or shout at him . . . or make love to him.

Of course, with Maddie, it could be some mad scheme his male mind couldn't comprehend—and probably was.

She stared with seeming fascination as he scraped his whiskers away, and when he wiped his face clean, she reached for him slowly and ran her fingertips over his now-smooth cheek.

Blast it. He wanted her again. He wanted more than her touch on his face. He wanted her hand on his chest. Her mouth on his cock. Her body rubbing on his. . . . She'd locked the door, and if she touched him again, he'd have her flat on her back, and to hell with his principles.

In a harsh voice, he asked, "So what did you come for?"

"To tell you . . . to give you this." Unhurriedly, she unbuttoned the first button of her elbow-length glove.

Incredulous, he stood frozen, the towel clutched in his fists, and watched as each tiny white satin-covered button slipped from its hole. Did she mean . . . ? Was she serious?

But her fingers trembled enough to make the task difficult, and her lips trembled, too. She kept glancing at him, then glancing back down, as if afraid to view his reaction too closely, and her bosom rose and fell in a wonderful, hypnotic motion.

For one moment, he was transported back to the day four years ago when she had slowly, erotically stripped off her glove. She hadn't been nervous then; she'd been taunting him, offering her body if he would only take advantage of her offer. She had been fresh, young, disciplined in every way—except with him. The wild desire between them had ignited as she revealed her smooth wrist and long fingers.

Then she called him back to the present by exclaiming, *"Merde!"* She had wrestled so hard with a button she broke it off, and it rolled across the floor to land at his feet.

That broke his paralysis. That made him realize what she was doing. What she meant by this.

She had declared him a victor in their war.

She had come to him, just as he demanded.

Striding forward, he pushed her hand away. "Let me."

A few of the buttons gaped open at her wrist. Lifting it to his lips, he kissed the blue vein that pulsed there. A slow kiss that lingered and tasted . . . tasted of fear, of daring, of remembered passion and hopes for yet more. "How many more buttons shall I undo?" he murmured against her skin, then looked into her eyes.

Her scent came off her in waves—fresh flowers and warm woman. "It depends on whether you wish to own the glove."

"Oh, I do."

"Then you take it"—she lifted her chin at him—"but I'm here on your command."

"Are you?"

"I've come to you."

He had her. He'd won her. He smiled at her, but without kindness. Without mercy. He opened the rest of the glove with ruthless efficiency. Stripping it away, he again kissed her wrist, then applied his teeth to the tender skin. "I've waited too long for this moment to be gentle."

"You don't have to be anything." Resting her bare palm flat on his chest, she pushed him backward. "Sit down. I'll do it all."

Chapter Twenty-three

 ❦

 $\mathcal{G}$ abriel went willingly, fascinated by the strength of Madeline's intention, the determination in her gaze.

 Sliding her arm around his waist, she pulled him to a stop in front of the armless vanity chair. Briefly, all too briefly, her breasts pressed against his chest.

 She didn't seem to enjoy the contact as he did, for she drew away without hesitation.

 Then he saw her flutter of eyelashes, and realized she was taunting him, giving him a brief taste of future pleasures, then withdrawing.

 "Do you think I'm going to put up with this?" he asked through his teeth.

 Again those eyelashes fluttered, and he caught a series of quick, coy glances from her blue eyes. "Yes, I think you will."

 She was correct.

 She said, "Stand right there," and her hand wandered down his stomach to his fly. There she toyed with the buttons, or perhaps she was as nervous now as she had been when she tried to remove her glove. Whatever the case, the backs of her fingers brushed him as she loosened his trousers from his hips, and each touch, accidental though it might be, brought him an agony of delight.

She eased his trousers open, and his cock sprang free. Her eyes, heated to the blue of the hottest part of fire, widened as she looked on him.

When she stared like that, as if his size amazed her, he wanted to strut like a peacock—but he couldn't move. He was as enthralled by her as she was intent on seducing him.

And he was willing to be seduced. Stepping out of the trousers, he stood nude before her.

"I love your"—she slid the flat of her hand along his thigh—"stomach. The ripples of the muscle fascinate me."

He gloried in her touch. "My stomach?"

"And your"—she slid her hand up his hip—"shoulders. They're so broad, I always feel protected when you're over me."

"My shoulders?"

Lifting her gaze to his, she teased him with false innocence. "And your hands." She caught one as he reached for her, and entwined their fingers. "What else should I admire?"

Her teasing, her admiration made him grow so hard his cock ached with the need to push inside her.

Her gaze dropped. "Of course, there is this."

He watched in absolute fascination as she wrapped her fingers around his length.

"I like this very much." The tip of her tongue lightly touched her lower lip. "The skin feels so . . . soft, and yet underneath it's firm and strong."

With grim humor, he said, "The skin ought to be callused from the use I've given it."

Startled, she tried to wrench her hand away.

Stopping her with his grip on her wrist, he said, "But the calluses are on my hands, instead." He showed her his palm.

She stared in confusion at the calluses on his hand, put there more by working on the ship than by self-indulgence. As she comprehended, her eyes lit up, and she giggled.

That was a sound he'd not heard for four years, that lighthearted, surprised merriment. That merriment gave him hope: that he could capture Rumbelow, that revenge would ease his sorrow at his brother's death, that he and Madeline would live happily ever after.

She gave him a last, gentle caress, then with her hands on his shoulders urged him down onto the low chair. Smiling at him, she ruffled his hair. "You're far too handsome for my peace of mind."

He liked to hear that. "Have I ruined your sleep?"

"And my waking. For four years, all my energies have been focused on forgetting you . . . and nothing ever worked."

He liked that even more. "Not even kissing those other men?"

"Especially not kissing those other men." Running her lips over his cheek, she murmured, "I very much like the way your face feels when it's freshly shaved."

"I'll shave twice a day."

"But I like this, too." She threaded her fingers through the hair on his chest. "It's brown and curly; when you're on top of me, it rubs my nipples. I like that."

Her bosom was on the level of his face and her nipples poked at the silky material. So. She was aroused. By their banter. By his body. Circling both lightly with his thumbs, he offered, "I can be on top of you, and in you, in two seconds."

"But then I can't be on top of you."

He wasn't yet ready to allow her to assume such a position. He still needed to be dominant, to forcefully show her his possession.

Yet she was a strong woman. She would have the same need. He wrestled with himself, wanting to do the right thing, to allow her to indulge herself in him, if that was what she wanted. With a sigh of both anticipation and resignation, he decided he must consent to allow her the freedom of his body. Just today. Just right now.

She went down on her knees before him, a gesture of obeisance that meant nothing, but that stimulated him yet more. He was so aroused he thought his eyes must be swollen. Certainly he could scarcely see.

Scraping her nails lightly down his abdomen, she asked, "Wouldn't you like me to be on top of you?"

His breath hissed from between his teeth.

"Where did you learn this? About women being on top, and on their knees and forceful?"

Leaning over, she kissed him on the thigh. "From all my continental lovers."

He knew she was lying, but the fury that roared through him accepted no such wisdom. Grasping her hair, he brought her head up.

She was smiling, a smile that mocked his alarm and enticed him yet more, and confessed, "When we were in Turkey, we were momentarily in the harem."

He groaned at the fear that struck in his heart.

She paid him no heed. "The women there told us how to bring a man to ecstasy."

This female delivered titillation and anxiety in equal doses. "Dear God, Maddie, how did you get away?"

"Do you really want to know . . . right now?" Her fingers trailed along his outer thigh, leading the way for her lips as she kissed her way up his thigh up . . . up . . . to the base of his cock.

He couldn't talk, and he dared not move for fear she would stop.

"Do you?" She cupped his balls, weighing them in her hand, rolling them within the hairy sack until he thought he would go mad.

He grunted rather than spoke. "Later."

She laughed. Air puffed over his privates, and even that light touch on the sensitive tissues was almost too much. He half rose off the stool.

She pressed him down with her hand on his belly. "We were fascinated, Eleanor and I, by the things the women told us. They said a man very much enjoys a kiss right here." She pressed her lips on the very cap of his penis, and drew away. Again her dark eyelashes fluttered, her blue eyes teased. "Is it true?"

Torn between frustration and delight, he said, "I don't know. Try again."

This time her lips were open just a little, and her tongue touched him. Wet, warm . . . he wanted to put his hand on her neck, to show her exactly what to do, but he also wanted her to learn, to experiment. "I like that."

"This?" Her mouth slipped over him, taking him all the way in her mouth. Her tongue licked at him, swirled around him. His toes curled with the effort of remaining still, of keeping control. "Mercy, Maddie. Show mercy."

Lifting her head, she asked, "What kind of mercy do you demand? Would you like me to suck on you like this?"

Closing his eyes, he clutched the sides of the chair while colors of red and black swelled behind his lids.

"Would you like me to hold you like this?" Her hands slid around to cup his buttocks. Her voice dropped to a husky whisper of pure feminine allure. "Tell me what you want and I'll do it."

Opening his eyes, he stared down at her. She was flirting, and yet she was serious. When she gave herself, her whole self, she was irresistible, like a wood nymph who seduced a man to madness. "I want you," he said, and he scarcely recognized his own voice. "I want you to take me."

She came to her feet in a sinuous rise that revealed her figure to him in slow increments. His heart beat in hard thuds as she clasped her skirt and lifted it up, revealing her white stocking-clad ankles, her strong calves, the plain dark garter at her knee. Then the pale flesh of her thighs. . . . She paused and sighed with delight as he slid his fingertips up the silky skin, reveling in the knowledge that she was his.

This time, she was completely his.

Impatient, he nudged at the hem of her skirt, seeking the place between her legs that gave him pleasure. That gave her pleasure. She gave a hum of anticipation, and the skirt resumed its journey upward. The first glimpse of dark curling hair both concealed her feminine folds and marked the juncture of her body, and his gut clenched in anticipation. Wrapping his hands around her hips, he brought her closer, knee to knee. "Put your legs around me," he instructed.

She hesitated. Perhaps a wisp of modesty held her in its grip. Perhaps she was teasing him again. He didn't care. He wanted—now. He guided her, not cruelly, but she couldn't escape him. Her buttocks flexed beneath his palm as he brought her close. He shifted her skirt out of the way, kissed her belly, her ribs. She moaned, softly, and he exulted in the proof she had aroused herself while she aroused him.

She dropped her hold on the skirt, enveloping him in the folds. In the darkness, he reveled in this special world composed of woman, heat and desire. Her hands wrapped around his head, holding him against her in an excess of affection.

Smoothing his hands down her belly, he threaded his fingers through the hair at her groin, remembering how sensitive she was to the lightest touch. She didn't move, said nothing, but he didn't make the mistake of thinking her indifferent, for when he swept his finger between her legs, he found the hair damp with her desire. Again he touched delicately, letting her anticipation build, and this time she gave the slightest gasp, and a faint moan. Still caught in the darkness and the bliss, he opened her to his touch, and explored within her folds. The silky skin, the sensitive nub, and finally, the entrance to her body. With leisurely intent, he entered her with his finger, allowing her to adjust to the intrusion, sensing her relax . . . then tense as anticipation whispered through her. Within her, he felt the pulse, the warmth, the rasp of her body, and he could think of nothing but how she would feel as she clasped him inside her.

He wanted that. He wanted it now. But still he withdrew his finger slowly, relishing in his eagerness, in the knowledge he had already brought her pleasure.

With a final kiss on her belly, he moved her skirt away. Her face was distant, concentrated on some inner joy that called him to join her.

"Maddie," he called. "Come back to me."

Looking down on him, she smiled. Leaning forward, she kissed him, sliding her tongue between his willing lips. He caught it, sucked on it, encouraged her as her hands traveled down his body and once again clasped him. Moving in such infinitesimal motions he was agonized with the waiting, she lowered herself onto him.

The hair between her legs teased him first, then she moved more attentively, absorbed in wonder.

His penis skimmed along her crease, seeking entrance. Laying his head back, he watched her, torn between the delight of his body and his delight in her.

Her eyes widened as she leaned against him. "Gabriel." Her voice contained a catch, as if the sensation were too much.

As it was. Yet it was not enough.

He moved to help her, lifting his hips to ease into her as she pressed, and pressed again.

God. Inside she was hot and tight. He wanted to plunge upward, to pound toward satisfaction. But he wouldn't. He would allow her her moment.

She rewarded him with a slight upward movement, then slipped down once more, taking more of him.

He breathed harshly, gasping for air.

She repeated the movement, up and down, up and down, and each time the *down* progressed a little farther. At last, at long last, she rested on his hips. She held his shoulders, her fingers digging into the skin, and stared at him with such an expression of worship, he wanted to bask in it forever.

But more, he wanted to move. "Ride me," he commanded.

"I don't ride well," she whispered.

"Your technique is flawless." With his hands cupping her thighs, he lifted her. "Ride me."

She did, rising and falling like a woman in the saddle. Her legs clasped his hips, her hair tickled his belly. Every time she slid down him, her pelvis pressed against his and he saw what the contact did to her. Each time her expression grew more fierce. Each time she grimaced with the onset of pleasure, and fought it away to continue.

He wanted to prolong their lovemaking, too. He wanted this ecstasy to go on forever. But with each swivel of her pelvis, his balls drew up, his moment grew closer, and he knew he wouldn't be able to contain himself any longer.

And each time he did. He had to continue for her, but with movement, his orgasm gathered strength. Sweat beaded his forehead, his chest.

Right before his eyes, her breasts bobbed up and down, silk-covered and glorious. Her head thrashed back and forth as her passion fought to peak.

Finally, when he thought he couldn't bear it anymore, she reached her climax.

She pressed hard against him, squirming, crying out, her head thrown back and her long, slender neck tense with release. Inside, orgasm clutched him, taunting him, making him crave more than he'd ever craved in his life.

He let her pummel him with her fists, rock on him until he lost his mind and his patience. He grasped her hard, moved her on him. Up and down, hard and fast, thrusting and moving until his seed spurted from him, making real his claim on her.

This time, this time she had made a promise. This time, she meant it.

This time, she would never leave him.

Gabriel held an exhausted Madeline against his chest. Slowly, his hand passed over her back, rubbing her in glorious appreciation. He hadn't liked letting her take the lead, but his restraint had made his reward all the sweeter.

He heard—felt—as she took a long breath of recovery. Without lifting her head, she kissed his neck. "I love you. I love you so much."

Ah. That was just what he wanted, needed, to hear. He hugged her tighter.

"I swear to you, I'm yours. No matter what happens in the future, I'll always be yours." She flung her arms wide. "I am the duchess of Magnus. A duchess of Magnus never breaks her vow. I am yours to command."

"You swear?"

Placing her hand over his heart, she said, "That is my solemn vow."

The dreadful tension in him relaxed a little. She truly understood now. She comprehended what he needed. What they both needed.

She asked, "Will you marry me?"

He stiffened. She had asked him to be her husband. That wasn't right.

Then he realized he suffered from affronted masculinity, and he chuckled at this reversal of roles. He had asked her last time; perhaps it was justice that she ask him now. Lifting her head, he gazed into her eyes. "I would be honored to be your husband. It's a role I've been waiting to play for four long years."

She must have seen something in his countenance that gave her pause. "We can put the past aside, can't we?"

"We will." They must.

With wobbly dignity, she stood, then backed away so he, too, could stand. "I'll do everything for you. You'll live like a king of old, with servants to do your every bidding, a castle or two, London in the spring, hunting in the fall. . . ."

Uneasiness crept over him. "Sounds delightful. What would I do?"

"Enjoy the wife who adores you and obeys your every wish."

"That's doing it up a little brown." He stood, also, and drew on his trousers. "I want to marry *you*, Madeline, not some stranger who resides in your body and fulfills my every wish."

She bowed to him as the maidens in the harem must have done to their master. "There. You see? You told me what you wished and I will obey you. I won't fulfill your every wish."

"That's better," he said with some humor. Yet

something was still not right. He pulled on his shirt and watched as she sprawled in the chair he had abandoned. "Maddie."

She rested her head against the back of the chair and smirked at him, to all appearances a woman sated and happy. "Yes, my love?"

Pressing his palms on either side of her face, he leaned toward her. "It's more urgent than ever that you leave now."

"I can't do that." Her smile lingered as if his anxiety were not important. As if he exaggerated the danger. "I can't leave you to do this alone."

Again that uneasiness swept through him. "You'll distract me."

"I'll help you. I'm really quite formidable, especially when I know I have you behind me."

Softly, he answered, "I have *you* behind *me*."

She laid her hands over his. "We're behind each other. When we've got this situation cleaned up, I'll go to London, rescue Eleanor and explain everything to Mr. Knight—"

"*You* will?"

"Then we'll send our announcement to the *Times*. I think I can have the wedding arranged in less than six weeks."

Now he knew what was wrong. Now he understood. He was marrying Madeline, the woman of fire and hidden passion . . . who cared for everything and everyone that was hers, because she didn't dare trust anyone else to do so. He straightened. "Do I understand this correctly? All you want is a man who's there when he says he will be, who'll do what he says he'll do, who'll keep his wedding vow till death do us part."

"Yes." She could barely breathe for joy.

"A man you can rely on."

"Yes."

"You've got one. Me."

She cocked her head, not comprehending his trepidation, not anticipating his ultimatum.

"But you're afraid that if you do try to lean on me, I'll step away and you'll fall on your face. It's what happened with your father, time and again."

At the mention of her father, her expression changed from carefree contentment to guarded unease. "No, I don't rely on Papa."

"Yet you still carry the bruises from the times you tried."

She stood, adjusted her gown, pressed at the wrinkles with the palms of her hands. "I don't know what you're saying."

He knew very well she did understand. She just didn't want to face the truth. "So you ran away from me rather than stay and see if I could hold up for the long run, and now . . . now you say you're mine, but you're still holding back."

She answered too quickly. "I'm not!"

He went after her, cornered her, when it would have been so much easier to just let the matter go. "Tell me, Madeline, what tasks will you trust me with at your estate?"

"What do you mean?"

"Shall I take over the responsibility of paying the servants?"

"Well . . . no, I do that. I've got a system worked out." She essayed a troubled smile, but she couldn't meet his eyes. "There's no need for you to bother yourself."

He pressed her harder. "Shall I buy the Twelfth Night presents for everyone? I'll make a list and take care of the matter."

"I always have that planned months in advance. There's no reason for you to—"

"Bother myself. I know."

She backed away as if he were a wolf and she a defenseless sheep.

"Look at you," he said softly. "Every guard has been raised. You've got your arms crossed across your belly and your brow is puckered. I'll wager your stomach hurts."

"I . . . just . . ."

He had almost believed her. For one brief, shining moment, he thought he'd achieved his dream—and his disappointment made him savage. Made him honest. "Everyone thinks you're so strong and self-confident, but inside you're a frightened child, waiting to suffer betrayal again from those who should love you most."

"That's not what I'm like!"

"I want everything, Madeline. Your heart, your soul, your thoughts, your dreams . . . I want to know you. I want to be with you. I want you to trust me." Coming to her, he kissed her forehead. "Come back when you can give me, not just your glove, but your hand."

Chapter Twenty-four

All Madeline had to do was make her way back to her bedchamber. Putting one foot in front of the other, she concentrated on thinking of nothing.

She met one of the Misses Greene; she smiled and nodded, forgetting that, as a companion, she should curtsy. Miss Greene stared, but didn't speak. Perhaps Madeline's expression was peculiar. Maybe she wobbled as she walked. She didn't know. She didn't care.

She met Lady Tabard, who told her that Thomasin had gone to her bedchamber after hearing the good news. "This very afternoon, before Lord Tabard could enter the game, Lord Hurth begged leave to ask Thomasin for her hand in marriage. There. What do you think of that?"

Madeline stared dully at Lady Tabard, then realized she should offer her congratulations.

Before she could speak, Lady Tabard cut her off. "Lord Tabard told her, and she didn't behave badly at all. She'll accept, I think. I really think she will. Surely she'll realize the great honor he has done her—and Lord Tabard says he's incredibly wealthy and will be a marquess on his father's death. Yes, this will put her off her infatuation with Jeffy, I'm sure. It's what I've always wanted for her." Lady Tabard grasped Madeline's hand. "Lord Tabard and I are cognizant of our debt to you, dear Miss de Lacy. It is through your efforts this wonderful opportunity has arisen. I have told Lord Tabard that we shall give you an extra day off next month."

Madeline didn't truly understand why this woman was gushing, barely recalling Hurth and Thomasin and the whole wretched matchmaking mess.

Lady Tabard added hastily, "And an increase in your wages, of course. We don't want to lose Thomasin's new companion!"

Giving a dry sob, Madeline pulled away. "Excuse me." Making her way to the bedchamber, she shut the door behind her and began to collapse, her back sliding against the wall.

She heard a snuffling from the bed, and froze. Of course. Lady Tabard said that Thomasin was in here. Madeline stared at the weeping lump flung across the counterpane. It would seem Thomasin wasn't happy about receiving a marriage proposal. Or perhaps she had some other silly problem that afflicts eighteen-year-olds.

Madeline would be expected to provide sympathy. She didn't think she could.

Lifting her head, Thomasin stared at Madeline. In a voice husky with weeping, she asked, "What's . . . wrong?"

The way Thomasin looked, miserable, yet concerned, took Madeline by surprise. The compassion overset her, and she blurted, "I have to get out of here. Lord Campion just . . . just . . ."

"Did he hurt you?"

Madeline shook her head.

"Did he yell at you? No, you wouldn't care." The truth dawned, and Thomasin sat up, her eyes red and puffy, her hands in fists at her side. "Did he reject you?"

Madeline nodded.

"That cad. How dare he?"

Madeline's fragile composure gave way to a burst of sobbing. She had never heard herself make such a noise in her life, not even when she was eight and her father forgot her at an inn. Stuffing her fists to her mouth, she tried to stop the raw desperation of the sound.

"You poor dear!" Thomasin leaped up and hurried to Madeline's side. Putting her arm around Madeline's waist, she said, "Come on. There's room enough for two on the bed."

Still crying pitifully, Madeline staggered forward and threw herself on the bed. For the first time, she opened her mind to the truth.

Gabriel didn't want her. She'd yielded him her whole being, and he didn't want her.

Clasping the covers in her hands, she cried, doubled over in pain.

Thomasin rubbed her shoulder. "Men are all louses, dirty, rotten, unscrupulous swine."

Madeline nodded and wept some more.

"You . . . you're really the duchess, aren't you?"

Madeline caught her breath, lifted her head and stared at Thomasin.

"Or rather . . . the marchioness of Sheridan and the future duchess." Thomasin pressed a handkerchief into her hand. "At first I thought you were the reason Her Grace and Lord Campion parted, but when I heard the rumor that you were in truth the duchess, I realized that that explained why you were so bad at being a companion and so good at directing just . . . everything else." Thomasin's eyes filled with tears once more. "Because of you, I'm a success. A huge success." With a wail, she threw herself back on the bed. "And I'm so ashamed!"

Struggling up on her elbows, Madeline took her turn patting Thomasin on the shoulder. "You don't have anything to be ashamed about."

"But I do. I'm having a good time, dancing and flirting, while poor Jeffy is home, alone and unhappy."

Madeline paused in mid-pat. "Oh. You're feeling guilty."

"Ye-es." Thomasin sobbed in the pillow. "And . . . and Lord Hurth asked Papa for my hand, and I en-enjoyed the attention."

"Of course you did. He's rich, and even if he has execrable taste in clothing, he's never proposed to anyone else in his life. It's a triumph."

"But Jeffy . . ."

Madeline's patience had evaporated in the heat of her own crisis. "Do you really think Jeffy's home pining for you? Or is he at some country dance right now courting another handsome female?"

Thomasin's crying stopped abruptly. Sitting straight up, she glared through red-rimmed eyes. "You've been talking to That Woman. She's never approved of Jeffy."

"Is that why you fell in love with him? To make your stepmama unhappy?"

Thomasin gave off outrage in waves. "Just because you're the duchess—"

"Doesn't mean I don't possess good sense." Madeline looked about for another handkerchief, and finally handed Thomasin a corner of the sheet. "Jeffy's not for you. You know it. If you really loved him, you wouldn't care who proposed. You would dance and frolic, secure in the knowledge you had found your true love—and that he was waiting for you to return. You haven't found him, yet, because Jeffy is just a boy of whom your parents disapprove."

The two women stared at each other.

"Have you found your true love?" Thomasin asked.

Madeline's lower lip trembled. "I have."

"Well, if that's true love, I don't want it," Thomasin said roundly.

Madeline slid back down onto the pillow. Tears squeezed out of her eyes, but they didn't ease the pain. "You're wise."

"Perhaps I'm not a duchess, and perhaps I don't have good sense"—Thomasin took a breath—"but when I watched you two together, I would have sworn he loved you, too."

Madeline struggled to answer without weeping bitterly. "He says he does, but he says I don't trust him."

"Do you?"

"Yes! Yes!" But he'd been so sure. And he hadn't looked happy about rejecting her. More weary and sad. Once more, Madeline buried her head in the covers. "I don't know. I think I do, but when he wants me to let him take responsibility for"—Madeline waved a hand—"anything, like hiring the gardeners, it makes me ill."

Thomasin patted Madeline's shoulder once more. "So Lord Campion didn't reject you. Not really. But to live with you, to marry you, he insists you give yourself to him completely. To trust him with your heart."

At this totally unnecessary and unasked-for clarification, Madeline sobbed anew.

Thomasin said defiantly, "You told me the truth. Why can't I tell you?"

What a stupid question! "Because I don't . . . wa-want . . . to hear it."

"Well, I didn't, either."

With tear-filled eyes, Madeline looked around the small bedchamber and thought about the evening to come, spent in the company of wives, sons and daughters while the men gamed. She thought about tomorrow, so dull. She thought about waiting, anticipating the next time she would see Gabriel.

She couldn't stand it. "We should leave."

Thomasin swallowed. "What?"

"We should leave here. Now. Tonight. I've got the queen's tiara. My father isn't here. You don't want to remain." And although Madeline couldn't rescue everyone from Mr. Rumbelow's nefarious plans, she'd grown fond of Thomasin. She could rescue her. She wanted to rescue her. "Let's go."

Thomasin slid off the bed and viewed Madeline with a mixture of confusion and hope. "Where?"

"To London to liberate my cousin, Eleanor."

At the name, Thomasin started. "We met her at the inn. She's the real companion."

"Yes. Very good." Madeline slid off the bed on the other side. "We'll leave a note, tell your parents who I am and where to find you when they're done with this party."

"They'll be furious with you."

"By the time this party is over, they'll thank me." Madeline could say no more. "I'll introduce you to the best hostesses as my special protégée. Lady Tabard will be thrilled."

With her hands clasped at her bosom, Thomasin stared into space. "Jeffy really doesn't love me, does he?"

"I don't know, dear. You know that answer better than anyone."

Thomasin's head dropped. "I might as well go."

Bitterly, Madeline added, "Gabriel wants me to leave, so this will make him happy."

Wetting her handkerchief, Thomasin wiped her streaked face. "Do you think that's why he rejected you? So you would leave?" She wet another handkerchief and offered it to Madeline.

Madeline's heart gave a quick, buoyant leap as she pressed the cool cloth to her hot cheeks. "Mayhap." She thought of that grieved, intense expression on his face, and hope failed her. "No. He doesn't want me as I am, and I can't be anybody else."

Thomasin considered Madeline critically. "I don't think he wants you to be someone else, I think he wants you to be . . . better."

"I'm fine as I am. I don't want to talk about it." Madeline grabbed her carpetbag and stuffed a handful of clothes inside. "Pack your bag. Let's go."

"I don't know how to pack a bag," Thomasin snapped.

"Neither do I. Whatever you can't fit in, the servants will send on later." Removing the box containing the tiara from under the bed, Madeline placed it carefully among the clothes. She put the black velvet holster, with its pistol, atop of that, and closed the bag.

Thomasin stuffed her valise so full of clothes and jewelry, Madeline had to help her close it. They hefted the bags. Thomasin gave a little moan at the weight. Then, quietly, the two women moved down the corridor, down the stairway and out the front door.

They met servants, but no guests; everyone was in their room making their preparations for the evening.

Twilight had turned the landscape into a pale, muddled tangle of trees and lawn, and changed the monstrosity of a house from a work of bad taste into a looming menace. The decision was made, and Madeline wanted to leave *now.*

MacAllister was right. Mr. Rumbelow was dangerous. Someone was going to die.

Madeline feared it would be an innocent, and . . . and Gabriel would not be distracted by Madeline if she were out of his way. It was true. She knew it. She just hated to leave him to face death alone.

Standing at the top of the stairs, Thomasin looked around as if expecting the carriage. "What do we do now?"

"We go to the stables—"

"The stables?"

"And instruct the hostler to prepare one of Mr. Rumbelow's carriages to drive us to London."

Thomasin stared at Madeline doubtfully. "Go all the way to the stables, carrying this bag?"

"Don't worry," Madeline assured her. "You have more strength than you give yourself credit for, and I've traveled all over the continent. Hostlers do as they're told."

But she was wrong.

In the stables, the lanterns had been lit, the horses were brushed and in their stalls, but when Madeline announced she wanted a carriage, Mr. Rumbelow's hostler shook his head. "Can't."

"I beg your pardon." Madeline couldn't believe the cheek of the man. Placing her carpetbag beside her feet, she rubbed her aching arm. "Lady Thomasin Charlford wishes to leave."

"Can't," he said again.

Madeline spoke in a firm tone meant to calm Thomasin. "My good man! You are the hostler, are you not? You do order the horses brought around, do you not? Do so at once!"

The hostler snapped his fingers, and when the stableboy came running, told him, "Run and get the master."

The master? "Mr. Rumbelow?"

"Nay. Me master."

Madeline had a bad feeling about this.

Thomasin put her bag down, too, and moved nervously beside her, looking around as if she'd never been inside a stable—which was certainly possible.

"I'll speak to your supervisor," Madeline said to the hostler. "We'll get this taken care of."

"Ye're goin' t' speak t' me, are ye?" Big Bill swaggered out of the shadows. "What are ye goin' t' tell me, Miss Swell Cove?"

Madeline's heart sank.

In the dim light of the stable, his thin, long face looked like a cadaver's, with hollowed cheeks and sunken eyes. His bow-shaped mouth sneered, black beard stubbled his chin and his body odor proved he hadn't bathed since they'd last met.

Tucking his thumbs into his suspenders, he spit a long stream of tobacco close enough to Madeline that some of the brown liquid splattered her skirt.

Sometime between yesterday's walk and to-night's escapade, Big Bill seemed to have lost his affection for Madeline.

Thomasin stepped in front of Madeline. "Watch what you're doing, you . . . man!"

Big Bill looked her up and down. "Aren't ye a 'andsome thing? Running away from yer folks, are ye?"

Thomasin shrank away from his insolence, but she boldly said, "What I do is none of your con-cern. You don't know your place."

Madeline put her hand on Thomasin's arm to restrain her. Thomasin, after all, thought him an insolent servant. Madeline knew him to be a mur-derer. "I'm Lady Thomasin's companion. I'm es-corting her to London."

"No, ye're not, because ye're not goin'. Neither one of ye."

That was bluntness indeed. "You're not in charge of the guests' travel," Madeline said.

He snapped his suspenders. "I guess I am. Or-ders are no one's t' leave 'ere until Rumbelow says so, and 'e ain't said so."

This was worse than Madeline could have imag-ined. She glanced around. The hostler watched, wide-eyed, and behind him a ring of grinning thugs waited on Big Bill's orders. Madeline had lingered too late to escape. Or perhaps they'd all been trapped from the first moment they'd arrived.

"That's ludicrous," Thomasin said. "Mr. Rumbelow wouldn't keep us here against our wishes."

"Ye don't want t' go anywhere with this piece anyways." Big Bill's gaze drilled into Madeline. "She's not a proper companion fer an innocent like yerself. She's gettin' above 'erself, swivin' a lord, when she could 'ave someone like me."

Obviously, Thomasin didn't understand what swiving was, or she would have been horrified. As it was, she strained at Madeline's grip. "She wouldn't have anything to do with you. She's really a duchess!"

"Thomasin, no!" Oh, no. That was the last thing Big Bill needed to know. Big Bill—and Mr. Rumbelow.

"A doochess? Is that wot she told ye?" Big Bill threw back his head and laughed, and all around them the other men laughed, too.

Thomasin glanced nervously from Big Bill to Madeline, out toward the others, and back to Madeline. "He's insolent," she said. "He's just a servant. He can't keep us here. That would be imprisonment, and he would be a criminal."

One of Big Bill's eyes drooped and twitched.

Madeline kept a close watch on him and said softly, "So he would."

"Rumbelow's orders," Big Bill repeated.

Still incredulous, Thomasin said, "But Madeline, that's impossible. This person must be mistaken. For Mr. Rumbelow to give such a command, he would have to be mad."

"Or also a criminal," Madeline said.

"Or both," Big Bill added helpfully.

"But . . . oh!" Thomasin put her hand over her mouth, and her large eyes stared between Big Bill and Madeline.

"Run back t' the 'ouse, now, and ye"—he pointed at Madeline—"make sure the little girl keeps her yap shut. Or I'll 'ave t' come after ye, and ye won't like that." Big Bill spit again, and this time he spit almost on Madeline's shoes.

Thomasin squealed and leaped back.

Madeline's usually quiescent temper stirred. She stared directly at him and didn't move.

When the disgusting brown had settled, she stepped up to Big Bill.

Much to the amusement of his compatriots, he grinned and made kissing sounds.

With a single swift gesture, she hit him under the chin with the flat of her hand.

His head snapped back. He swallowed the whole, disgusting wad of tobacco.

She leaped back.

He clutched his stomach and gagged.

Grabbing up both of their carpetbags, she handed one to Thomasin and said, "Come on, dear. We need to get back to the house before we're missed."

Chapter Twenty-five

As the men laughed at Bill, Madeline and Thomasin hurried out, shoulder to shoulder.

As soon as they were free of the stable, Madeline said, "*Merde!* I shouldn't have done that. Big Bill will be . . . vicious. *More* vicious."

"You can't be sorry. He's a dreadful man. He spoke ill of you, and imagined himself on your level, and—what did he mean? When he said he'd come after us, what did he mean?" Thomasin stomped toward the house. "I need to tell my papa, right now!"

"No." Madeline glanced behind her, but didn't slow down. "You can't. That would ruin everything."

"Ruin what? Mr. Rumbelow's party? I hate to tell you this, but it's already ruined for me." Thomasin had developed a sturdy backbone. "Am I supposed to dance and laugh for the next two days knowing that man has virtually de-

clared I cannot leave? I'm a guest. I'm an aristocrat. He can't do that."

"Yet he seems to have."

The sky had faded to a silver-gray in the west,
leaving the landscape shrouded in shadow. A
wind kicked up off the sea, and the groaning of the
trees masked any sound from behind them.
Thomasin stumbled over a tuft of grass; Madeline
caught her arm and helped her get her balance, but
they never slowed. Danger lurked behind them.

"And why should you make sure I keep my . . .
my yap shut?" Thomasin was breathing hard,
from indignation and exercise. "Are you in
charge?"

"He means if you or I raise the alarm, he'll hurt
me."

"He can't do that."

Exasperated, Madeline said, "Thomasin, did
you look around in there? There were a great
many men holding a great many guns, and none
of them were huntsmen who had lost the fox."
She waited while that sank in. "We're isolated.
The game has started. None of the ladies or the
sons and daughters are going to believe us if we
tell them what happened. They'll want to know
why we were trying to leave."

Thomasin was struck dumb by the logic. "But
we can't just let Mr. Rumbelow hold us here. He
must be planning a mischief." She struck her fist
in her palm. "I never did trust him!"

Madeline wanted to laugh, but the situation

was too serious. "If you will trust me, I'll tell someone who'll know what to do." She hoped.

"Who? All the gentlemen are in the game."

"Lord Campion's valet. He'll believe me." If she had to pound the truth into his head.

They mounted the stairs and opened the front door. "In the meantime . . ."

"In the meantime, you and I shall go and enjoy the gathering Mr. Rumbelow has arranged for the wives and children."

Thomasin looked down at her crumpled day dress, then up at Madeline.

"Before, you were fashionably late." They hurried up to their bedchamber and thrust their bags beneath the bed. "Tonight, we shall be *very* fashionably late."

Armed only with a silver-backed garment brush, MacAllister stood in Gabriel's bedroom and looked dumbstruck at Madeline's news. "How in bluidy hell did ye find that out?"

"I tried to leave, as Gabriel instructed."

"Couldn't ye have tried a wee bit sooner, before his lordship went int' the dowager's house?" MacAllister tapped his palm with the brush. "Ye're sure that's what they meant? Rumbelow won't let anyone leave withoot his permission?"

Madeline enunciated clearly and with exasperation. "The men had guns."

"Ach, I've wanted t' shoot ye a time or two myself."

"This is no time for jests."

"That it is na'. I wish I could tell his lordship, but there's no stopping the game now."

"Can you deliver a message to him?" If MacAllister didn't do something, she would.

"Rumbelow's na' allowing the gentlemen's own servants t' wait on him. He says so there'll be no cheating, but we know better." MacAllister stroked his chin. "So I ken I'd best start hoofing it toward the village where his lordship's men are waiting."

"He has men waiting to come in?" For the first time in hours, Madeline relaxed. "Thank heavens."

"Ye didn't think he'd try t' capture a scoundrel like that by himself, did ye? A scoundrel with his own private army?" MacAllister snorted. "His lordship's na' so big a fool."

"That's a matter of opinion," Madeline said tartly.

"Aye, missie, he's na' happy with ye. What did ye do now?"

Stung by the injustice, Madeline replied, "He doesn't wish to marry me."

"Nay, 'tisn't true."

"I assure you, it is very true."

"Four years of moping after ye, and just today I give him my blessing—and now he dunna want ye?" MacAllister pulled a long, disbelieving face. "Ye must have done something wrong."

"Apparently I did a great many things wrong, including—" Abruptly, the pain caught at her again. For a few moments, in the barn and in her rush to inform MacAllister of this new development, she had forgotten Gabriel's rebuff. Now the memory swamped her, and she turned her head away.

"Here, now. Ye're na' weeping, are ye?" MacAllister walked around to view the evidence.

She glared at him defiantly, and wiped her cheeks. "I'm just leaking a little bit."

"So ye finally grew a woman's heart."

"What did you think?" she snapped. "That I had a dog's heart?"

"Nay, dogs are true. Thought yer heart was more possibly a badger's."

No one dared talk to Madeline that way—except MacAllister. The old man was incorrigible, interfering, cantankerous—and right now, the only hope of everyone here at this party.

He examined her as if she were an unusual specimen of fungus and he a botanist. "I wonder what madness has possessed his lordship now."

"I don't know, but I'm not discussing the matter with his valet." She put MacAllister firmly in his place, not that he seemed to notice. "Do you have a way of protecting yourself if you meet with any of Mr. Rumbelow's men?"

"I've got my knives."

"Gabriel has knives, too."

"Who do ye think taught him how t' use them?" MacAllister shook his head. "Daft female. Ye dinna know nothing."

* * *

Five tables, placed close together. Ten hardback chairs.

Four footmen of disreputable origins.

Claret-colored walls. Bottle-green drapes, closed over the tall windows. Bookshelves empty of contents.

Ten gentlemen, gamblers all, who noticed neither the isolation nor the fact that the footmen stood before the doors like prison guards.

A Turkish carpet of green and black. Smoke rising from the occasional cigar. The gaming room silent, the air still.

The clock striking midnight.

Gabriel could hear the wind gusting outside as a storm moved in off the sea.

In the gaming room, the gentlemen sat, hunched over their cards and concentrating as if their lives depended upon it. Only the occasional expletive or exclamation of triumph broke the quiet.

Even Rumbelow focused totally on his hand, remaining absolutely still and never speaking unnecessarily.

So Gabriel spoke. He had to. He was a man who gambled to win, and winning involved strategy. Not just card strategy, but the kind of strategy that interrupted the other men's concentration.

Actually, it was rather fun to make them writhe in annoyance. It was a break from the deliberation involved in winning the game. And he had to win the game.

Or not. He would decide as the stakes, and the circumstances, became clear.

At the end of his hand with Mr. Payborn— Gabriel won, of course, and he'd be surprised if Payborn hadn't lost everything by the morning— he said, "We should open the window. The wind will clear some of the stuffiness from the room."

No one responded. A few men shifted their cards in their hands. Lord Tabard sucked on his cigar.

"Rumbelow, is it all right with you if I have the window opened?" Gabriel insisted.

Seated at a nearby table, Rumbelow waved a negligent hand. "Yes, yes, do whatever you wish."

Ah. Rumbelow didn't like to be interrupted when he was playing cards. "I hesitate to command your servant. May I?" Gabriel asked.

"Yes! For God's sake, whatever you wish!" Raising his head, Rumbelow glared.

Gabriel scrutinized him; the heightened color, the tight lips, the flared nostrils, all proof that Rumbelow could be prodded into revealing his feelings, and possibly his cards.

Then Rumbelow caught himself. Relaxing, he smiled, using all his charm. "You're a sly one, Campion, but you shan't provoke me again."

The table with Lord Tabard and Monsieur Vavasseur ignored the ruckus, slapping cards down in blatant disgust at this interruption.

"Yes. I will." Gabriel challenged Rumbelow with his gaze, and again wondered: What drove

Rumbelow to play these hands when he planned to abscond with the ante? Did he seek a challenge? He'd always outsmarted the best lawmen in England. Did he want to brag he'd outplayed the best gamblers in England, too?

Had he grown arrogant?

Rumbelow glanced down at his hand, then back at Gabriel. "No one catches Thurston Rumbelow."

If Rumbelow was seeking a challenge, Gabriel was willing to give it to him. With one hand, Gabriel expertly shuffled the deck—a show-off gesture, but one that served its purpose. "Until now."

Rumbelow observed the expert precision Gabriel used with the cards. He saw the other men looking at him, and at Gabriel. "Talk's cheap," he said. "When we play, we'll see who catches who—if you're not eliminated by one of these fine gamblers before I have a chance to play you."

In a gesture of indolence, Gabriel crossed his boot across his knee and watched his own hand work the cards. "Or if you don't throw a game and run away to escape humiliation first." A challenge. One he thought Rumbelow would accept.

"Perhaps there's a way to make this more interesting," Rumbelow said. "A side wager, between you and me."

Gabriel's gaze flicked to the safe, black, metal, heavy and sealed with a padlock. "A side wager. But I haven't yet seen proof that your part of the wager exists."

"What?" Rumbelow snapped. "Are you calling me a cheat? Are you saying I didn't deposit my ten thousand pounds in the safe with yours?"

"I would like to see the cash. I find I concentrate on my game with more acumen if I'm assured I will have what I win." Gabriel enjoyed the rise of color in Rumbelow's cheeks. A thief, a swindler and he wasn't impervious to insult. Fascinating.

By now everyone was watching with interest, and a few of the men were tactless enough to nod.

Rumbelow put down his hand in precise, irritated motions. Rising to his feet, he strode to the safe. He showed them the key that hung around his belt. "There's one other key, but it's in London in my bank." He knelt beside the safe, opened it and inside Gabriel saw nine stacks, each tied in string. Rumbelow removed one and showed them the thousand-pound note on either end. "Satisfied?" he asked Gabriel.

Forgery, perhaps? Or a real note to camouflage the sheaves of blank paper cut precisely to pound-note size? "I am satisfied." And if his men were here, and if the ship that waited to take Rumbelow away was waiting, he would challenge him now. "A side wager is an excellent idea." He nodded toward the stacks of bills. "I like the look of those. So—we wager ten thousand pounds more."

"That's what *you* want. I want something different. Something unique." Rumbelow's gaze spoke only too eloquently. "Something you . . . own."

Gabriel shouldn't have been surprised, but he was. Something he owned?

Oh. He knew what Rumbelow wanted.

Yet he didn't hesitate. "Whatever you name is yours. I will deliver my possession into your hands, regardless of the anguish such an improbable loss would present." He needed to think about this new development. Would this give him an advantage? Or not?

Rumbelow's smile was brilliant and charming—and oh, so cruel. "It's a wager. Everyone here is witness. If Campion and I play the final game, the stakes are ten thousand pounds from me, and any one of Campion's possessions that I desire."

"Damned stupid bet, Campion," Mr. Greene said. "He could take Campion Court."

"He has to win first." Gabriel cast his gaze over the other gamblers. "What man has ever bragged he had beat me?" Snapping his fingers at one of Rumbelow's ruffian footmen, he commanded, "Open the window. Let's get some air in here."

"Are we going to chat, or are we going to play cards?" Lord Achard glared at Gabriel.

"Indeed, let us play cards." Gabriel dealt another hand.

Chapter Twenty-six

It was after midnight when the Mademoiselles Vavasseur finished their song, curtsied and received their applause.

Lady Tabard spoke slowly and loudly to Madame Vavasseur, sure that, despite proof otherwise, Madame couldn't understand English spoken in any other manner. "How excessively talented your daughters are."

Madame Vavasseur's eyes twinkled merrily and in accented, but excellent, English replied, "Thank you, my lady. Your own daughter, the charming Lady Thomasin, plays the pianoforte most excellently for them."

"Lady Thomasin is indeed endowed with great gifts, and you know"—Lady Tabard leaned close to Madame Vavasseur, but Madeline heard every word quite clearly—"today she received an offer from Lord Hurth."

Madeline wanted to groan aloud. Glancing around the crowded music room, she saw more than one person had eavesdropped on Lady Tabard's announcement. Not that they didn't want society to know that Thomasin had made such an important conquest, but the matter should be handled subtly, and after Thomasin had rejected him—which, despite Lady Tabard's hopes, Madeline knew would inevitably occur.

Lady Tabard didn't know the meaning of subtle.

Lady Achard clapped her gloved hands to get everyone's attention. "Which lovely girl shall we hear from next?"

"Josephine, you play the harp gloriously," Mrs. Greene said. "Gift us with a tune."

Lady Achard blushed becomingly, made the proper protestations and, on being begged to perform, removed her gloves and commanded the servants to place the harp in front of the huge black marble mantelpiece.

Madeline chewed her lower lip and listened to the wind that rattled the windows. How soon would MacAllister be back with the men? Though Madeline felt grief at Gabriel's rejection, she feared for him, alone in the dowager's house with Mr. Rumbelow and the other gamblers. Would Mr. Rumbelow even allow the game to be played? Was he even now robbing the men, beating them . . . killing them?

But no. That made no sense. He could have done that anytime these last few days. His plan was more intricate than that, and Madeline did believe Gabriel was more than a match for him . . . but Gabriel needed reinforcements.

Yet everywhere Madeline gazed, Mr. Rumbelow's disreputable footmen lurked about the music room, dressed in elegant livery but looking coarse and out of place. No one else noticed, except Thomasin, and from the way she eyed the villain by the door, Madeline feared she was close to bursting forth with the tale of their flight and Big Bill's maltreatment. Madeline thought the only thing that had stopped her thus far was the evening of lighthearted gaiety, arranged by Mr. Rumbelow so the young ladies could display their musical talents.

But even among the other guests, an undercurrent of intensity ran beneath the cheerfulness. Everyone was waiting for a report of the game.

As Thomasin walked away from the pianoforte, she was stopped every few feet to receive whispered congratulations and praise for her talent. She was a properly raised young lady, and disclaimed and blushed, but Madeline saw the panicked expression in her eyes and rose to intercept her, Big Bill's warning ringing in her ears.

Hurth got there first. Resplendent in a waistcoat of quilted lavender silk and a jacket of light blue velvet, he bowed and smiled, and indicated he would like to speak to Thomasin in private.

She shook her head, but Lady Tabard boomed, "Go with him, girl! You have my permission." She cast a coy smirk around at the other ladies.

As Lady Achard seated herself to play, Hurth tucked Thomasin's hand into his arm and led her into the corridor.

She cast an anguished glance at Madeline.

Madeline hurried out after them, and slipped into the library before he could close the door.

He glared.

She curtsied and went to sit in a dim corner. She had a right and a duty to be here. She was, after all, the companion.

With a toss of his curled, coiffed head, Hurth indicated a low sofa. "Please, Lady Thomasin, if you would have a seat."

"I'd rather stand, thank you," Thomasin said truculently.

Bound up in his own importance, Hurth didn't notice the truculence, or the way she watched him, as if he were a dentist and she a patient with a toothache. "Please, I insist." He gestured at the sofa again.

Sighing loudly, Thomasin seated herself with a flounce.

Madeline bit her lip to hold back her grin. If she weren't so worried about Gabriel and MacAllister and death and disaster, this would be one of the comic highlights of her life.

With a creak of his corset, Hurth lowered himself onto one knee. He arranged his trousers to sit correctly over his knee, then tried once more to take one of Thomasin's hands.

She sat on them.

Undeterred, Hurth launched into speech.

"First, I wish to assure you that I spoke to your father today, and I have his permission for this discourse which must otherwise seem like the greatest of brashness in your eyes."

Thomasin hurried into speech. "Lord Hurth, I've been told of your suit, and I wish to save us both pain and—"

He interrupted as if she had never spoken. "Despite the fact your stepmother is an undesirable connection, I find myself drawn to you."

Thomasin stiffened.

Madeline wondered how any man could be so bad at courtship. It was as if he'd taken a class on how to infuriate and repulse a woman.

"The attentions I've paid to you, marked as they are, have undoubtedly flattered you and made you aware of my deepest regard."

"Flattered me? Lord Hurth, I am not—"

"I would like to make you my wife." He blinked rapidly and settled back, waiting for Thomasin's exclamations of rapture.

Yet Thomasin didn't speak. She barely seemed to breathe. Madeline suspected she was grinding her teeth.

Finally, when Lord Hurth began to show signs of discomfort, Thomasin managed, "Your attentions are indeed flattering, my lord, and it is with the deepest regret that I must refuse your gratifying proposal."

Hurth shook his head slightly as if he couldn't believe what he'd heard. "Lady Thomasin, you are perhaps overwhelmed at the chance to wed into my family, but I assure you, your manners are impeccable—well, except for an occasional unseemly exuberance which daily exposure to my mother would cure—and you have a fine bloodline. In short, you are worthy to bear the next Hurth heir."

"Would you like to check the state of my teeth?" Thomasin asked frostily.

Madeline snorted. When both sets of eyes turned her way, one set reproachful, the other disapproving, she whipped out her handkerchief and lowered her face into it. Laughing at such a momentous occasion was perhaps a *faux pas*.

With a lowering brow, Hurth said, "Lady Thomasin, you also suffer from occasional bouts of levity. It is those bouts which made my mother question my choice of bride, but I assured her you had a superior understanding and would easily learn your place."

Thomasin rose. "Would, in fact, be broken to bridle with ease?"

The references to horses were too much for Madeline's gravity, and she had to stifle her giggles in her handkerchief.

Hurth rose also, but he groaned a little as he straightened his knee. "I suspect you're once again using your humor to deal with what is a very crucial decision. Remembering that your father gave his blessing to my suit and, perhaps more important, that my parents have also agreed you would be acceptable, will you be my wife?"

"Lord Hurth, I already gave you my answer," Thomasin snapped. "No, thank you. I will not be your wife."

Indignation brought a mottled color to his cheeks. "Don't I deserve more of an explanation than a simple denial?"

Thomasin's eyes narrowed; her fists clenched and rose. Madeline recognized the signs. Thomasin was about to lose her temper.

Hastily coming to her feet, Madeline said, "Lady Thomasin!"

With a glance at Madeline, Thomasin controlled herself and turned back to Hurth. "We do not suit, my lord. We have nothing in common."

He pulled a long face. "We don't need to have anything in common. What a vulgar idea. We're going to be married!"

Madeline brought the handkerchief to her mouth again.

This time, Thomasin dimpled with amusement, too. "I don't love you," she said with some finality.

"I blame your stepmother for such notions," Hurth said. "Love is for peasants!"

"Then I am a peasant, for I'll have love when I wed or I won't wed at all," Thomasin retorted.

Gratitude, Madeline mouthed to her.

Thomasin nodded, then turned to Hurth. "If you'll excuse my companion and I, we'll repair to the ladies' retiring chamber, where I'll try to deal with the blow of having done what I know is the right thing." Placing the back of her hand to her forehead, Thomasin said in dramatic tones,

"Someday, my lord, when you're married to the right lady, you'll thank me for this."

His rouged lips thinned with irritation. "What poppycock!"

As if to say, *I tried,* Thomasin shrugged slightly at Madeline and strode toward the door.

With another quick curtsy at the choleric Hurth, Madeline hurried after her. They walked into the retiring chamber, looked at each other and burst into laughter.

When Thomasin had gained control of herself, she seated herself before the mirror and buried her head in her hands. "That was so dreadful. And That Woman will be livid with me for turning him down."

Remembering how Lady Tabard had revealed her affection for Thomasin, Madeline said, "Oh, Lady Tabard isn't so dreadful as you imagine."

Thomasin's head came up. "She's a merchant's daughter."

"With a good heart."

"And a bold, brassy manner."

"There are worse things. I've seen stepmothers who turn their stepdaughters into drudges, who beat their stepdaughters with a rod and feed them bread and water . . . who try to force them to marry the first man who proposes."

"You're making that up." Thomasin half laughed. "That's a fairy tale."

"It's not, I assure you," Madeline said. "Lady Tabard does have your best interests at heart. She simply expresses herself poorly."

"That she does."

"I think if you try, you'll find you can talk to her. She's a powerful personality. She'll help you achieve whatever you wish."

Thomasin viewed Madeline thoughtfully. "She *is* powerful."

An uneasiness stirred in Madeline. What was Thomasin thinking?

Then, in a normal tone of voice, Thomasin asked, "Why do girls like receiving proposals?"

"Most proposals aren't that dreadful." Madeline seated herself beside Thomasin and patted her hand. "Most of the time, the gentleman talks about how much he adores you, not how you should feel privileged to adore him."

"Is that what your proposal was like from Lord Campion?"

Madeline tried to remember that first proposal, four years ago, but the events of earlier today kept intruding. She'd proposed to him, and he'd spurned her. Spurned her, and now she suffered a deep-seated ache that never left her. Not when she laughed, not when she concentrated on Thomasin, not when she listened to Lady Tabard. Never.

Would the pain ever leave her again?

"I'm sorry. I shouldn't have reminded you." Wetting a towel, Thomasin handed it to Madeline. "You're so unhappy. Can't you change yourself to be what he wants? It seems he wants so little. A chance to labor for you. A wife he knows will give herself wholly into his keeping."

Hopelessly, Madeline dabbed her face. "He shouldn't expect me to change."

"You expect *him* to change."

"Yes, well, but . . . but for the better. I want him to eschew gambling."

Thomasin sailed on, undeterred by Madeline's feeble protestation. "You expect him to never accept any responsibility on your estates, and I think he's a man who takes his responsibilities seriously." She stared hard at Madeline. "Isn't he?"

"Yes, but . . ." Thomasin waited for Madeline to finish, but this time Madeline couldn't even think of a retort.

"Perhaps you could change for him, because you know you truly can trust him?" Thomasin insisted.

"It's too hard." Yet how easily Madeline had trusted that Gabriel would get justice for Jerry, dispose of Mr. Rumbelow and keep the guests safe.

"So is being a companion, but you've made a triumph of that," Thomasin said shrewdly.

Madeline blinked at Thomasin. "That's true. I have been a triumph, haven't I?"

"You've done wonders with me."

"Maybe—"

But before Madeline could complete her thought, Lady Tabard rolled in like a great, ornate mail coach. Fixing her eye on Thomasin, she said, "There you are, young lady."

Thomasin came to her feet. "Mama, I need to tell you something." Casting a defiant glance at

Madeline, she added, "About what happened earlier today."

What had Madeline told Thomasin? *Lady Tabard is a powerful personality. She'll help you achieve whatever you wish.*

Thomasin was going to tell her about Big Bill. Coming to her feet, Madeline said, "Thomasin, no!"

Thomasin ignored her. "Mama, earlier Madeline and I were outside—"

"Is that when you decided to refuse Lord Hurth's suit?" Lady Tabard flapped her hands at Thomasin as if dismissing her. "I am most grieved with you, Thomasin. Most grieved. Any other young lady would recognize the chance she had to be a great lady."

"Mama, that's not important right now. What is important is—"

"Not important! What else is important, but a chance to wed a rich man who has a title and dresses well, too. But no, not you. You love your Jeffy." Lady Tabard imbued his name with such scorn, even Madeline cringed and wished herself elsewhere. "Jeffy. A more worthless, silly, unfaithful young man you could never find. For him, you gave up a man who'll someday be a marquess."

All of Thomasin's burning intent died under the barrage of Lady Tabard's disapproval, and anger took its place. "I didn't give up Lord Hurth for Jeffy. I gave him up because I don't like him, and I won't marry a man I don't like."

Lady Tabard seethed with impatience. "Why not, girl?"

"Because my mother did, and she and my father were miserable every day of their lives." Thomasin stared right at Lady Tabard. "That's why Papa took you as his mistress and, when my mother died, as his wife. Is it not?"

Madeline watched in fascination as Lady Tabard shriveled into a white-faced, middle-aged woman of no particular appeal and a shamefaced expression. "Young lady, that's not a matter for you . . . to . . ." Taking a quivering breath, Lady Tabard searched for, and found, her dignity. "Lady Thomasin, what did you want to tell me?"

With no expression whatsoever, Thomasin said, "Nothing, ma'am. Absolutely nothing."

In relief, Madeline collapsed into the chair and watched Lady Tabard leave the retiring chamber. Into the silence that crackled with Thomasin's temper, she said, "You were very hard on her."

"She deserves it." Thomasin's bosom heaved. "She took my mother's place and I'm supposed to pretend I don't know."

"Your father is equally guilty."

Rubbing her forehead, Thomasin said, "I know. I know. But he doesn't bother with me much."

"So you can't hurt him, because he isn't there to hurt." Madeline understood that. Her own father was just like that—and where was he now? It was not that she wanted him involved in this game, but now she worried about him because he allowed a game to take place without him. Where was he?

"That Woman is a fool," Thomasin said.

"Yes, she is." And Madeline was grateful, for now Thomasin would never tell her stepmother what had happened in the stables. "Shall we go back to the party?"

Thomasin bristled with hostility. "Must we?"

Madeline thought about rallying Thomasin with an appeal to her pride, but the young lady had suffered through enough challenges today. "I beg that you go with me. Mr. Rumbelow promised us a report on the game, and I'd like to know how it is going."

"You mean—whether Lord Campion is winning."

"Yes. That's what I mean."

With a nod, Thomasin led the way back into the music room.

It was very late. The party was ready to break up. Everyone waited on only one thing—the same thing Madeline wished to hear. The report on the game.

At last, Big Bill stepped into the music room, fortified by an air of importance. Clearing his throat, he waited while the clamor died. In a formal manner quite at odds with his street accent and his prizefighter face, he said, "Mr. Rumbelow sends 'is respects, and 'ere's the first night report. Mr. Payborn lost 'is first partie. Lord Achard lost. Mr. Rumbelow won. Lord Campion won. Mr. Greene won. Mr. Darnel won. Monsieur Vavasseur lost." The chamber grew deathly silent as he recited the names and their positions on the list. Finally, he grinned, showing brown teeth that too forcibly reminded Madeline of yesterday, and tonight. "Mr. Rumbelow begs t' tell ye there 'as been a side wager between 'imself and Lord Campion. If Lord Campion wins the final round, Mr. Rumbelow shall pay 'im an additional ten thousand pounds. If Mr. Rumbelow wins, Lord Campion shall give 'im any one o' Lord Campion's possessions that Mr. Rumbelow desires."

An amazed chatter broke out.

Big Bill held up his hand. "One more thing. The entertainment tomorrow in the village 'as been canceled due t' the fact Mr. Rumbelow thinks it might could possibly 'ave inclement weather, and he don't want any of 'is guests t' catch their deaths of cold. So until Mr. Rumbelow tells ye any different, ye're not t' try and leave Chalice Hall. None o' ye. After all"—his beady black eyes narrowed on Madeline—"we don't want ye t' get sick. We don't want ye t' die."

Chapter Twenty-seven

"It is my considered opinion that Lord Campion has overreached his confidence with this nefarious wager," Lady Tabard announced as she puffed toward the dowager's house. The other guests—*all* of the other guests—walked with her, and most nodded their heads in agreement. "Ten thousand pounds against anything he owns. I can't imagine what is in his mind."

Madeline thought she knew. Gabriel wanted Rumbelow off balance, desperate to win—and here. For MacAllister hadn't yet arrived with the reinforcements, and he'd left more than thirty-six hours ago. Thirty-six hours of gusting wind, of intermittent rain . . . of constant worry. Madeline had listened to the servants' gossip, hoping to hear if MacAllister had been captured, but no one spoke of him. No one noticed he was gone.

Yesterday, during the long daylight hours, everyone had lamented the fact they couldn't go into the village and eat at the Two Friends Tearoom. A few of the younger gentlemen wished to take their chances with the weather; they had been rather rudely dissuaded by the footmen. That put a strain on the company, one they didn't comprehend, but one that cast a gloom over the house.

Mr. Rumbelow had arranged for traveling actors to perform *King Lear,* a poor choice of entertainment in Madeline's opinion. All in all, last night had been subdued, and after Big Bill came in with his report of the game, everyone had gone to bed.

"Is Papa really eliminated from the play?" one of the younger Lady Achards asked plaintively. "Because if he is, I don't understand why we can't leave. I don't like it here anymore."

Glancing toward Thomasin, Madeline caught the young lady watching her. She gave her an encouraging nod, and Thomasin, unsmiling, gave her one back. Thomasin had grown up in these last few days.

Madeline wondered if someone might say she herself had, too.

"I presume your father wants us to watch the last of the gaming so we can tell the tale of the Game of the Century." But Lady Achard's brow puckered in a puzzled frown as she tucked her shawl tighter around her hair and struggled against the wind.

Madeline found herself wanting to run toward the dowager's house to see that Gabriel was alive and well. A hunger gnawed at her. How had she imagined she could leave him here, alone and facing an army of felons?

Just because he rejected her . . .

But Thomasin said he hadn't. Thomasin suggested Madeline could change and become what he wished—a woman who was utterly his.

"But why do all of us have to go?" Mademoiselle Vavasseur wailed. "And so early? I could have slept another two hours."

It was true. The call to come to the dowager's house had arrived at nine in the morning, a time when most of the guests had not yet opened their eyes. The demand that they attend had been quite stringent, and quite specific. All the families were to come to view the end of the game.

"So it's down to Mr. Rumbelow and Lord Campion?" Hurth sniffed, and used his handkerchief to blot his dripping nose. "Mr. Rumbelow hasn't a chance against Lord Campion. Everyone knows Lord Campion has the devil's own luck, and the skill to go with it. I don't know why we didn't just give him the money and forget about the game."

"Spoken like a man who cares nothing for gambling," Thomasin observed.

Hurth gazed on her as if she were some sort of vermin beneath his notice, but he never passed up the opportunity to break into speech. "Not about cards, of course not." He sniffed again.

His mother said loftily, "As far as I'm concerned, there's nothing to match a wager on a good horse race."

"Of course not," Thomasin said faintly.

Taking a deep breath of the brisk air, Madeline assured herself trusting Gabriel was not so much a matter of dependence, but of courage. Her own. Gabriel called her a coward. Perhaps she had been, but no longer. He generously gave of himself; she had to learn to do the same. Perhaps it wasn't fair for him to take all the chances in this love affair.

"Here we are." Lady Tabard stepped into the foyer of the dowager's house and threw back her shawl. Looking around, she said in surprise, "Quite a pleasant place, this is, after the oppressive decorations of Chalice House." Then she glanced sideways at Madeline, as if expecting her to point out that, when they had first driven up, Lady Tabard had declared Chalice House to be grand.

Madeline was too busy peeling off her pelisse and handing it to one of those rough-looking footmen. She wanted to see Gabriel. She wanted to see him now.

Another footman held the door and nodded toward the gaming room. Madeline recognized nothing; last time she'd been here it had been dark. She'd come in the back door. And when she left in the early dawn, she'd been dizzy with the residuals of passion.

"The families, Mr. Rumbelow," one of the tallest footmen announced.

"Thank you, Lorne," Mr. Rumbelow answered.

The ladies and their children filed into the room and saw the gray, tired faces of the gamblers.

Madeline suspected most of them had gone without sleep the whole time, surviving on brandy and excitement until they were eliminated. Now they sat around the room in armchairs, silently watching the middle of the room, where one remaining table had been placed.

There, at the center of attention, Gabriel and Mr. Rumbelow faced each other, cards in hand.

Madeline drank in the sight of Gabriel, noting the casual posture, the calm expression, the steady hand. He must have taken a break at some point, for his white cravat appeared to be crisp and his black coat pressed. He wore only one ring, his signet ring, and that focused her attention on his hands—long-fingered, precise, and steady. He played for one hundred thousand pounds in the same manner in which he played for ten shillings: coolly, without visible signs of strain.

He didn't look at her. He didn't look at anyone. But she knew he was aware of her, of all of them, as they filed into the room.

Looking at him, being in the same room as him, brought such a wave of love through her body she could barely refrain from going to him, throwing her arms around him and declaring he was hers.

A dozen footmen followed the guests in, and stationed themselves about the room like guards at Newgate.

Madeline's uneasiness gathered strength. This moment, this finale, was the reason why Mr. Rumbelow had insisted no one leave the estate, but what did he have planned? Simple robbery? Or gruesome murder?

Within the gaming chamber, the drapes and carpets muffled every sound. The players sat quietly. The gamblers were hushed. As the families made their way to their men, a profound silence fell.

The wives leaned down and kissed their husbands, and murmured a pretense that it mattered not that they'd wagered a year or more's income on a single game. The subdued offspring gathered around the chairs, and all eyes turned to the players.

The atmosphere in the gaming chamber was brittle with tension. The onlookers leaned forward with every play, watching, counting. Madeline saw the other gamblers' hands twitch every time a card was thrown, their lips move every time they added a point.

She hated it when her father gambled, when he abandoned the real world for a place where glory and riches hovered elusively out of reach. Magnus wasn't here, but she observed the same greed and desperation in each of these men, and she knew, she *knew* danger lurked right under their noses, and they were too involved to notice. Too absorbed to care.

Madeline thought . . . it now seemed . . . she might have no choice but to give Gabriel her trust, for she didn't know if she could live without him. Which sounded dramatic, but, in this case, she'd already tried the alternative. She'd found it was not living, but merely surviving.

She waited for a signal from Gabriel, indicating she should approach him.

He never looked in her direction, but lolled in his chair as if indifferent to her presence.

Big Bill wasn't indifferent to her presence. He brought up the rear of the crowd, shut the door behind them and stood, arms crossed, guarding the entrance. He watched her with a hostility that made her want to reach for her pistol—but her pistol was still in her valise. She had encouraged him on their walk, then rejected him in the most evident manner possible, by taking another lover. She had smacked him under the chin and made him a laughingstock among his peers.

Satisfying, but definitely unwise. In his hostile gaze, she saw her fate should he get his hands on her. He would hurt her. He would enjoy hurting her.

"Madeline!" Thomasin called her in a low, strained voice. "Come and stand with us."

Madeline obeyed, and Thomasin deliberately placed Madeline behind Lady Tabard's ample form, out of Big Bill's sight.

Looking around, Madeline realized she wasn't the only family retainer in the gaming chamber. It had never occurred to her she shouldn't come; it had never occurred to anyone to forbid her. But why was Mr. Darnel's valet in here? The young man looked troubled and out of place, and spoke to Mr. Darnel in a low, urgent voice. Mr. Darnel stared at Mr. Rumbelow with narrowed eyes, as if displeased.

Mr. Rumbelow took no notice. Why should he? No one could touch him here.

The steady slap of cards resumed. Unlike Gabriel, Mr. Rumbelow showed wear from the extended game. His blond hair was damp on his forehead. A fine sheen of grayish sweat covered his face. His blue coat showed damp rings under the armpits.

Madeline was glad. She hoped he suffered for each point he lost. She hoped he agonized over each play. She hoped . . . She glanced around at the footmen. At Lorne, hulking and ominous. At Big Bill, who had moved enough to watch her. Reality slapped her in the face.

It didn't matter what she hoped. It didn't matter if Mr. Rumbelow really lost. Somehow, he had plotted to win all, and she feared to imagine how.

Gabriel had a plan, but that plan had included a company of men under MacAllister's command moving in to take prisoners. What was Gabriel going to do now?

What could she do to help?

Gabriel laid down his hand.

Mr. Rumbelow did the same.

Mr. Greene counted the score, then added up the total. With a quiver of excitement, he announced, "We have only the last hand to play, and they're tied!"

"Incredible." "Unusual." "Amazing." The whispers swept the room.

"Demmed impossible," Lord Tabard muttered. "Campion was ahead the whole time. Either his luck has changed, or . . ."

Madeline didn't know what the *or* meant, but

an air of expectation now permeated the stuffy room. The gamblers leaned forward, watching intently as Gabriel shuffled the cards.

"Is this where the auxiliary wager is played?" Thomasin asked her father.

He nodded. "An extra ten thousand from Rumbelow, or anything that Campion owns."

Placing the deck of cards face down, Gabriel lifted them, then let them shower back onto the table—and into a perfect deck once more. His voice mocked the lines of strain on Mr. Rumbelow's face, the intensity of his concentration. "It's time to declare what your winnings shall be."

Mr. Rumbelow stared at Gabriel, and for the briefest moment, Madeline saw the ravenous wolf beneath his civilized exterior. Then his charming smile flashed out. It was the smile that had beguiled her on her arrival, and he lavished it on each of the ladies in the room.

But it didn't beguile now. Each of the ladies shrank back as if sensing an uncleanness beneath the geniality. At last, his gaze reached Madeline, and came to rest. "Ah, Campion, you know what I want."

"Indeed I do. I'll see your ten thousand, and raise you one duchess." As Madeline watched, incredulous, Gabriel took her glove from his coat pocket. He flung it on the table between him and Mr. Rumbelow. "If you win her, she's yours."

Chapter Twenty-eight

Madeline's knees gave way. She caught Thomasin's arm for support.

Just like her father. Gabriel was just like her father, tossing her into a game as if she were no more than a coin or a jewel.

When he'd refused her proposal, when he'd shredded her character, not viciously but sorrowfully, she'd thought she would perish from the torment. But that pain was nothing compared to this. This was the worst thing that could ever happen to her.

Her lover had betrayed her.

Thomasin put her arm around her. "What is it?" she whispered. "I don't understand."

Neither did anyone else. A murmur of confusion swept the room.

At the table, Gabriel waited, back straight, expression disinterested.

He waited for her.

But Gabriel had said he was not like her father.

He demanded that she trust him. And she had promised him she was his, to do with as he wished.

Did she trust him? Would she honor her promise?

How could she not? Whether or not he really wanted her, she was the duchess of Magnus. She had given her word.

She couldn't break it again. She wouldn't.

"It's my glove." Madeline could scarcely get the words out, and Thomasin had to lean close to hear her. More loudly, Madeline said, "It's my glove. Lord Campion bet me against the ten thousand pounds."

A murmur of surprise swept the room.

"What do you mean?" Lady Tabard asked. "Miss de Lacy, that's absurd. Why would either one of them be interested in *you*?"

Thomasin shot Gabriel an outraged glance. "He can't do that."

"He can if I let him." Madeline used all of her strength to remain calm, but her hands trembled, and so did her voice.

Mr. Rumbelow's gaze lingered on her, and that overpowering smile made Madeline's scalp crawl. With the flare of a Vauxhall magician, he announced, "I have long known we had an imposter in our midst, and have watched with much amusement as she tried to fit the mold of Lady Thomasin's companion. Yes, my friends, it's true. Miss de Lacy *is* a de Lacy, but in addition, she is the marchioness of Sheridan and the future duchess of Magnus."

Every eye in the room turned on Madeline. The whispers started, thin, hissing sounds she recognized from the first time she'd created a scandal. This time it was worse. This time she didn't have her fury to buffer the embarrassment. Her skin heated, took fire, until she felt her cheeks turn red and splotchy.

"I knew it!" Monsieur Vavasseur turned to his wife. "Didn't I tell you she was the duchess of Magnus?"

Madame Vavasseur gave a murmur of agreement.

Madeline couldn't tear her gaze away from Gabriel's profile. She could almost hear his voice give the command. *Come to me.*

Lady Tabard craned around to stare at Madeline. "She is not! She's the cousin of . . ." Something struck her: the events of the last few days, Madeline's demeanor, Gabriel's absolute stillness. Lady Tabard's eyes popped as she realized who she had so roundly abused.

Did Madeline trust Gabriel to take care of her, be her lover, be her husband . . . be her partner in all things? Because if she did, she had to trust he had a higher purpose in mind than to hurt her. She had to trust this wasn't the act of vindictiveness or, worse, thoughtlessness, but a well-thought-out strategy. For what reason, she couldn't guess. But trust was without reason, without logic.

Big Bill straightened away from the door. "What're ye doin', Thurston? Play fer the ten thousand, don't play fer 'er. She's no doochess."

The ladies and gentlemen goggled at the servant who dared chide his master, and Madeline saw the waves of uneasiness wash over them.

Did she trust Gabriel? For if she didn't trust now, she knew she would never get another chance.

Mr. Rumbelow held up his hands like a priest giving a blessing. "I assure you, she is the duchess of Magnus. I recognized her at once. If she had recognized me, she would have saved everyone here a great deal of grief."

The families murmured and pulled closer together, viewing Madeline with suspicion or pity—or horror.

Mr. Darnel spoke up. "See here. If she's really the duchess of Magnus, you can't play for her as if she were a . . . a guinea."

"Why not?" Mr. Rumbelow asked. "Her father did."

Another thrust of pain, almost as great as the moment when she realized Gabriel had wagered her . . . but fading quickly. Only Gabriel mattered now. *Did she trust him?*

"Yes, that's another thing. She's betrothed to that American." Mr. Payborn was indignant as only a true gambler could be. "If we are agreed Her Grace is a piece of property, Campion doesn't . . . doesn't own her, Knight does. And if Knight relinquished his claim, her father's claim would once more be in effect."

"She's here now, and Campion made his claim on her two nights ago in that bedchamber where some of you gentlemen washed and changed." Mr. Rumbelow smiled at her with all the charm of a collector viewing a particularly fine snuffbox.

Madeline's teeth snapped together. How good of Mr. Rumbelow to tell everyone *that*.

The Mademoiselles Vavasseur started giggling and couldn't stop, despite their mother's attempt to hush them. Nervous giggles.

Lady Tabard snapped, "I hope that is an untruth, Your Grace, for you had charge of my daughter!"

Lord and Lady Achard were whispering furiously to each other, and murmurs of outrage sped through the room.

At last Gabriel turned his head to gaze on Madeline. His features were still indifferent, his gaze heavy-lidded. Without the slightest tone of affection, he said, "Madeline, come to me."

Come to me.

Madeline's feet felt as heavy as anvils as she lifted first one, then the other, taking the first steps toward him. As she walked, it became easier. She breathed more calmly. Her color faded.

She was the duchess of Magnus. She had made her choice of mate. Now she would trust him, and let the chips fall where they may.

Unbuttoning her glove, she stripped it off. As she reached Gabriel, she slowly and with great ceremony offered him her bare hand.

He stared at the curl of her fingers, her pale, lined palm, the wrist where the blue veins crossed. He looked up, and in his eyes she saw a flaring triumph and a bittersweet weariness that shook her to the bone.

"Gabriel?" she whispered. She had given him what he wanted. Why did he look so sad?

Cupping her hand, he lifted it to his lips and kissed the very center of the palm.

The pureness of the gesture soothed her fears and renewed her faith. He might be using her, but only to get justice for his brother. He wouldn't sacrifice her, also. He wouldn't.

Taking her hand, he placed it on his shoulder and faced Mr. Rumbelow. "Very well. Let us play the last partie."

Gabriel dealt the cards, twelve apiece, and placed the remainder in the middle of the table.

Mr. Rumbelow exchanged first, then, as Gabriel exchanged, Mr. Rumbelow said, "Tell me, Your Grace, what you intend to do when I win you."

She allowed her gaze to flick him with so much scorn, he reddened. "If I were you, I would be more concerned with how to fund ten thousand pounds."

"She is so loyal to you, Campion," Mr. Rumbelow marveled. "Point of five."

"Not good," Gabriel replied to Mr. Rumbelow's play.

"Trio of aces. So few men own their women's souls as well as their bodies. It will be a great pleasure to take her from you."

Gabriel answered only to piquet. "Good."

"Three." Mr. Rumbelow led the king of hearts. "Four."

Madeline stared at the far wall, as humiliated by Mr. Rumbelow's comments—and Gabriel's indifference—as ever she'd been in her life. Yet she would get through this. Gabriel would win her. He would wed her. And she would spend the rest of their lives reminding him what he owed her.

The humiliation was temporary, she reminded herself. Justice would be sweet. Justice for Jerry. Justice for everyone here who had been so duped by this shyster who called himself Mr. Rumbelow.

The play continued. Slowly, the circle of ladies and gentlemen closed in around the players, the suspense of the outcome holding them in its clawed grip.

Madeline tried not to watch. She tried to put all her faith in Gabriel's skill. But how could she not see every move when she stood right at Gabriel's shoulder? How could she not know . . . that things were going badly for Gabriel?

When the last card was thrown, a dreadful silence gripped the room.

Mr. Rumbelow had won the last trick.

Gabriel had lost the partie, the game—and her.

Chapter Twenty-nine

"I won. I won!" Throwing back his head, Mr. Rumbelow cackled with glee.

Madeline struggled to breathe. To believe.

"I actually won, fair and square. Who would have thought? I have the hundred thousand without stealing it." Mr. Rumbelow laughed again, and the maniacal sound brought everyone to attention.

"Stealing it?" Lord Achard came to his feet. "Why would you steal it? You organized this game."

Mr. Greene's mouth gaped unattractively. "You don't mean you were planning some kind of uncouth heist?"

Madeline's hand remained on Gabriel's shoulder. She felt his warmth, his steadiness beneath her hand. And she couldn't believe he had done this.

He took her hand. He raised it to his lips. Once more, he kissed the palm.

The tenderness of his gesture made his betrayal seem like delusion.

Then he offered her hand to Mr. Rumbelow. "She's yours."

The world had gone insane. *Gabriel* had gone insane.

"She can't go with him," Lady Tabard stated in her imperious tone. "We don't know who his people are."

Madeline stared at Mr. Rumbelow and shuddered in disbelief. In revulsion. She tried to pull her hand back, but Gabriel held her firmly by the wrist.

"She's the future duchess of Magnus, not some racehorse," Hurth said.

How had this happened? Madeline couldn't understand it. Gabriel had never lost, never, and now he had failed in this, the most important game of his life. Of her life.

"Outrageous!" Monsieur Vavasseur stroked his luxuriant mustache. "Unthinkable."

Thomasin stepped right up to the table and said fiercely, "You can't do this. You . . . you men . . ."

Gabriel stood so suddenly, he knocked his chair down. "I lost." He leaned over the table toward Mr. Rumbelow. "I lost her, so you'd better take care of her."

Did Madeline trust Gabriel? She either did or she didn't. She had made the decision to depend on him. Nothinghad changed from a few moments ago. If Gabriel had lost her, he must have a plan.

If Gabriel had done this, he needed her help.

"Oh, I will." Mr. Rumbelow reached across the table for her hand. "Believe me, I will."

How could Madeline help Gabriel?

Calmly, she plucked her glove off of the table and handed it to Mr. Rumbelow.

Not her hand, but her glove.

He understood she had agreed she was his, and insulted him, all at the same time, and she saw the feral creature beneath the civilized mask.

Leaning forward again, Gabriel blocked her view of him. "You'll let her pack a bag."

In a lofty tone at odds with his red-eyed fury, Mr. Rumbelow said, "Of course. I'm not an unciv-ilized man."

"Lady Thomasin." Gabriel caught Thomasin's arm. "Pack Madeline a bag. Make sure she has all the necessities for a long journey. The necessities a lady needs for a dangerous journey."

At that moment, in Madeline's mind, it all clicked. She knew what Gabriel wanted. She understood—at least a little—what he planned.

Thomasin's eyes flashed. "I most certainly will not!"

Pandemonium erupted as everyone spoke at once. "You can't—" "She can't—" "Shocking!" "Deplorable!"

Madeline stopped them with a gesture. "My valise is already packed. Thomasin and I tried to leave the day before yesterday, and were forbid-den by Mr. Rumbelow's men."

The voices started again, high and low, male and female, some directed at Mr. Rumbelow, some at Madeline, some at Gabriel.

Madeline spoke slowly and seriously to Thomasin. "Please bring me the bag that I packed."

Thomasin stared at her as if she'd run mad. "You don't mean to go through with this?"

The rumpus faded as everyone strained to hear what they were saying.

"I agreed to be wagered. I'll fulfill my part." Placing her hand on Thomasin's shoulder, Madeline pressed it firmly. "Now you, my friend, must bring me my bag."

Thomasin was slack-jawed with bewilderment. "Please, Madeline, you can't . . . he's . . ." She glanced at Mr. Rumbelow. "He's horrible. He's always been horrible, and now he's . . . You just can't!"

With the sincerity formed of desperation, Madeline said, "Thomasin, if you are my friend, please do as I ask."

Reluctantly, Thomasin nodded and darted toward the door.

One of the footmen stepped into her path.

"Let her go," Mr. Rumbelow instructed. "And Lady Thomasin?"

She faced him.

"The servants are mine. If you try anything, I'll kill your parents."

Thomasin's wide eyes grew wider, and she pressed her fist to her lips.

"What do you mean, you'll kill us?" Lord Tabard's florid complexion turned alarmingly bright.

"Please, Thomasin, hurry," Madeline begged.

Thomasin ran from the room.

"Are we prisoners?" Mr. Payborn asked in his booming voice.

"What did Her Grace mean when she said they couldn't leave yesterday?" Mr. Darnel demanded.

Lady Tabard turned on Madeline. "Why did you try to leave? With my daughter?"

"Yes, Rumbelow, and what's the meaning of all these men?" Lord Achard demanded.

Now they noticed the men and the danger, Madeline thought in disgust. Why hadn't they noticed as Mr. Rumbelow had them herded in like cattle to the slaughter?

Reaching under the table, Mr. Rumbelow pulled out a pistol and pointed it at Mr. Payborn. "A prisoner? Worse. Unless you do as you're told, you're on execution row."

One of the Misses Achard screamed.

"Papa." Miss Payborn flattened herself against her father.

Mr. Rumbelow's pistol moved to point steadily at her. "If you want your daughter to stay alive, Payborn, she'll hand over those pearls she's wearing around her scrawny neck."

Mr. Payborn and his daughter seemed frozen, staring at the ugly black eye of the pistol as if transfixed.

Lady Tabard intervened, her bosom quivering

with her indrawn breath. "Mr. . . . Rumbelow! Whatever do you mean by pointing a pistol at that young girl?"

As if he'd been possessed by a demon, Mr. Rumbelow's lips drew back, his eyes narrowed. "Get them to me now!"

Miss Payborn gasped and reached around for the clasp.

Mr. Payborn pushed her behind him. "See here, Rumbelow, I don't know what you think you're doing, but—"

Mr. Rumbelow pointed the gun at him. "The rings. The snuffbox. Now."

"I beg your pardon!" Mr. Payborn's double chins swung as he gobbled in indignation.

"So you should." Mr. Rumbelow nodded to his men, and around the room, a dozen pistols appeared.

Monsieur Vavasseur embraced his family as if he could protect all of them with his skinny body. "This is the act of a villain."

"Yes. I'm a thief and an imposter—and you never knew." Rumbelow's contempt overflowed and scorched them all like acid. "You bunch of bloody morons—"

Lady Tabard still had it in her to be horrified. "Mr. Rumbelow, watch your tongue!"

"Shut your yap, you stupid old boot." The pistol swung around the circle that surrounded him. "You fools thought I was so fine. Just like you. Now you're going to pay." With a smile, he indicated the crowd with the stock of his pistol.

"Strip 'em clean, boys. This is as easy as it gets."

With a growl, the footmen moved in, demanding every piece of jewelry.

The young ladies were crying.

Hurth raised a fist to protect his mother. For his pains, he received the butt of the pistol to his head. He fell to the ground, unconscious. Kneeling beside him, Lady Margerison wailed as she removed her rings, while Lord Margerison tried to bribe the footman to leave them alone. The footman was taking the money, but he wasn't going away.

In every corner of the chamber, the footmen were pilfering and the aristocrats were providing.

In the middle of the ugly scene, Gabriel moved closely behind Madeline. "MacAllister?" he breathed in her ear.

Turning her head, she said, "Left night before last. No sign of him."

"Damn."

Thomasin came panting back, Madeline's bag banging against her knee. She paused in the doorway, petrified by the sight of so much violence, until Mr. Rumbelow gestured to her. "Let me see what's inside," he ordered.

Thomasin trudged to him and handed over the carpetbag.

Madeline took a long, slow breath and watched as he placed it on the table. In a voice heavy with mockery, she inquired, "Will you approve my stockings, Mr. Rumbelow?"

"If I wish." Opening it, he looked inside. "Ah."

Rummaging around, he brought out the box containing the queen's tiara. "Campion gave it to you. Good."

Placing it on the table, he produced a key.

"You had it all along!" Madeline said.

"Yes. So I did." He fit the key into the lock and lifted the lid.

She stared at the incredible creation of gold and diamonds, rubies and emeralds. A heavy crown. A royal crown.

An unfamiliar crown. "What's that?" she croaked.

Gabriel did a double take and stared at her.

Mr. Rumbelow's long fingers caressed the jewels. "It's the Crown of Reynard."

Madeline's shock was as great now as at any point in the evening. "That's not *my* tiara!"

"For God's sake," Gabriel muttered.

Mr. Rumbelow laughed again, one of those laughs that started slow and grew in intensity. "You thought it was yours? You thought your father sent it? Is that what you're doing here in that miserable excuse for a disguise? The prince of Reyard sent it, and I suppose the English blockade prevented his arrival."

Madeline knew Mr. Rumbelow was dangerous. She knew he was cruel, unprincipled and probably mad. But no one laughed at the duchess of Magnus. She lifted her hands to box his ears.

Gabriel caught her wrists.

She whipped her head around and glared. "Let me," she demanded.

"I need you alive," he murmured just loud enough to be heard over the cacophony of screaming women and shouting men.

Of course he did. Still her temper raged, and she tugged against Gabriel's grip.

"Let her go!" Mr. Rumbelow wrenched Gabriel away from her. "She's mine."

In that instant, Madeline saw Gabriel's face contort, saw his body spring to attention and thought she was going to have to stop Gabriel from attacking Mr. Rumbelow.

But Gabriel backed away. "I said she was."

Mr. Rumbelow wrapped his arm around her shoulders. "Don't touch her again."

Gabriel nodded.

"Lord Campion!" Thomasin quivered with indignation. "How can you let this happen?"

Madeline swallowed hard. It was one thing to decide to trust Gabriel, quite another to allow Mr. Rumbelow to touch her. This was worse than when those other men had kissed her. She could feel the viciousness, desperation and victory that drove Mr. Rumbelow. He had been the cause of so much death and so much disaster. She feared him almost as much as she despised him.

Gabriel pointed toward her bag. "Have you got enough packed, Your Grace? I suppose you'll be leaving the country."

Mr. Rumbelow stuffed the crown back in the bag. "On a French ship. What an adventure for you, my dear duchess."

"Hm. Yes." Rummaging in the carpetbag,

Madeline searched for the black velvet holster that contained her pistol. For one horrible moment, she thought it had vanished, and her heart beat so hard she thought Mr. Rumbelow would hear it. Then she placed her hand on the black velvet, and she breathed a sigh of relief.

"What've you got there?" Mr. Rumbelow asked, his tone sharp with suspicion.

"My reticule." She lifted it up and showed him. "I trust that's all right with you?" The query ridiculed his concern. "Or did you think *I* could carry something inside that would hurt *you*?"

He didn't answer that, but she smelled the faint scent of sweat and fear emanating from him. Now that he'd come so far, he wanted to escape before this became a trap—for him. "What do you need a reticule for?" he asked.

She looked him squarely in the eye. "I am a woman. Once a month, I—"

"All right." Mr. Rumbelow blanched. "All right! Keep it."

Sometimes—only too seldom—being a woman had its advantages.

"Your Grace, that was a little too frank," Lady Tabard objected, but feebly, as she handed over her diamonds.

Madeline slipped the holster over her wrist, holding it like a woman who used her purse for nothing more than storing a handkerchief and a few coins. But the weight of the pistol comforted her, and no matter what happened to the carpetbag, she now had the gun.

She looked at Gabriel, who slowly dipped his head. Just once. In reassurance.

As she faced disaster and possibly death, she realized—she didn't want reassurance. She didn't want him to feel guilty about the way he had betrayed her. She wanted only one thing from Gabriel—his love. And she didn't know if she had it.

"Wait a minute." Lorne pointed his pistol at Mr. Rumbelow. "That crown's to be divided with the rest of the loot."

With a gesture both vulgar and expressive, Mr. Rumbelow said, "First I'm taking the duchess to the bedchamber for a quick toss."

Madeline looked desperately at Gabriel—who had the gall to look relieved.

"Don't look at him." Mr. Rumbelow shook her arm. "He can't save you."

Then I'll have to save myself.

Chapter Thirty

❦

That was the question Madeline should be asking herself. *Did Gabriel love her?*

Lorne still pointed the gun at Mr. Rumbelow. "I want me part o' the crown."

"Do you think I can tear it apart with my hands? Do what you're supposed to, and point that thing at one of them." Mr. Rumbelow jerked his thumb toward the desperate aristocrats. "It's not as if I can leave the bedchamber without being seen. I'll be back soon enough. Here." He handed the valise to Madeline, and said to Lorne, "Just in case you get any ideas about making off with the spoils."

"Ye can't take it!" Lorne objected.

Big Bill walked up behind Lorne and smacked him on the back of the head.

Lorne turned on him, but Big Bill planted him a facer, and when Lorne went down like a rock, Big Bill kicked the pistol away. "Rumbelow's goin' t' take his pleasure." He glared at Madeline. "Then we'll all 'ave a toss o' that."

Madeline's hand crept toward her throat.

Rubbing his bloody nose, Lorne mumbled, "I don't want no toss. I want me money."

"I'll be back out soon to open the safe and divide the cash." Mr. Rumbelow's tone changed from informative to sarcastic. "You can place a guard at the door if you like."

As Gabriel watched, Rumbelow led Madeline toward the door. Her gait was long and relaxed. She moved as she always did, with a bone-deep sensuality and the confidence of a woman born to a position of wealth and privilege. She seemed unaware of—or unconcerned about—the peril she was in.

Yet Gabriel knew her. Knew she comprehended the danger Rumbelow posed to her. To everyone. And she would do whatever was needed to save lives and bring Rumbelow to justice.

She was the bravest woman—the bravest person—he'd ever met. As he watched her disappear through the entry, he wanted to chase after her, to take her away from Rumbelow, to kill the man for daring to lay hands on Gabriel's woman. The only thing that stopped Gabriel was a bone-deep desire for revenge for Jerry, the need to capture the French ship that prowled their shores with impunity and the knowledge that Maddie would box his ears for faltering now.

He'd told her to trust him. Now he had to trust her to do her part to capture Rumbelow. She was the only help he had.

The gaming chamber was a melee of weeping

ladies, of indignant lords and jubilant thieves.

Gabriel noted one brute of a footman had a crying Miss Greene backed into a corner while he stripped her of jewels in a most lascivious manner. His hands wandered over her body with a freedom that made her cringe and sob. It was too much for Gabriel, seeing that, knowing that the same thing might be happening to Madeline, wondering if he would hear a gunshot . . . wondering if she would be the one behind the pistol or in front of it.

Gabriel knew he had to give Rumbelow enough time to escape through the tunnel. Not too much time. Just enough of a head start so he could lead him to the French ship. In the meantime, Gabriel couldn't stand it anymore. Slipping his blade from the sleeve of his jacket, he stepped up behind the footman and pressed it to his neck. "Let her go," he murmured, "and give me your gun."

The burly footman laughed. "Who ye tryin' t' scare with that little sticker?"

"No one." Gabriel smacked his knuckles hard into the blackguard's Adam's apple, and when the man doubled over, choking, Gabriel picked up a small table and knocked him in the back of the head.

The pistol went flying. The fellow fell face first onto the hard floor. Gabriel heard the sound as his nose broke, saw the splatter of blood.

One of the other footmen saw the violence and

took a step toward Gabriel. Gabriel faced him, knife held in fighter's stance. "Come on," Gabriel urged. "I'm itching for a fight."

The footman backed away. Robbing the women was easier. He wanted only easy pickings.

Picking up the pistol, Gabriel tucked it into his waistband and started for the door.

He passed Big Bill, pistol cocked, watching the action in the gaming room and keeping an eye on the door of the bedchamber. So. Big Bill's faith in his master was failing. Big Bill could be used. He could be valuable. "Come on, then," Gabriel said to him.

Big Bill started, then pointed his pistol at Gabriel. " 'Ey, where ye goin'? Get back in there. We're robbin' ye."

"Rumbelow's not really in there."

Gabriel had Big Bill's full attention. "Aye, 'e is."

"No, he's not." Gabriel walked backward down the corridor and considered Big Bill like a compatriot.

Mouth open, Big Bill thought about it, then stepped into the corridor and followed Gabriel. "Why the 'ell would I listen t' ye? Ye stole me woman."

"She's a duchess." Gabriel kept a wary eye on that gun. "She was never your woman."

Big Bill bared rotting teeth. "I know wot a woman wants, and she wanted me."

Leaning his ear against the door, Gabriel heard nothing. Not a wisp of sound. Not a scream. Not a shot. "How long have they been gone?" he asked.

"I . . . dunno," Big Bill stammered. "Ten minutes."

"That seems right." In that ten minutes, Rumbelow had used his knife to slit open the wallpaper and open the passage. Madeline was giving him no trouble, so depending on the condition below ground, they would be moving swiftly. They would exit by the stable, have the horses brought around and be off toward the rendezvous with the ship.

Straightening away from the door, Gabriel asked Big Bill, "Do you hear anything?"

Staring at Gabriel as if he'd run mad, Big Bill pressed his ear to the door. "Nay."

"Is Rumbelow always so quiet when he takes his pleasure?"

Big Bill lifted his head. "Nay, there's usually some screamin' and cryin', and it ain't 'is."

"They're gone." Gabriel watched as bewilderment and suspicion fought for possession of Big Bill. "Escaped out the passage."

"Passage? There's no . . ." Big Bill's bloodshot eyes showed white around the irises.

"Rumbelow figured out a way to keep everyone busy while he got away."

Big Bill spit a brown stream of tobacco onto the polished wood floor. "He wouldn't leave one hundred thousand quid. 'Tis still in the safe."

"Really?" Gabriel drawled. "Do you think so?"

Big Bill had trusted the wrong man, but he

wasn't stupid. He aimed his pistol at the handle.

Gabriel covered his ears.

Big Bill shot off the lock. The report echoed up and down the hall. Kicking open the door, Big Bill stormed in. Stopped. Gasped.

A man-sized black hole gaped in the wall, opening onto the black depths of the underground corridor.

Madeline was gone. Vanished in the custody of a lawless, immoral thief.

Just as Gabriel had planned. Guilt, worry and fear chased through his veins. Had he done the wrong thing? Was revenge for Jerry worth Madeline's life?

Yet how could Gabriel falter, when Rumbelow had done so much wrong, and so richly deserved to be removed from this world?

Cursing viciously, Big Bill stormed back toward the gaming chamber.

Gabriel followed close on his heels.

The scene had changed since they'd left. Lord Achard slashed at two of the footmen with his wicked cane-sword, leaving them howling and bleeding. Lady Tabard hid Thomasin behind her ample girth, and under the lash of her tongue, their attacker was so cowed he backed away and pulled his forelock. Mr. Darnel's valet lay bleeding on the floor, felled by a blow to the face. Mr. Darnel stood over him, protecting him with the kind of pugilism usually seen only in the auspices of the prizefighting ring.

In a furious undertone, Big Bill declared, "I tol' Rumbelow this wouldn't work. I tol' 'im they'd fight back if their loved ones was attacked."

As one footman lifted his pistol to shoot Lord Achard, Big Bill grabbed a gun from another of his cohorts and shot the fellow in the back. The footman fell forward, sprawled in the agony of death. The explosion brought the room to a shocked silence. Smoke from the pistol wreathed Big Bill's head as he scowled. "Ye don't shoot a nobleman, ye fools. They'll hunt ye down and hang ye fer sure."

The thieves shuffled their feet and hung their heads.

Satisfied they'd been properly intimidated, Big Bill rushed to the safe and knelt beside it. He pulled a key from his pocket—so much for Rumbelow's claim there were only two keys. Opened the door. Pawing the bundles of money out on the floor, he ripped the ties off . . . and found blank sheets of paper.

Every person in the room stared.

"Where's the cash?" Mr. Payborn asked.

One of the other footmen stepped up. "That's what I want t' know. Where's the bleedin' money?"

"Bastard," Big Bill muttered.

"The money's gone. Long gone." Fixing them all with a cool glance that threatened them with the hangman's rope, Gabriel said, "You might want to be long gone, too."

One of the footmen dropped the jewelry he had in his hand. "I knew it. 'Twas too easy." Lifting the window, he jumped out.

The fighting between the gentlemen and the thieves began anew, but the balance had changed. The gentlemen knew the footmen wouldn't dare shoot them. The footmen knew they were outnumbered.

"Bastard," Big Bill said again. With a disgusted glance around, he headed toward the door.

Gabriel followed hard on his heels. Big Bill knew where to go. Now—if they could only get there on time.

Chapter Thirty-one

Did Gabriel love her?

Madeline and Rumbelow emerged from the dark tunnel covered in dust and cobwebs. Madeline coughed as she drew in her first breath of fresh air, but Mr. Rumbelow gave her no time to dust herself off. He marched her along at a brisk pace, heading toward the stables.

Gabriel would come after her, she had no doubt of that. He was an honorable man who had demanded her trust, and earned it. She trusted him to come after her, but why? Because it was the honorable thing to do? Because he wanted to catch Mr. Rumbelow and get revenge for Jerry? Or because he couldn't bear to leave her in Mr. Rumbelow's hands?

Did Gabriel love her?

Would she ever know? For one of them could die.

Her bag banged on her shin. A sparse rain fell from the lowering gray clouds, and the overcast sky matched her mood.

She knew everything that Gabriel wanted as clearly as if he'd told her. He wanted her to go with Mr. Rumbelow to the rendezvous place so Gabriel's men could capture Mr. Rumbelow, deliver him to justice, *and* capture the ship that waited for him. She understood all of that, but if something went wrong—and she recalled far too many things already had—and she was killed, would Gabriel weep? Would he remember her with affection, or as the greatest calamity to visit his life?

She wanted, she needed the assurance that this gut-wrenching need to be near him, this longing, this desire, was reciprocated. The *everything* he demanded from her, she wanted from him.

When they reached the stables, Mr. Rumbelow shook the hostler awake. "Hey! Hitch up the cabriolet. Use Campion's matched grays. Now!"

The hostler looked out at the rain, then back at Mr. Rumbelow as if he were insane. But he clambered to his feet. "Aye, Mr. Rumbelow, sir. Whatever ye say."

As the hostler led the horses from their stalls, Mr. Rumbelow leaned against the wall and beamed at Madeline. "Clever, what? I recognized you the first time I saw you."

Madeline set the heavy bag down and rubbed her aching arm. "Very clever."

"I knew I could make use of you somehow, but I never imagined I'd win you." He loomed over her so suddenly she jumped. "Give us a kiss."

In the brisk tone she used to dissuade her father from his wildest schemes, she said, "Let's get on the road first. Gabriel's no fool. He'll be after us soon."

"He'll have to break down the door to the bed-chamber, and he'll not do that for a good long while. My footmen will keep him busy."

Pressing her hand to Mr. Rumbelow's chest, she looked up at him with tacit admiration. "You planned that very well, I think. A stroke of genius, I would call it."

"Genius?" He nuzzled her neck.

"Distract the footmen with promise of jewelry provided by the families of the very gamblers you're stealing from." She had to restrain herself from smacking him under the chin, just as she had smacked Big Bill. Instead, she kept talking. "The gamblers are so concerned with their family's safety that they don't dare fight back, and the footmen are having so much fun robbing a bunch of rich sitting ducks, they don't know you've stolen the ante."

Lifting his head, Mr. Rumbelow subsided against the wall, a flattered smile playing around his lips. "You are a smart one. How did you know I had the ante?"

She hadn't, until he confirmed her suspicions. "You're clever. You never intended to leave it."

The hostler stepped around the corner. "Yer cabriolet is ready, sir, but even with the top up, ye're going t' get wet." He craned his neck to look at the sky. "If I know me weather, and I do, it's about t' do more than spit."

"No matter. Let's go." Mr. Rumbelow took Madeline's arm and shoved her toward the door.

She resisted. "My bag. The crown's inside."

"Bring it."

She snatched up the carpetbag—after all, perhaps she could use a sash to tie him up, if ever she got the chance—and hurried beside him to the waiting two-wheeled open carriage.

Mr. Rumbelow helped her up.

"Will ye drive yerself, sir?" the hostler asked.

"Of course." Mr. Rumbelow climbed in and, standing, took the ribbons. With a brisk flick of the whip, they were off.

They moved swiftly down the road, splashing through the puddles. As they left Chalice Hall behind, Mr. Rumbelow glanced toward the dowager's house as if he feared they would be seen.

Good. He worried someone would follow them, and driving would keep his hands busy.

"Where are we going?" Madeline ignored the light spatter of rain that flew beneath the leather top, and looked about the inside of the carriage.

"To Adrian's Cove. My ship's waiting just out of sight, the longboat's at the beach. We'll be in France by nightfall."

He wore a pistol shoved into his belt and had tucked a rifle into a long, slender pocket close to his right hand, protected from the rain. In a particularly nasty tone of voice, he said, "That's not a very handsome reticule. Perhaps, if you please me, I'll buy you a new wardrobe in Paris."

Paris? Not Paris. "They'll put me in prison in Paris."

Mr. Rumbelow whisked a fake tear from his

eye. "Into every life a little rain must fall."

So he schemed to use her and be done with her within days. Did he plan to sell her to the French authorities? They would probably pay well to hold an English duchess, and in turn ransom her back to her father—who had promised her to Mr. Knight.

"You've planned this very well." He possessed no other weapons that she could see. He had two shots. She had one. But he didn't suspect she had even that. An advantage, to her mind, but one that scarcely offset his larger size and street-smart brutality.

Whatever plan Gabriel had in mind, he had better bring it to fruition soon. She said, "I don't understand—why didn't you steal the ante the first night? Why bother with so much pretense?"

"I enjoyed it. Charming everyone, making them think I liked them, that I ran a clean game." Mr. Rumbelow used the reins with a kind of elegant gratification, as if his own skill enthralled him. "It was fun."

"I can see that would amuse you. But to wait until the last minute to leave! That seems . . . risky." As they rounded a corner, the wheels sank into the mud. The cabriolet tilted. She tensed, prepared to jump if they overturned.

Flogging the horses mercilessly, Mr. Rumbelow shouted, "Get going, ye slackers!"

Madeline flinched, wanting to yank the whip from his hand.

With a jerk, the grays pulled the carriage free. "That's better," he told them. Then, in a normal tone of voice, he said to her, "Not risky at all. Big Bill's the only one of my men who knows me well enough to suspect a trick, and the fool thinks of me like a brother."

The salt-scented breeze blew in her face. "You've never betrayed him before."

"Never. But when he started courting you, I knew he had developed airs."

"And you're the only one who's allowed to put on airs." She saw Mr. Rumbelow's flash of temper, and knew a moment of fear, followed by a moment of triumph. She wanted Mr. Rumbelow on the defensive. She wanted him concentrating on anything but pursuit and capture.

Shaking off the rage, he flashed one of those blinding smiles. "Yes, I'm the only one who's allowed to put on airs." He stroked her cheek. "Don't worry, little duchess. You'll come to like me."

His conceit had risen to frightening proportions. Turning her face away, she watched the wind-tossed trees, looked in the brush, hoping to catch a glimpse of MacAllister and his men. Where were they? What had happened to MacAllister?

They were very close to the coast now. They would be at Adrian's Cove soon.

She couldn't get on that French ship. She had to keep Mr. Rumbelow talking until . . . until Gabriel got here. *Hurry, Gabriel. Hurry.* "You played the whole game all the way to the end just to prove you could beat all those gamblers, didn't you?"

Mr. Rumbelow laughed, that same maniacal cackle.

Madeline found the sound as frightening now as before.

"Especially Campion. I beat your old lover, the best gamester in England, and I took his woman." Mr. Rumbelow pressed her shoulder. Caressed her shoulder. "I'll be a legend now. It was good to win, and it'll be almost as good to take you. A duchess, just for me."

Nausea swept her, but she would not give in to such weakness now.

"And you're not hideous!" he said.

"Your compliments will turn my head." She needed to change the subject. "Where's the ante?"

"I took it out of the safe almost as soon as it was placed there." He gestured behind them. "It's padlocked in the boot."

She turned, but could see nothing except the dark leather of the top. "No wonder you wouldn't allow anyone to depart. They might have used the cabriolet, and where would that leave you?"

"Quite right." In a patronizing tone, he said, "You're rather smart for an aristocrat."

The tone, the words, infuriated her. She smiled with all the chilly weight of family, nobility and history behind her. "You're rather impertinent for a footpad."

His hand flashed out toward her face.

She impeded the blow with a solid block of her arm. The horses danced sideways, jerking the cabriolet back and forth. The black velvet reticule swung up and smacked him on the elbow with all the solid weight of the pistol inside. "Watch your driving!" she commanded, but too late. Nothing would distract him.

Cruelly, he jerked the horses to a halt and wrapped the ribbons around the rein guide. "What's in that?" He snatched at the reticule. "Give it to me."

Swinging the black velvet holster fiercely, she had the delight of feeling the heavy metal pistol connect solidly with his ribs.

He fell back with an audible, "Oof."

Heart in her throat, she leaped for the step.

He grabbed at her skirt, caught a handful of material.

The gathers at the waist tore. Off balance, she missed her footing and fell out of the carriage. She put her hands out to break her fall. She hit hard on her stomach. Mud softened the fall, but she gasped, trying to get air.

Close, too close, the horses pranced, their hooves splashing her with muck. The wheels wrenched back and forth. Inside her head, she could hear the thrumming of other horses. Or perhaps the fall had addled her brains. She rolled onto her back. She scrambled to her feet. Reaching into the reticule, she grasped the pistol and brought it up.

Mr. Rumbelow stood in the carriage, struggling to draw his rifle.

The wind shook the trees. The rain fell, dripping into her face.

"Drop it!" she commanded. "Put your hands up."

She hadn't freed the pistol from its elegant holster. He looked. He laughed. "What're you going to do, shoot me with your reticule?"

In a long, smooth movement, he brought his rifle to his shoulder.

Dear heavens, she was going to have to kill him. Pulling back the hammer, she sighted over her hand and aimed at his heart.

And around the bend, Big Bill rode on a great roan stallion. "Bastard!" he roared at Mr. Rumbelow, waving a pistol. "Damned thieving bastard."

The rifle smoothly turned. Mr. Rumbelow shot Big Bill right in the gut.

Crimson blossomed beneath Big Bill's ribs. He screamed, an incoherent shriek of pain and rage. He flung his arms wide, as if to embrace death, and toppled off the horse into the grass at the side of the road.

The stallion reared, jumped over the body and galloped right at Madeline. Dodging into the brush, she scrambled to get out of the way. The stallion thundered past her, so close his heat brushed her face.

She staggered. She recovered.

She'd lost her pistol.

Mr. Rumbelow laughed again, and this time he didn't stop.

The sound of awful merriment went on and on until she wanted to cover her ears.

He pulled his pistol free of his waistband.

She searched frantically. Saw the black velvet on a tangle of brush. Saw the pistol free of the holster. She dove for it, but she knew . . . she knew she was too late.

Still Mr. Rumbelow laughed. He sighted the pistol on her, and he laughed.

She was going to die. *Gabriel!*

A shot rang out. But she felt nothing. No searing pain, no disability. Rumbelow's laughter stopped. He swayed. Grasping her pistol, she cocked the hammer, lifted and aimed—and saw Mr. Rumbelow fall, a wound in his chest, an expression of surprise on his handsome face.

She didn't understand.

Then Gabriel cantered into the middle of the road, and she did understand. He tossed away his smoking gun, and sat slumped on a bare-backed gray gelding, his chest heaving.

He'd killed Mr. Rumbelow. He killed him, and saved her life. Now he stared at her as if she were the embodiment of his every dream.

"Gabriel." Her muscles, cramped with tension, ached as she slowly lowered her pistol. She stumbled toward him. "Gabriel."

He slid out of the saddle and strode toward her.

They met in the middle of the muddy road. The wind whistled about them, the rain fell in ever-increasing torrents, but they didn't notice. They'd avenged Jerry. They'd rid the world of a black-hearted villain. They were alive. And they had each other.

Gabriel swept her into his arms, holding her so tightly she could scarcely breathe.

She didn't need to breathe. She just needed Gabriel.

Tilting her head, she pressed frantic, open kisses along his jawline. Rain ran into her mouth. She could have drowned, but she didn't care. As long as they were together. He caught her lips with his, he kissed her as if she were his heart, his soul, as if he couldn't survive without her.

She wanted to talk, to tell him how she felt. Instead she reveled in the taste of Gabriel, the scent of Gabriel, the glorious warmth and closeness of Gabriel.

At long last, he stared down at her. "I'd be happier if you'd put that pistol down."

"What? Oh." She looked at the pistol, still clenched in her white-knuckled fingers. She could scarcely believe it was over. "I've been afraid to let go."

Low and intense, he said, "Maddie, I don't care how good a shot you are, I don't care if you are a duchess and the most capable woman I've ever met, next time we find ourselves facing a villain, any kind of villain at all, I want you to scream and faint."

She giggled.

He was *not* smiling. He was *not* jesting. "At least then I'll know where you are. At least then I know I can protect you."

Sobering, she stroked his damp cheek. "Were you worried?"

"Worried?" He laughed harshly. "Do you realize I lost that game on purpose?"

"I suspected you did. I was standing behind you, remember?" She shook her head. "You'll never know what it took for me not to shout at you for playing so badly."

"I can imagine." He still wasn't smiling. "I threw the game knowing you would keep your word to me and go with him."

She stiffened, no longer amused. "Were you so sure?"

"You vowed that you were mine to command. You vowed that four years ago. You vowed that last night. And you are the duchess of Magnus." Gabriel looked away from her as if he couldn't bear to see what was in her face. "I knew you wouldn't break your word."

Gently, she brought his face back. "Just as I knew you had a plan."

"A plan! I suppose you could call it that. I needed help, and with MacAllister gone, you were my only hope."

"Your only hope?" She smiled. "I like that."

"I didn't. To depend on my woman, to send her into danger, because I knew she owned a pistol and she knew how to use it!" He shook his head, horror and despair mingling on his countenance.

"Really. I didn't mind." Now that it was over and all had ended well, she found she *didn't* mind. "You wanted me to go with Rumbelow to the French ship and hold him until you and your men got there. I could have done it."

"Thank God you didn't have to."

"Gabriel, truly, I knew you wouldn't wager me, and lose me, unless it was necessary to stop Mr. Rumbelow. I had faith in you, Gabriel."

"When I lost you, you had your doubts."

She hesitated to answer, but honesty compelled her. "You told me you weren't like my father. And you're not. You're completely different. You're dependable, and everything I've ever dreamed of."

He stared down at her, then nodded abruptly, accepting her affirmation. "I am dependable, but do you know how frightened I was? Riding bareback on a gelding like some impoverished knight to the rescue? Wondering if I would get here on time? Whether I would find you hurt or dead?" Gripping her hand, he kissed her fingertips. "Wondering if you would forgive me for gambling you, for losing you, for sending you into danger armed only with one little pistol? My God, Maddie, how can I ever tell you—"

A faint noise came from behind them.

Gabriel stiffened, looked over her shoulder.

"Wha . . . ?" She looked, too.

Big Bill had rolled, crawled, lifted himself—and now he sighted his pistol right at Madeline. "Bitch," he whispered.

Lifting her pistol, she pulled her trigger.

Big Bill pulled his trigger.

Gabriel swung himself in front of her.

The guns roared in unison.

Gabriel's body jolted against hers. Catching him in her arms, she dropped slowly to her knees, his weight bearing her down.

He'd been hit. Dear God, Gabriel had been hit.

Chapter Thirty-two

"Gabriel!" Madeline knelt with her knees folded beneath her, held him in her lap, struggled to hold him out of the mud. "Gabriel!" Pressing her hand to his chest, she felt it rise and fall. He was alive. But . . . groping along his back, she found the wound high on his right shoulder, small and horrible. Blood smeared her hand, blood swiftly washed away by the rain. "Please, Gabriel."

His lips moved.

Bending close to his face, she turned her ear to his lips. "What? Tell me."

Softly he said, "Stop . . . yelling. I'm . . . fine."

She sat up straight. "I'm not yelling. And you're not fine."

"It could be worse." Opening his eyes, he looked up at the thunderous gray sky. "It could rain."

Unknotting his cravat, she gently removed it from around his neck. "You're not funny." But he was talking, at least. He was going to live, at least—if she could just get this bleeding stopped.

"No sense of humor." He took a laborious breath. "Did you kill him?"

She didn't even have to look at the body sprawled in the brush. "Oh, yes."

"That's my girl." Another one of those painful breaths shuddered through Gabriel. "I'd kill for you, too."

"You did."

"I'd die for you."

"Don't . . . you . . . dare." She wrapped his cravat around his wound and tied it tightly. "Don't you dare." She glanced about her. She needed help. There was none. "Damn MacAllister! Why couldn't he be around the one time I want him?"

Gabriel wheezed with laughter.

"If I assist you, can you get into the carriage?"

"If you assist me." His eyes were slits of pain. "Stay with me."

"Of course I'll stay with you."

"Forever."

"Forever." Silly tears gathered in her eyes. "And forever is a damned long time, so you'd better survive to see it."

"That's my girl." He smiled and slowly lifted his left hand to stroke her sopping hair out of her face. "So you do forgive me for wagering you? And losing you?"

"I understood what you were doing." What a stupid thing to worry about now, when they'd both faced death and he was reclining in the mud in the road with a gunshot wound in his shoulder.

"I don't give a damn about understanding. I want forgiveness."

"I forgive you!"

Tugging at her hair, he brought her head closer and looked into her eyes. "Maddie, I love you."

She saw bright red blood seeping up through the white linen, and she cursed.

His eyes opened wide. "Does that mean you don't love me?"

"I adore you. I love you." She stripped off her sash and tied it atop of the cravat. "I will even be thrilled and excited that you love me—when we have you on a bed and a doctor taking that bullet out of your shoulder."

"So you do love me."

She wanted to tell Gabriel to shut up, to save his breath for living, but right now, things needed to be said. "I've always loved you. Did you think I would do those things . . . with you . . . if I didn't?"

He sounded a little slurred, but he was smiling again. "What things would those be?"

"I'll show you when you're better."

"I'm a fast healer."

"You'd better be." Because she couldn't resist any longer, she leaned down and pressed her lips to his. Both Gabriel and Madeline were wet and muddy. And his lips were warm and generous— and alive. "I love you," she murmured. "I love you. I love you."

"Will you marry me?"

"Yes." But she'd said yes before, and hadn't. She waited to see if he would question her, doubt her.

Instead he smiled. "Today."

Apparently he planned to live long enough to make it to the church, and a bit of her tension seeped away. If Gabriel had decided he would live, then he would live. "They have to call the banns. It'll be four weeks at least."

He watched her with that bone-melting intensity that made her breathless. "I've got a special license."

"A special license?" She stared blankly. "When did you get that?"

"Four years ago, and I've carried it everywhere, waiting for the day you came home to me." He had to be in pain, but he seemed not to think of that as he watched her, his beautiful, dark-fringed eyes serious. "Marry me today."

She wanted to say a lot of things. She wanted to accuse him of overconfidence. She wanted to say she hadn't come home to him. She wanted to rescue the pride he had shredded so completely with his arrogant wager.

Madeline tucked her chilly fingers into his. "Today."

Outside Chalice Hall, lightning struck and thunder roared. The wind howled around the gargoyles and sent the smoke puffing back down the chimneys, and the rain fell in torrents that filled the streams and made the roads a quagmire.

In the corridor, the clock struck midnight. Madeline sat in a chair beside the bed, twisting Gabriel's signet ring on her finger and watching her husband as he slept. The candlelight flickered on his drawn face. He was in pain and would be for days, but—she touched his cool forehead—he showed no signs of infection.

Never taking her gaze from him, she seated herself again. Pulling her legs under her, she tucked her white nightgown tightly about her feet and tugged the cashmere shawl around her shoulders.

She was glad to be inside on a night like this. She'd had enough of rain and wind earlier today as she held Gabriel in her lap and they pledged their love.

They'd been rudely interrupted by MacAllister, who was limping from the accident that had made him so late. Cantankerous as always, he complained the whole time he helped Gabriel to his feet and into the carriage. MacAllister had been searching all over the countryside for them, he said. The king's men had the French ship in custody. Except for a few hoodlums' bodies and a few hysterical women, all was well at Chalice Hall. As he set the horses in motion, he groused, "But evidently, I canna leave *ye* two alone without ye getting in trooble."

The bullet extraction had been relatively easy. With absolute bed rest for a fortnight and plenty of beef broth and red wine, the doctor had promised a full recovery for Gabriel.

The elderly clergyman had been less pleased to perform a marriage on the authority of a time-worn paper dated four years ago, but an ample donation to his orphanage had convinced him to perform the ceremony. MacAllister had stood up for Gabriel. Thomasin had stood up for Madeline. And as many of the bruised, shocked guests as could fit in the bedchamber had served as witnesses.

As soon as the storm let up, they would leave, their antes safely in their pockets, to spread the tale of the marvelous game and how Lord Campion had lost a card game in order to defeat a blackguard, capture a French ship—and wed, at last, the duchess of Magnus.

A smile played around Madeline's face. Married. To Gabriel. That ridiculous wager of her father's was now null and void. Mr. Knight would be annoyed, of course, but she would explain and . . . No. Gabriel would insist it was his task to explain matters to Mr. Knight, and Madeline would welcome him taking that responsibility. She trusted him to manage the difficulty well.

A ruckus in the corridor brought a frown to her face. Didn't everyone know Gabriel needed his rest?

The sound came closer and, donning her robe, she hurried to the door to quell it. MacAllister limped up to her, extending a sealed sheet of paper. "Yer Grace, this came for ye this minute, delivered by your groom. He's soaked through to the skin, is Dickie, and he wouldna' listen when I said ye were asleep. He broke down in the mud, walked most of the way, and he wouldna' go away until ye have read this."

Madeline recognized the handwriting on the

paper. "Eleanor." Was she ill? Dead? Had Mr. Knight done her a harm? Dread filled Madeline as she tore the sheet open.

When she had read the brief note, she lifted her head to see Gabriel awake and staring at her in concern.

"What is it, love?" he asked.

"It's Eleanor. She says unless I come at once, she'll be married to Mr. Knight tomorrow at noon."